A Dish to Die For

Also available by Lucy Burdette

Key West Food Critic Mysteries

A Scone of Contention

The Key Lime Crime

A Deadly Feast

Death on the Menu

Killer Takeout

Fatal Reservations

Death With All the Trimmings

Murder With Ganache

Topped Chef

Death in Four Courses

An Appetite for Murder

Other Novels

Unsafe Haven

A Dish to Die For

A KEY WEST FOOD CRITIC MYSTERY

Lucy Burdette

CROOKED LANE

NEW YORK

Published in the United States by Crooked Lane Books, an imprint of The Quick Brown Fox & Company LLC.

Crooked Lane Books and its logo are trademarks of The Quick Brown Fox & Company LLC.

Library of Congress Catalog-in-Publication data available upon request.

ISBN (hardcover): 978-1-63910-072-9
ISBN (ebook): 978-1-63910-073-6

Cover illustration by Griesbach/Martucci

Printed in the United States.

www.crookedlanebooks.com

Crooked Lane Books
34 West 27th St., 10th Floor
New York, NY 10001

First Edition: August 2022

10 9 8 7 6 5 4 3 2 1

For Steve Torrence and John Hernandez, with love, gratitude, and admiration for their dedication to the people of Key West

Chapter One

One more question, Doctor: would it be possible to introduce a fatal dose of poison into a chocolate?

—Agatha Christie, *The Chocolate Box*

As much as I loved the island of Key West, my home for the last handful of years, some days I felt I'd go mad if I didn't get off this rock, as the locals called it. Today was one of those days. Happily, my psychologist friend Eric Altman had invited me and my husband Nathan's min pin, Ziggy Stardust, to accompany him and his two dogs to Boca Chica Beach, located on a small key eleven miles north in the string of islands above Key West. The dogs could run without leashes, and we'd be off the concrete, away from the hustle and bustle of our town. And, if I was being honest, away from the streak of negativity that I had sensed bobbing along the surface and in the undercurrents of the community since the pandemic had been declared vanquished last year.

Key West wasn't the only place where problems had been left behind like an ugly surge of plastic junk and fishing line after a high tide. But since this was where I lived and worked as a food critic for *Key Zest*, it was the particular negativity that I knew best. If I had to guess, I'd say a good quarter of the businesses on the island had gone belly-up over the year we'd suffered with the virus. Cruise ships were no longer arriving several times a day at the docks near Margaritaville, now the Opal Key Resort, and Mallory Square, which some residents celebrated and others despised. And my two bosses were tussling like vultures on carrion. Should we focus on the losses, the Caribbean sandwiches and bowls we'd never again order from Paseo's—aka Bien—and the steaks and bloody Marys we couldn't sample at Michael's? (Wally's point of view—he'd always been a bit of an Eeyore.) Or should our tone be light and airy, as if this new version of Key West was exactly the same as the last, or quite possibly better? (That was Palamina, who had a brighter outlook in general than Wally.) Things *were* getting better, in my mind, and I sure hoped that trend would continue. All that said, as we drove out of town, I felt a weight lifting from my shoulders. It had rained hard in the night, a rain that came more often in the summer than early November. We had felt the wind kick up the waves underneath our houseboat, which made it a little harder to sleep. But the storm had cleared the air, and the temperature felt a little cooler. Perfect weather for the beach.

Boca Chica Beach on Geiger Key stretched along the eastern edge of the naval air base, separated from the base by a chain-link fence. We parked with a few other cars at the end of the road near the Jersey barriers protecting the entrance. Though a sign plainly said U.S. GOVERNMENT PROPERTY—NO TRESPASSING, Eric assured me that people were welcome to swim and dogs welcome to run on this little stretch of seaweed, sand, and mangroves. Soon after, we passed a concrete column on which NUDE BEACH had been written, just above a line drawing of a naked lady.

"It's probably not official," Eric said with a grin, "and definitely not obligatory." He leaned down to unsnap the leashes from the collars of his Havanese, Chester, and his terrier, Barclay. I did the same for Ziggy, who was dancing and whining with excitement.

This beach did not resemble a Caribbean resort—that is, no manicured white sand bordered stretches of turquoise water. Boca Chica Beach was narrow and rimmed with coral rock. The rain and wind in the night had washed up a thick line of seaweed and pocked the sand all the way up to the high-tide line like an old-fashioned popcorn ceiling. We stopped to admire a handful of rock cairns built of chunks of coral. I remembered from our recent trip to Scotland that such stacks of balanced stones could mean the builder had been practicing patience and gratefulness, or offering up prayers for someone in need.

We hiked in about a half mile and set up our low beach chairs in the mottled shade of a buttonwood tree. A series of small waves followed one after the other, rushing against the rocks that edged the beach, humming like the white-noise machine Nathan and I kept beside our bed on Houseboat Row. I could pretty much sleep through anything unless I had a particularly sharp worry, but my husband, a police detective competing for an upcoming vacancy as captain, had a mind that circled problems like a laboratory rat on a wheel. I'd bought that machine because I hated for the hubbub of our houseboat community to wake him up too early and start his cycle of worrying.

"This is beautiful," I said to Eric, watching the three dogs frolic in and out of the water. "This would've been so good for Nathan."

He leaned over to squeeze my shoulder. "It'll be good for you too. And I picked us up sandwiches from Bad Boy Burrito as a special treat."

My mouth watered, and I closed my eyes. "Don't tell me. Chicken, beans and rice, jalapeños, cabbage, cilantro, cheese, sour cream, tomatillo salsa."

I opened my eyes as a parade of birds flew by overhead, in perfect formation.

"You nailed it," he said, laughing. "Plus pico de gallo on the side. I also brought chew bones for the dogs so they won't pester us."

He opened the brown bag that he'd extracted from his pack and handed me a burrito wrapped in white paper. We ate in silence, appreciating the perfect mix of ingredients and concentrating on catching every bit of juice before it ran down our chins. Bad Boy Burrito was one of the restaurants that had sunk under the weight of expenses and too few customers over the past year and a half. Happily, it had resurfaced with a new owner and a smaller storefront and the same high-quality food, and I was thrilled to support them. "This is amazing, thank you," I said, smiling at my friend.

I closed my eyes and leaned back in the chair, not even bothered by the one aluminum leg listing left into the sand. With the breeze picking up and the sound of the waves and the smell of seaweed, I could almost imagine myself at the shore in New Jersey. For which, oddly enough, I'd been yearning.

"I know you've been feeling a little down," Eric said.

I looked up sharply. He was one of the few people in my life who could read me as though I were transparent. "I feel like I'm missing home," I said. "Even though I live here and Nathan's here and my mom lives here too, I feel homesick. I don't even know for what."

He nodded slowly. "The pandemic touched all of us. Even if we weren't on the front lines or sick as dogs, we've ended up with PTSD. Something honest and optimistic and hopeful that we took for granted has been taken away. We have to feel our way through what's left until the light gets brighter. But it's going to, I promise." He put a hand on my forearm and squeezed gently. "I promise."

"I hope you're right." My forehead felt tight with worry, and I smoothed my furrowed eyebrows with my fingers. "I've also been thinking . . . have you noticed that I take on a lot? If someone I love has a problem, it affects me almost as much as it does them." I tapped my heart with my fist. Of course, Eric would have noticed, but I knew he'd be kind.

"That's part of what people love about you," Eric said. "You want to take care of everyone. But boundaries are important too. You don't want to end up like an international porter or an Everest Sherpa, carrying everyone else's baggage while they frolic."

I laughed. "Easier said than done. You're so smart. You should be a shrink." I grinned and looked out across the water, watching sailboats and shrimpers bob slowly in the distance and listening to small black birds chittering on a rock that protruded from the surf. Already I felt lighter than when we'd come. Chester and Barclay emerged from wading in the water and lay beside Eric in the sand, pink tongues lolling. They had bits of dried sponge tangled in their fur that would be hell to comb out. I suddenly realized that Nathan's Ziggy was not with them.

"Where's Ziggy?" I asked, looking at the other dogs as if they might answer.

Off in the distance, I could hear a few sharp yips. Eric started to get up.

"You stay here and relax," I said. "I better go see what that little rascal's gotten into."

I trotted along the beach, weaving in and out of the skeletal remains of mangrove trees and into the brush along the chain-link fence, calling for Ziggy. He was pretty good at coming when called, but right now he sounded more excited than usual. I paused to listen. The yips had grown louder, so I kept walking in their direction.

I jogged until I reached a hut built from piles of flat white stones and pieces of driftwood, bleached pale gray in the sun. According to Eric, rumor had it that a homeless man had built this place and lived here until he was finally evicted by the authorities. It was decorated with weathered buoys, beer and wine bottles woven into sections of fishing net, old shoes, and sheets of metal that hung from the overhead branches and played a dissonant drumbeat when the wind picked up. It almost looked as though the driftwood structure had been divided into rooms, one of them kitchen-like with a fire pit and a large metal bowl. I suspected it was a very popular spot for teen parties.

Beyond the kitchen, I saw our sleek little black dog digging frantically in the sand. I called him again and huffed with exasperation when he didn't respond. Nathan and I were going to have to have a chat about obedience training. Ziggy did exactly what Nathan told him to do, and they'd never taken a class. But I was like the stepparent whose kid announced *You're not my mother* when asked to do something that didn't suit him. I could picture Ziggy with paws on hips and lower lip jutted out, if that was possible with a small dog. I approached him, leash in hand, prepared to scoop him up and scold him.

But as I got closer, I could see that inside the shallow hole he'd dug, he'd uncovered a piece of denim. And then, oh good gravy, what looked like the fingers on a man's hand. He took hold of the loose denim and shook it hard, growling. Then I noticed that some of the sand around the right of the man's head had been stained dark. The color of blood. My heart began to pound and my knees felt wobbly. But I needed to appear calm if I wanted a chance of getting him away from his prize.

"Good boy, Ziggeroo," I said, squatting down to his level, hoping to lure him over before he destroyed what surely looked like a crime scene.

Chapter Two

It's not that the problem is the occasional French fry dropped by a tourist. It's the people who show up with 50-pound bags of chicken feed. Some of them even dress up as chickens.

—Clayton Lopez, *Key West Citizen*

I sucked in a big breath to get the guts to move closer so I could see what was really going on and get control of the dog. Ziggy had dug out enough of a trench that he'd shaken loose much of the sand blown over the top of the body. I could now see the shape of a man's head—a strong nose, short dark hair with only a few strands of gray woven in, full lips covered in sand as if he'd applied textured lip gloss. I didn't think the man had been buried. It looked more like the wind in the night had blasted sand over parts of him. I pulled a treat out of my pocket and called the dog again. He was smart enough to be able to hear desperation in my voice when he discovered something I found disgusting. He wouldn't drop anything super interesting unless bribed.

"I'll trade you, buddy," I said in a voice that sounded too high and too tight. The light brown of his doggy eyebrows shifted higher, as if he doubted any trade I offered would be worth it. "Come on, Zig, it's salmon." I waved his favorite dried treat, which I kept for emergencies. Sinking to my haunches, I squatted on a piece of fallen driftwood, attempting to look nonchalant. At last, he dropped his prize—the piece of denim—and trotted over. I snapped the leash onto his collar and fed him the treat, then dialed Eric.

"What's up?"

"Ziggy's found what looks like a body. Could you leash the dogs and come this way? I'll call the cops and Nathan."

I hung up, called 911, and described the situation. As I talked, it occurred to me to wonder whether the Key West Police had jurisdiction over a crime committed on this beach. Probably not. It was outside the city limits for sure and ran parallel to the Navy base, marked off with a tall chain-link fence. But it wasn't my job to figure that out.

"I'm putting you through to the sheriff's department. Please hold."

"Help is on the way," a new voice said, after I'd described the scene a second time. "Are you certain this person is deceased?"

Honestly, I was certain. Dead certain. But I took a few steps closer and held my hand over the sandy lips. Nothing. Then I touched my fingers to his neck. "No signs of breath or pulse," I said.

The dispatcher instructed me to remain where I was and not touch anything, which I already knew. But I moved a good twenty yards downwind so I wouldn't have to see—or, possibly even worse, smell—the body while still keeping watch. I had no idea how long this person had been here and what condition the remains might be in. Then I called Nathan and spilled out what I'd seen in a frantic rush of words.

"Is it someone you know? Is there anyone else around? How recently do you think this happened? You could be in danger." His voice held an edge of panic.

"No, no, I have no idea, and I know," I said, feeling the muscles in my neck tighten. "The sheriff's department will be here shortly, and Eric is on his way. He was a quarter mile up the beach from where I am." Then I started to cry.

"I'll get there as soon as I can."

"I'll be fine, really," I assured him, snuffling back the tears. "It was a shock. And I know you're busy. Please don't drop what you're doing, I just needed to hear your voice. And I didn't want you to hear about this from someone else."

I scrambled to reassure him, almost wishing I hadn't made that call. I refused to be the kind of wife who leaned heavily on her hub at the slightest disturbance in her energy field. Although to be fair to me, in this instance the disturbance in the field was a death, not a minor problem. Besides, it would take him at least a half hour to get here, and by then, hopefully the whole mess would be wrapped up. Optimistic timeline, I knew from past unfortunate experience. But a girl could hope.

Eric and his dogs showed up minutes later, all of them huffing with the pace. "Are you okay?" Eric asked, pulling me into a hug while keeping a tight grip on the dogs' leashes.

"Sort of," I said. I sank down to the sand and sat cross-legged, feeling weak with the shock. "I'll feel better when the cops get here."

I explained about Ziggy digging alongside the body.

"He found bones?"

"Unfortunately, more than bones," I said. I described spotting the denim shirt, and then my horror when I recognized blue-tinged fingers, and then how the features of the face had taken shape in my mind like the colorful shards of a kaleidoscope.

Through the brush, from the direction opposite the parking lot, we saw a man in khaki hiking pants and a faded denim bucket hat approach. He had binoculars around his neck, a day pack on his back, and white cream smeared over his nose. As he drew closer, I could see his face under the sunscreen was tan and lined, as though he'd spent a lot of time outdoors.

"Greetings on a beautiful day," he said, a huge smile on his face. "I hope you got the chance to see the belted kingfisher."

Then he frowned, noticing the three dogs. "Though most likely your animals scared him off."

"Please don't come any nearer." I stood up and held my hand out with what I hoped was a commanding presence. "Unfortunately, you're probably approaching a crime scene." I explained once more about Ziggy finding the body and told him the authorities were on the way. "Did you pass anyone going the other direction in a big hurry?"

"No one could escape that way," he said, gesturing toward the brush and a clump of buttonwoods. "There's a tidal stream crossing the beach up a half mile or so. They'd sink up to their thighs in lime mud, and the cops could scoop them up like trash collectors on Thursday mornings."

He chuckled to himself, then glanced toward the chain-link fence that marked off the narrow stretch of beach from the Navy property.

"I suppose the perpetrator could have gone over the fence, but I suspect the military monitors this boundary carefully. They don't welcome interlopers on Navy property. And their runway is right there." He gestured at the expanse of cement that we glimpsed through the brush.

Even though I had asked the bird watcher to stay away from the body, he approached the dead man and squatted down to observe. "It looks like someone's been digging around the edges," he said, looking up at me.

"This little someone," I said, pointing at the dog. "Ziggy. You haven't seen anyone today who looked out of place?"

"There are some regulars on this beach," he said. "One guy comes most days because you can sunbathe nude without the cops hassling you. Not that I would be showing the equipment he's got to the world at large." He chuckled again. "And from time to time we get teenagers, but usually they come later in the day or at night. And there are a couple of homeless who spend time here, depending on whether they can get a ride and have enough food to tide them over. And then I see random visitors who've gotten tired of the party scene in Key West and need a dose of nature to chill out."

From the man's report, I could see that this crime scene was going to be difficult, trampled by a lot of feet and a lot of possible suspects. Besides that, the storm had probably blown a lot of the evidence away. It occurred to me that this man seemed to be a regular also. And he was cool as a cucumber. And he knew an awful lot about the possibilities.

"And bird watchers too," he continued. He removed his sweaty hat and smoothed his hair before replacing it. "We get all sorts of people who come up from Key West when they realize there's not much green space on that island. Lots of birds fly in and out here, and those are a big attraction." He dropped down on his hands and knees and crawled even closer to the body. "It looks like he sustained a blow to the head," he said. "He's got a big knot on his forehead. Notice how some of the sand is stained a darker color?"

"You probably ought to stay away," I said in a sharp voice, feeling nauseous and out of control. "The authorities are coming, and they're going to have a devil of a time as it is figuring out who might be responsible for this man's death and who might have been innocent bystanders."

He glanced up at me, adjusted the unfashionable bucket hat, and squatted back on his heels. About to argue, I thought. Instead, he said, "I know this guy. And he's not someone who spends much time on this beach appreciating nature, you can be pretty sure of that." He scrambled to his feet.

I gulped and took a step away. "Who is it?"

"You might recognize him too. He's been in the paper a lot over the past year and a half. A rabble-rouser, I'd say. He owns three or four restaurants on Duval and Greene Streets and a bunch of property on Stock Island."

Stock Island was the next island up from Key West, where the golf course, our community college, the sheriff's department, and so-called Mount Trashmore were located. And most important, the humane society where my former roommate Miss Gloria's ginger kitty T-Bone had been acquired. Property was cheaper there than in Key West proper. There'd been recent attempts to spiff up the rougher patches of the island to draw in some of the tourist trade that its more desirable sister enjoyed.

"He had dollar signs in his eyes instead of pupils," the bird watcher continued. "If you were paying attention to the arguments in the *Citizen* about opening the city during the pandemic and allowing cruise ships back in, he was always the gadfly. In my mind, there might be a lot of people who would want to do him in." He must have read my inquisitive expression. "Gerald Garcia," he added. "Spelled with a *G*, not a *J*. He goes—went—by GG."

As he talked, my mind buzzed around the question of how this man knew quite so much about Geiger Key and its visitors, and how he had happened to recognize this GG fellow in his current very sandy condition. Who was he, really?

Chapter Three

In tonight's performance, the role of the duck will be played by a beet, doing things no root vegetable should be asked to do.

—Pete Wells, "Eleven Madison Park Explores the Plant Kingdom's Uncanny Valley," *The New York Times*, September 28, 2021

Not long after I'd called in my horrifying discovery, we heard the wail of sirens in the distance. Shortly after, a swarm of sheriff's department deputies dressed in green trotted down the beach and arrived on the scene. They clustered around the dead man half-buried in the sand, a few squatting to see the situation up close. A woman emerged from the pack and came toward me. She had an air of authority and blonde hair pulled back in a stubby ponytail that stuck through the hole in the back of her ball cap.

"I'm Deputy Darcy Rogers. You phoned this in?"

"Yes." I opened my mouth to repeat the story. The bird watcher started to speak at the same time.

She nodded briskly and held her hand up, cutting both of us off before we could explain anything further. "Stay right where are you are. I'll be with you in a moment." She turned back to the other deputies and instructed several men to rope off the area so they could canvass the site for clues, another to take photographs, and one to phone the county coroner. When these assignments seemed to be proceeding to her satisfaction, she approached us again.

"And you are . . ." Her gaze bored into me, her eyes the color of a pair of prized jeans that I'd had in college, bleached to a light blue.

"This is my good friend Eric Altman, and I'm Hayley Snow." I wondered these days whether I should identify myself as wife of Key West Police detective Nathan Bransford or let someone figure that out on their own. Before I could decide, the bird watcher piped up.

"I'm Davis Jager. We just now met. She found the body," he added, pointing at me. "I was merely looking for birds." He flashed a wide grin and held up the pair of binoculars that hung around his neck as evidence of his veracity.

Something about that struck me wrong, as if he was saying I'd come out looking for trouble instead of seeking calm and a little distance from the hectic nature of everyday life. Or that I was flat out lying.

"What was your business here?" Deputy Rogers asked me.

"I came up from Key West for lunch with my friend Eric. We needed time for relaxation, and the dogs needed to run." I gulped, thinking that most likely it wasn't legal for dogs to run without a leash on this beach. Probably not legal to sunbathe in the nude either. Maybe not even legal to be here at all, or so the sign at the end of the road read. Suddenly, in her fierce presence, I felt guilty about everything, even the things I hadn't done.

"Walk me through it," she said briskly. "How did you happen to find the man, and what did you notice along the way?"

For the third time, I explained about Ziggy's misadventure.

Then the bird watcher butted back in. "The man's name is GG, aka Gerald Garcia, spelled with a *G*, not a *J*. I'm sure you've seen him in the news. Everybody has. He's pretty much come out in favor of anything the bread-and-butter locals hate—giant cruise ships dumping sewage in the harbor, any restrictive noise ordinance, let those gas-powered leaf blowers run, certainly no masks during Covid." He scratched a finger over the reddish stubble on his chin. "Well, maybe the chamber of commerce types liked him, I'll grant you that."

Deputy Rogers stared at him. "Where were you when"—she glanced at her notes—"Miss Snow found the body?"

"Looking for birds," he said, rolling his eyes as though that should have been obvious. "Several of my colleagues reported spotting a flock of fulvous whistling duck out this way. They tend to like swampy habitats, but we only see them here occasionally. Their coloring is gorgeous—a rich caramel. And they make a whistling sound, hence the name." He puckered his lips to imitate their whistle, then laughed. "You get the idea. I was hoping to confirm the sighting. However, I did see a belted kingfisher."

The deputy was watching him carefully, her eyes squinted against the sharp early-afternoon sun. "I take it you would have passed by this area as you proceeded to your duck watching. Did you not notice anything awry on the way out to the point?"

The bird watcher tapped a fist to his chest and widened his eyes, almost as if he thought she was accusing him of something. And maybe she was. Ignorance, maybe, or poor observational skills at best. Which would be death to a bird specialist, right?

"You heard the lady; she said her dog dug up the corpse. No way I would have noticed anything wrong before that because I arrived early in the morning, and it was barely light. Besides, I have passed this hut a thousand times, so I hardly see it anymore. I'm focused on what's ahead."

His story struck me as possibly true—I wouldn't have noticed the body tucked behind the driftwood hut had it not been for Ziggy.

But then he added, "I bet you do the same thing in your line of work. You see what you expect to see and miss the rest. Except you might miss some important and obvious clues and torpedo your case. And in the case of murder, the stakes would be very high." He seemed to be taunting her now underneath his jovial tone and his smile. Her lips tightened into an angry line, but she didn't take his bait.

"We're talking about you, Mr. Jager. I'd like your contact information so we can speak with you again later if we need to. Both of you."

I recited my phone number and address, and the bird watcher did the same.

"We've called the medical examiner in, but he works in Duck Key, so it will take some time for him to get here. We won't ask you to stay, but you'll need to be available for a follow-up if needed. Got it, Mr. Jager?"

"Got it," said Davis Jager.

Then she asked me to show her exactly where Ziggy had dug and think back to whether I'd seen anyone else on the beach, either coming or going. Finally, she asked Eric to describe anything he'd seen or heard while I was chasing down the dog. None of our answers seemed to add anything useful.

Within the hour, our interviews had been wrapped up and we were on our way home. Nathan texted me twice to see if I needed him there, but both times I reassured him that I was fine and would see him at the houseboat. I reminded him that he was on his own for dinner, as I had a girls' night out date with my mother, Miss Gloria, and her best friend, Mrs. Dubisson, to eat at Matt's Stock Island Kitchen and Bar. It was an early birthday celebration for Miss Gloria, who preferred to keep her eighty-third low-key.

Even though we lived near each other, we were all busy enough that we were looking forward to catching up—and laughing. I could also knock off the first stop for my article for *Key Zest* focusing on restaurants off the rock, aka islands north of Key West. It all felt a little surreal, planning the night's fun with a man murdered just up the keys. I decided I'd feel better if I could talk to my husband on the phone again. He picked up right away.

"Are you all right?" he asked, sounding guilty. "I should have come up to help."

"I'm fine," I said. "It was unpleasant and spooky and tragic, but honestly, it was better that you didn't come. I know you're busy and the sheriff's department was thorough, and they weren't unkind with their questions. I feel badly that I won't be home for dinner. I could make you something if you'd like—it wouldn't be any trouble. I have chicken in the fridge—"

He cut me off. "Please don't worry about it. Remember my father has arrived in town and we're having dinner with the chief? I'll see you around nine o'clock. Have fun with your girls."

Oh lordy, the fact of his father arriving on the island for his first visit ever had totally slipped my mind. I had yet to meet him, and Nathan hadn't seen him in years. He had announced earlier this week that he'd be coming down on police business. I was puzzled about Nathan's father and the relationships he had or didn't have with his family, but Nathan had clammed up the few times I'd asked what his father was like. I knew that he'd been devastated about Nathan's sister's kidnapping and that somehow his wife Helen, Nathan's mother, had blamed him for not finding her more quickly. That traumatic event and its emotional fallout had contributed to their divorce. I also knew he loved golf and that Nathan's teenage rebellion had consisted of throwing away family-heirloom clubs. That was the sum total of what I knew about my father-in-law. Except the ways that he was reflected in my husband, including those traits I had yet to identify.

"I feel awful about this. If it wasn't Miss Gloria's birthday, and if we hadn't had this scheduled for ages—"

Nathan cut me off. "This plan is fine. It will give us a little time to make a connection after a long time apart. Although," he added, "if you and your mother and Miss Gloria were there, I would not worry one bit about how to carry the conversation along."

"I believe you might be saying we talk too much?" I asked, laughing. "Love you. See you tonight."

I was glad Eric was driving so I could lean my head back, close my eyes, and try to quiet my spinning brain. My phone buzzed with a message, ruining that plan instantly. It was from Davis Jager, the bird watcher. First of all, how had he gotten my phone number? Second, why would he be contacting me?

I meant to say you can find me at happy hour at the Geiger Key Fish Camp almost every night. From the little I saw of you, I suspect you're not done with this murder case.

But I wanted to be done with it. I didn't want to be involved with it in the first place.

"Nope. Boundaries," I said to myself firmly, not realizing I had spoken out loud. And then I deleted the number. There was nothing more we needed to discuss.

Eric said, "What did you say?"

"Boundaries," I repeated with a snicker. "I swear to God I'm working on that right now."

On the drive home from Geiger Key to Key West, my heart wanted to believe that. But (a), I *was* intensely curious about how that poor man had ended up dead and half-covered with sand. Chances were he had been killed right there, not done in somewhere else and dragged to that site. Because it was far enough from the parking area that hauling a dead body on foot would have been both a heavy burden and quite obvious to anybody watching. Plus, I'd seen no sign of anything being dragged—no obvious telltale divots or scrapes in sand.

And (b), the part of me that felt obligated to help anyone in trouble had surged to the forefront—a knee-jerk reaction that would be hard to quash. "What do you know about this Gerald Garcia?" I asked Eric. "The name sounds familiar. I have the idea he was arrested for breaking some kind of curfew during the pandemic."

Eric glanced over at me. "Remember back at the beginning of that time when the keys were shut down to anyone who didn't live here?"

"Of course," I said. "It felt like the apocalypse had arrived. I will never forget seeing the Southernmost Point Buoy wrapped in blue plastic. I had the creepy feeling they'd find a body underneath the plastic when they finally unwrapped it."

Eric's eyes bulged. "Your mind works in strange ways sometimes, girlfriend. Garcia refused to close his restaurants and bars," he added. "Everybody else had complied with the mayor's recommendations for safety, but not him. Plus I've heard that he was the fellow who bankrolled the lobbying outfit in favor of cruise ships, the more and the bigger the better." He glanced over at me and frowned. "Don't ask me where I heard that, because it's confidential. In fact, please don't say anything about that to anybody else."

This meant his information had come from one of his therapy patients and was privileged. I held up my crossed fingers. "Pinkie swear, my lips are sealed."

Chapter Four

You want happy endings, read cookbooks.

—Dean Young

Eric dropped me off at Houseboat Row at twenty to three. Ziggy, exhausted from the fun he'd had at the beach, immediately settled into his dog bed. I scooped up Evinrude the cat and brought him out on to the deck to sit in the sun. "It was a nightmare," I told him. "But you don't need all the gory details. Just be glad we didn't take you along."

Of course, I'd never take a cat to the beach, but it would be bad form to rub that in. I spent a few minutes stroking the cat, eyes closed, as I listened to him purr—feeling the calm of that raspy rumble seeping through my body. Beyond that, I absorbed the sounds of my neighborhood—water slapping the hull, the whining of a saw, and Mrs. Renhart's wind chimes from two doors down. I'd started to notice them more since complaints about disruptive chimes had begun to pile up in our newspaper's Citizens' Voice, comparing that sound to the roar of jets overhead and gas-powered leaf blowers. It had never occurred to me or Miss Gloria to complain to the

Renharts—unusual sounds and smells were part of our life on Houseboat Row. I hoped I'd grow into the kind of gracious spunky old lady Miss Gloria had become, rather than a crabby curmudgeon carping anonymously about my annoying neighbors in the newspaper.

An alert buzzed on my phone, reminding me that I was due at the Key West Library in fifteen minutes. The Friends of the Library received many used book donations for their monthly book sales, and the librarian had recruited me to be trained to sort through any food-related books to make sure we weren't overlooking something valuable. Today, musty cookbooks might help take my mind off the vision of the corpse in the sand that felt as though it had been burned into my retinas. I'd seen other bodies in the past, but the sight of a lifeless human come to a violent end always disturbed me deeply. I washed my face and changed my shirt and headed downtown on my scooter.

Our library was located in a cute pink stucco building on Fleming Street. Perhaps its best feature was the adjoining palm garden with its brick patio, benches to read on, and a beautiful selection of tropical palm trees. It was no accident that the Friends had chosen this setting for their monthly used book sales. But today I would be working inside, in the less charming book collection shed. Annette Holmstrom, my bookish mentor, was already busy.

"Good afternoon," she said, grinning broadly. She was a short woman wearing red glasses, blonde bangs held in place with a wide pink headband, and a big smile. "If it's okay, I'll give you the overview of how I go through the donations to find books that might be worth selling separately. I won't expect you to remember all of it, because then we'll move on to on-the-job training."

"Sure, I'll do my best." I took a seat on the folding metal chair beside her. Books were stacked all around her in teetering, musty piles. And there were more behind her—shelves and shelves of them stashed in moldering boxes. I felt my eyes widening and beginning to water.

She laughed and patted my knee. "Like eating an elephant, we take it one book at a time. For sorting through your cooking section, I'd err on the side of optimism, so you don't miss something valuable." She turned to the pile next to her and took the top three from it. "I chose a few examples to illustrate what I'm saying." She held up a hardcover copy of *The Louie's Backyard Cookbook*.

"I look for five things." She ticked them off on her left hand. "Condition, edition or print run, whether or not it's signed by the author, rarity, and demand. Cookbooks can be less perfect, since people expect them to have been used, but an unread book in pristine condition is most valuable. As an aside, I hate this aspect of the business, because once I started collecting, I hesitated to read books that I thought might increase in value. Serious bummer for a reader. Now I purchase a used copy too and read that. Isn't that nuts?"

"Makes sense to me," I said, thinking this job might change the way I looked at my own small collection.

Annette pulled on a pair of white gloves. "For the book's condition, I look for shelf wear, fading, tears, scribbles—all the things you would expect to find with cookbooks, plus spills and stains, of course." She flipped carefully through the cookbook to show me a couple of dog-eared pages and scattered food stains. But all things considered, it didn't look well used.

I couldn't help wondering who had bought the book in the first place, whether they'd made any of the recipes from it, and why they'd given it away. Had it belonged to someone who'd died? Or left Key West for good? Or had it been a gift to someone who didn't cook? The recipes made me hungry, and the questions left me a little sad.

Annette continued her tutorial. "First edition, first printing, are most valuable. This information is usually found on the copyright page but not always—sometimes I have to dig. The library's signed Obama book, *Audacity of Hope*, is a first edition, twentieth printing, so only worth a hundred dollars or so. Their copy of *Dreams From My Father*, which is a signed first edition/first printing that I found earlier this week, will be worth a couple thousand."

"Wow," I said. "I had no idea."

She nodded, grinning and pushing her glasses up her nose. "Another thing that increases the value is if a book is signed by the author, preferably on the title page.

"We also consider how many copies were printed. Obviously, if there are fewer copies, they're worth more. The library has a signed Tim Dorsey book in pristine condition, for example, but since he signs so many and he's not competing for the top literary prizes, a used signed copy is not worth that much."

"So commercial fiction isn't worth as much to collectors as literary?"

"Sometimes," she said. "It has to do with both numbers printed and literary prizes. Next, I consider how many people want a certain book. Everyone interested in food wants to own

Julia Child's *Mastering the Art of French Cooking*, and a signed first/first in great condition is worth between five and seven thousand dollars. And some books you might not think should be valuable are. I sought out a favorite childhood book, for instance, and it turned out it was quite collectible, since so many other baby boomers loved the book and wanted to collect it. You never know."

She crossed her hands in her lap. "Did I overwhelm you? Do you feel like you have enough information to get started? You can set any books aside that you're not sure about, and I'll check those over."

"I think I'm good, though it feels like a lot of responsibility."

She patted my shoulder and smiled. "I'll check your work. By the way," she added, "keep an eye out for loose papers in the books. I've found love letters—both received and unsent—receipts, and once an uncashed check for a thousand dollars. We were able to track the owner down and return it, to much gratitude. I'll leave you to it—have fun and give a shout with questions, okay?"

I begin to sift through the pile of cookbooks. I put two aside that had been signed by a local celebrity chef who'd since moved off the island. Underneath those, I found many copies of the Sunset cooking series (probably worth something at the time but not these days), a stained and obviously well-loved copy of Jell-O recipes (really?), and at the bottom of the box, a cookbook from the Key West Woman's Club published in 1949. The recipes had been written in longhand and then copied, printed, and spiral bound. Quite irresistible.

I glanced at the table of contents, then flipped to the section listing soups. One caught my eye: green turtle soup from the Garcia family. The green turtles, the introduction read, were named not after the color of their shells but the layer of fat underlying those shells. That color varied according to what they ate. The list of ingredients began with two pounds turtle flippers. I felt instantly queasy. I had recently been reading about the history of green turtles on our island, thinking of pitching an article with a historical angle. I would have to remind myself that an ingredient that struck me as horrifying today was perfectly normal back then.

Green turtle stock had been in huge demand in the late 1800s, not only in local restaurants but across the nation. Key West fishermen were major suppliers, as the turtles were plentiful and easy to catch. The State Department had declared the green turtle an endangered species in the 1970s, and people stopped using it. By then, it was almost too late.

It occurred to me that this cookbook could make a very good article for *Key Zest*, with a bit of history, a few photos of the pages originally written in longhand, plus my attempts to recreate a few of the recipes. I could probably get my mother to help with the cooking if I needed her. We would not make turtle soup, of course.

I stuck my head into Michael the librarian's back office. He was sitting at his computer, in front of a wall of bookcases bursting with books and behind a big white sign that read *America's Most Beloved Librarian*.

"Do you mind if I borrow this for a week or so?" As I asked the question, I realized how much I wanted to own this cookbook. "Or better yet, once we figure out what it's worth, I'd love to buy it. It's giving me an idea for an article, maybe more than one. I'll treat it with kid gloves. Literally."

Too late, I noticed Michael was on the phone. He waved and nodded, then covered the mouthpiece. "Sure, take it. Unless Annette determines it's worth a small fortune, you've earned it. See you later this week."

* * *

Back at home, I paged through the cookbook again, wondering if I should whip something up for Nathan and his father—it felt wrong not to be making a big foodie fuss to welcome him. Chicken piccata, maybe? My husband always enjoyed my lemony version, and it was innocuous enough to suit most palates because the capers could be pushed aside by conscientious objectors. Or I could pull something out of the freezer? Sweet potato soup and Melissa Clark's buttery corn muffins?

There were no simple chicken recipes in the old cookbook—most of them began with whole fryers, either fried or consigned to pressure cookers. I didn't have the time or ingredients to do them justice. I scanned the green turtle recipes again. Aside from several versions of soup, there were instructions for making baked turtle sliced thinly and rolled like eggplant, breaded turtle steaks, Phoebe's turtle, steamed turtle. The woman who'd provided the baked turtle had ended her instructions with *This is a very rewarding recipe.* Likewise, the steamed turtle offering ended with a poem about the turtle being introverted, *content to live within his shell.* It finally sunk in that the author of several turtle recipes was Mrs. Gerald Garcia Sr. Could she have been related to the man I found on the beach?

I began to feel very excited about researching and writing about this little cookbook but less excited about cooking, at least right now. In the end, I knew Nathan had meant it, he didn't need me to cook. He would be eating out with his father and a few colleagues and my food would end up in the refrigerator or, worst case, the trash. As far as he'd told me, his father wasn't even coming to our boat.

Not cooking could be my first very small step toward setting boundaries—taking care of myself rather than attempting to fix the possible unhappiness or angst of all the people around me. I could take a leisurely shower and even put on a little makeup for Miss Gloria's dinner. Instead of cooking, I wrote Nathan a little love note saying how much I was looking forward to seeing him later and really, really, really hoped the reunion with his father had gone well. I added hearts and lips and went to get dressed for dinner.

Chapter Five

Estelle knew no better way of saying that she cared about people than to ask if they were hungry.
—Fredrik Backman, *Anxious People*

Matt's Stock Island Kitchen and Bar was attached to the newish Perry Hotel right on the harbor. You could spend a lifetime in Key West and never see this restaurant, tucked away as it was off a side street. It would be hard to describe the drive out to the restaurant on Stock Island as scenic. We took the highway past the golf course, then turned right off the main drag. The route twisted through several streets lined with industrial buildings and homeowners' trailers before finally ending at the harbor. There was a reason the cost of living on this island was lower than in Key West.

The ladies chattered all the way out, perhaps wondering why I was a little quiet. But I determined that I wouldn't talk about finding the dead man until we had a glass of champagne in our hands. And maybe not even then. We parked near the harbor, enjoying the short stroll past a few houseboats sprinkled among party boats and yachts. A clutch of young women with very short shorts and even smaller tops passed us, giggling. One of them applied mascara while holding up her phone—using her makeup mirror app, I guessed.

The hostess showed us to a table out on the veranda overlooking the water.

"This is lovely," said Mrs. Dubisson with a big sigh of happiness. She smoothed over her lap the pink dress I'd seen her wear on other special occasions. "Thank goodness it's your birthday."

Miss Gloria beamed, radiating joy from every cell in her body. She too wore pink, a sweatshirt with a birthday cake outlined in sequins. She had insisted she didn't want a fuss made over her day, but now that I saw how much she was enjoying this outing, I was beginning to regret not planning a big party. A waitress appeared with a pitcher of icy water and four glasses.

"Anything to drink for you ladies besides water?"

"You betcha," said my mother. "We thought you'd never ask. We'd like a bottle of your very best champagne."

"Fifty dollars is our limit," added Miss Gloria, and we all laughed. "And bring the wine list while you're at it."

Once the waitress had filled the glasses with bubbly, the birthday had been thoroughly toasted, and white wine had been ordered for later, I couldn't help myself: the horror of the day began to sink into my being, heavier and heavier. Miss Gloria turned to me.

"I hate to hound you, but you seem a little bit gloomy. Are you worried about your father-in-law? Really, we could have postponed this if you thought it would be a problem. When you're as old as I am, you can celebrate a birthday any day."

I took her hand and squeezed gently, aware of her slender fingers and papery skin. "No way we were going to postpone celebrating you. As for my father-in-law, I'm super curious about him but not so much worried. Though I am worried about Nathan. He's very wound up about his dad's visit."

"Knowing him as I do, that's his natural state," Miss Gloria added, starting to laugh, but she cut that off when she saw my face. Nathan and I had lived with Miss Gloria while we were waiting for our houseboat renovations to be finished, so she knew him intimately—and had teasing rights, too. And she was correct: Nathan's baseline state was tightly wound. His work at the police department was filled with difficult challenges—homeless folks, drunken tourists, reckless motorists. Public opinion of police departments had suffered over the past few years as well, and that bothered him. He thought they could do better, at least in Key West. Finally, he worried constantly about how to keep my mother and Miss Gloria and me safe. His estranged father's visit was the icing on his cake.

"Anyway, in-law problems are the least of it," I said. Then I told them about the outing with Eric and finding the deceased GG Garcia.

Miss Gloria literally gasped. "Garcia? I thought he was invincible. I knew he was well hated, but I never thought someone would have the nerve to actually kill him off."

My mother reached across the table and laced my fingers with hers. "This sounds so distressing for you."

I did not want to ruin the party by starting to cry. "It wasn't great, but it was a lot worse for Mr. Garcia." We all broke into uncomfortable laughter.

"I catered GG and Andi's anniversary party about a month ago," my mother said. "Thirty years they were together. I guess she must have loved him, even if others in town found him to be an opinionated bully. In some ways, thirty years seems like a long time to me. Hayley's father and I sure didn't get there." She shook off an expression of regret. "Anyway, the party was lovely—we set up in the backyard on their estate, with fairy lights and candles everywhere and the dreamiest band. The liquor flowed, the food was amazing, and people were dancing . . . She must be so sad. And his mother—oh my gosh, he was her only child, and she will be devastated. Who would have imagined her son would go before she did? It's so awful to think their next party will be a funeral reception."

Who else but a caterer would think of the aftermath of a death in those terms? "How do you know these people?" I asked. I'd been on the island a few years longer than she had, and they certainly weren't in my circle of friends.

"Charitable events," she said. "My bread and butter. I did a southern lunch at the Woman's Club about six months back—hot biscuits, creamy chicken salad, sweet tea, the whole works. Andi couldn't stop raving. The person doing her anniversary party food left town suddenly, and I was able to fill in. She's called me several times since then to save dates for future parties. She knows I can pivot on a dime, and that's a very good quality in a caterer."

"One of many," I said with a wide grin. "Your food also tastes amazing and doesn't cost a bloody fortune."

My mother's new husband, Sam, had helped her when she was starting out in this business. She wanted everything perfect and had gotten carried away by sourcing exotic and top-quality ingredients. But she couldn't charge enough to cover her expenses, and that caused her business to sink into the red ink.

"What about her husband GG? Did he love your food as well?" I asked.

"He never said much more than hello," Mom told us. "I got the sense he left that sort of thing to her because he didn't really care about food."

"Did you notice any particular tension between them?" I asked.

"You know how it is when you're working an event—you don't have much time to be studying people." She paused for a minute to think. "They didn't spend a lot of time together at the party. But there were a lot of guests—important Key West luminaries as well as lots of family and friends—and I imagine they felt as though their first obligation was to act the host and hostess. There was a champagne toast, and he called her . . ." She paused again and crinkled her nose. "I'll have to remember. I did think the way he described her and their marriage to be a little odd, maybe bordering on mean-spirited. Sam mentioned it later too."

The waitress appeared with our dinners, platters of fried chicken for me and Mrs. Dubisson, the fish of the day with cornbread mash for Miss Gloria, and a lovely steak with smashed potatoes and roasted asparagus for my mother. Finally, she delivered a big bowl of salty, delicious-looking fries. I opened my mouth to tell her we hadn't ordered these.

"For the table," she said, with a wink, "as a gift from that man over there."

She pointed across the open patio to the table nearest the bar. David Sloan, a man I'd met when covering a key lime pie contest, gave a little wave. "He said to tell you to stop by on your way out." She leaned in a little closer. "I think he's curious about the murder."

I dropped my head into my hands, a little shocked at how quickly that news had spread through town. Plus, my reputation for amateur sleuthing—aka pure nosiness—was going to be hard to shed. The waitress was still standing there, looking as if she hoped I'd talk more about finding a dead man. Instead, I thanked her, waved a hand at David Sloan's table, and then focused on tucking into dinner.

"I've heard of a guy sending over drinks to the ladies," said Miss Gloria. Her gaze had followed my hand and now lingered on David Sloan. "But salty bacon fries are a first. And that trend is not half-bad, in my book."

We spent a few minutes savoring the food in near silence, and then I jotted down comments from my tablemates' opinions about their meals. I worked my way slowly through the plate of fried chicken and fries in front of me. As the waitress had warned when I ordered, this was an entire half chicken and a huge plate of French fries, never mind the extra potatoes David Sloane had sent to the table. But honestly, after the day I'd had, I felt as though I deserved every greasy, crispy, salty bite.

"What are you going to do about it?" asked Miss Gloria.

"Do about what?" I asked. "The chicken? I can't possibly eat it all, so I'll ask for a to-go box."

"No, don't be silly. I meant figuring out who killed that poor man," said Miss Gloria, patting her lips with her napkin. "You were in the perfect position to see and hear things that no one else could have. I bet they would really appreciate your input."

"Nothing," I said, setting my cutlery on the plate to emphasize the point. "I'm going to do nothing. The case belongs to the sheriff's department. They interviewed me thoroughly. They called the medical examiner. They had the site cordoned off. And they have my contact information if they think of more questions. They did everything right, and I'm pretty sure they would hate me butting in even more than the Key West Police Department would."

The ladies laughed. My mother said, "I think you're right about that. Men in uniforms don't appreciate being told what they're doing wrong or how a woman thinks they could improve it. Except for Sam, of course; he takes constructive criticism like a champ when he's wearing an apron." Sam had retired from his business in New Jersey, married my mother, and fallen happily into the job of sous-chef for her catering company.

"Sam's an anomaly. He's pretty much perfect, and I don't think you'll ever find fault with him or lose that honeymoon glow. But in fact," I said, "in this case, the officer in charge was a woman. A very competent and fierce woman."

"So interesting," said my mother. "I wonder how she chose that line of work and how she got to be in that kind of powerful post."

"I wasn't really in a position to be asking anything about that," I said with a grin. "Maybe next time, if there has to be a next time."

We finished up dinner by singing "Happy Birthday" to Miss Gloria and sharing a piece of key lime pie and a caramel cookie tart with bacon maple ice cream. I had offered to make a birthday cake, with candles and presents and streamers, but she'd demurred. "I'm very old," she'd told me. "I've had a lot of parties, and dinner for four is just the ticket this time."

My mother and I picked up the check and, after paying, stopped to chat with David Sloan on the way out. He had an empty martini glass in front of him along with a half-eaten slice of key lime pie. He laughed as he saw my gaze land on the dessert. He was known in the Florida Keys as a key lime pie aficionado, very proud of his own recipe. I wouldn't have expected him to be ordering that pie while dining out.

"I know, coals to Newcastle, right?"

"Thank you for the extra bacon fries," I said, "though my waistline does not thank you."

"They say the way to a woman's heart is through potatoes," he said, grinning at my mother. "One chef to another, haven't you found that to be so?"

She laughed in agreement. "The customers often tell me they and their friends are on a diet, so don't make a lot of carbs. I've learned to pay no attention to that, because those are the first empty bowls in a buffet."

"So," he said, glancing at me, "another body, eh? Coconut telegraph tells me it was GG Garcia." His eyebrows peaked as if to ask for my confirmation.

"Unfortunately, yes. And lest you think I go out looking for murder, this time it was a complete fluke. I was at the beach, and Nathan's dog started digging . . ." I left off there, thinking it prudent to not describe the gory details. I'd be better off leaving that to the authorities.

"Have they said anything about who killed him or why?"

"If they know anything, they are definitely not sharing it with me," I said. But then I couldn't help adding, "Why, have you heard something?"

"I'd heard he was making plans to develop Geiger Key. Which, as you know, is one of the few open spaces between Key West and Marathon. Buildable, anyway, and reasonably close to Key West. He's been involved in lots of fighting over beach rights and eminent domain and was positioning himself to knock down the trailers in the vicinity."

"Eminent domain?" my mother asked. "Isn't that where the state or county takes over a piece of property for what's considered necessary government needs? How could that possibly apply to a private party and Geiger Key?"

David Sloan shrugged, lifting his shoulders easily to show his disdain for government process. "Sometimes our leadership skips over what's best for the people and actually legal and focuses on what's good for their wallets."

Which struck me as needlessly pessimistic but probably not something he'd be talked out of easily. "Thanks again for the extra fries," I said, placing my hand on my mother's back. "We better get our elderly ladies back home."

"Don't let them hear you call them old," she said, winking at me. "Nice to see you, Mr. Sloan. Let me know when you're ready to take on another bartending gig."

Once we were walking along the dock toward the car, she asked, "What was all that about? Did he have some special connection to Garcia, or is he simply nosy?"

"I have no idea," I said.

My mother dropped the three of us back off at Houseboat Row with my promises to let her know if she'd get the opportunity to meet Nathan's father and tell her if I heard any more about the demise of GG Garcia. I walked each of the ladies to her houseboat—Mrs. Dubisson's a square, bright-blue rig at the far end of the dock, Miss Gloria's a small, comfortable yellow floating home right next door to me. Then I returned to my own residence to walk the dog and wait for Nathan.

I wrote up some notes about the dinner at Matt's while I waited. I'd learned over the last few years of being a food critic that it was best to write the reviews, at least in draft form, as close to the dinner as possible. I ate enough meals out that sometimes details did tend to run together.

After drafting an introduction about the differences between Stock Island and Key West and their restaurants, I emphasized the high points of the meal: the setting, the cheerful waitstaff, the solid dinner choices. Ziggy began to woof with excitement, and I knew Nathan had arrived. I got up from my desk and hurried out to the deck to throw my arms around him, grateful for his strength and warmth. "Boy, am I glad to see you. It's been quite a day. How is your father? How did it feel to see him again?"

"Fine." For a minute my husband was silent, hugging me and resting his chin on my head. "He asked if you'd be willing to have lunch with him. Alone." He let go of me and took a step back. He had a funny look on his face that I'd never seen. Sort of guilty, sort of pleading, and a little bit annoyed.

What could I say but yes? "Of course I'll take him to lunch. Where should I take him? What does he like to eat?"

Nathan groaned. "He doesn't eat fish, he loathes tapas, he objects on principle to anything modern or chichi. And he doesn't want to share his plate with anyone except his dog.

Although his dog died years ago. He likes southern food, and he likes it fried until it's certainly dead. And he hates most of all when servers are too friendly or rush him through a meal." He pressed his palm to his forehead. "And PS, you're going to think I'm joking, but I'm not. Don't sweep the crumbs away from his place at the table—it makes him feel like you think he's messy. And don't refill his water glass when it's half-empty. He wasn't done with that water!"

This description pushed me into fits of giggling because it ruled out so many options. Obviously, I wasn't going to take him to the Oasis, with its delicious falafel wraps and fried eggplant salad and other Middle Eastern favorites. And I wouldn't take him to Santiago's Bodega with its tapas plates for the table. And I wouldn't take him to 7 Fish or any of the other great seafood restaurants on the island. Definitely not to the few restaurants on our island with pretensions toward fine dining.

"How about Firefly?" I asked. "He can order a fried chicken sandwich or a cheeseburger. And I definitely won't ask him for a bite. The upstairs porch is quite private, and no one's going to rush him out of there. Although honestly, I can't think of what we could say to each other over a long lunch. Have you figured out why he's here?"

Nathan looked a little hurt.

I hurried to try to fix that. "I mean besides coming to see you, and maybe the tiniest bit of curiosity about your new wife. And by the way, how is the conference going?"

"There is no conference." Nathan barely smiled. "I had gotten the idea he'd retired, but he's not retired at all. Turns out my information about him was completely out-of-date. He's here to conduct the practice session for our department's three-year accreditation."

Now I was truly confused. "How can a Georgia police officer investigate the Key West Police Department?"

Nathan sighed, and I could see the shadows under his eyes as he turned his head toward the streetlight on our dock. "He lives in Tallahassee now. And it's not an investigation. His job is to study over two hundred policies and make sure we're following them. If he finds issues, he shares them with us so we can correct them before the official accreditation. Today he met with Chief Brandenberg and interviewed a lot of our staff. Apparently, they are finding him to be something of a cold fish, which I could have told them in advance. I'll tell you that I'm not looking forward to his time on our island. It was tough when my mother came, but this," he said, shaking his head slowly, "this will be worse. The pits."

Honestly, that sounded awkward: evaluating your own son's department. How had he been chosen for this job? But it seemed like a bad idea to doubt my father-in-law before I'd even met him. And Nathan was clearly ready to be finished with this conversation, even though I was bursting with questions about his father. Was anyone in the family in touch with him? Did he talk with my mother-in-law, Helen, his ex-wife? I doubted that Vera had much to do with him.

"Are you okay?" he asked, hugging me. "You had a rough day. Want to talk about it?"

"Not really, I think I've told you everything I know."

We were both exhausted and fell into bed shortly afterward. I was a little bit tipsy as well and counted on going right off to sleep. But there was too much crammed into my poor brain for me to relax. My mind kept circling the image of that sandy body—the lips, the nose, the fingers.

On top of all that, now I was nervous about meeting Nathan's father, feeling a little sad about what kind of man he might be. I was pretty sure I was beginning to understand why my husband simply didn't care about food the way I did. Some significant part of how a person turned out in the foodie realm had to do with the way they were raised, I thought. I'd already met his mother several times, and as he'd warned me, she simply didn't care that much about eating. She knew she needed to eat, and she did, but to make a fuss over it? Not going to happen. It sounded like his father was not too different and possibly worse. Why was the man's relationship to food so important to me? Because I felt it was a window into his relationships with the rest of the world, including with Nathan and me.

Chapter Six

What Keats could have done with the lovely names of our tropical fruits . . . papaya and guava, sapodilla and sugar-apple, persimmon and pomegranate, mango, tamarind, carissa . . . But Keats is long gone, and so we must say what you can do with them . . . not the lovely names, but the fruits themselves, and their accompaniments.

—*The Key West Cookbook* by the Members of the Key West Woman's Club, 1949

Nathan had risen ahead of me, allowing me to sleep an extra forty-five minutes. He'd left a sweet note on the kitchen table saying the pets had been fed and Ziggy walked, and he so appreciated me having lunch with his father. He would confirm with him the reservation at Firefly at twelve thirty, but he assumed that would be fine. He also reminded me he would not be home for dinner, as he was again entertaining his father with the top brass at the police department. "I'll make it up to you, I'll swear. I would a million times more prefer to be eating at home with you." Followed by an *xox*, which was positively effusive for Nathan.

Checking my phone, I saw I had also received a text message from an unknown number. Only a few words in, I figured out that it belonged to the bird watcher I'd met on the beach yesterday, Davis Jager. The number I'd deleted yesterday.

Hoping you might meet me at the Geiger Key Fish Camp tonight at happy hour. I feel like we bonded over our shared traumatic event. And I have a few things to talk over with you. No one else will understand the shock. And I apologize if I seemed glib yesterday, sometimes a tragedy has that effect on me.

My first reaction was *absolutely not.* I had absolutely not bonded with him and couldn't imagine what gave him that impression. I didn't like him having my phone number.

Sorry, no, I texted back.

They are trying to frame me. I know you're good at solving puzzles, everyone says so. I hoped you'd be willing to help.

Why would I agree to help a man I didn't know and hadn't really liked? I texted my regrets. Another text came in.

David Sloan suggested I ask. We can sit right at the bar with dozens of witnesses. Ask David, he'll tell you I'm harmless. Anyway, I'll be there in case you change your mind.

I texted David Sloan as he'd suggested.

What's up with Davis Jager?

He replied quickly. *He's not a bad guy, but a little awkward. Sounds like he's being railroaded by the sheriff's department. I told him you were good at that stuff.*

We texted back and forth a few more times, with David Sloan insisting that Jager wasn't capable of murder, and gradually, my definite no morphed to a maybe. I wouldn't spend an evening drinking with Jager, but I could have one drink with him and then move to a table by myself to enjoy a plate of shrimp tacos or fish and chips. I could include that meal in my "off the rock eateries" article, due at the end of the week. As one of my bosses, Wally aka His Grumpiness, had often told me, one restaurant review did not make a roundup.

Maybe this dude really did have some information about the murder. Meanwhile, I could get to Boca Chica Beach early and try to remember details of what I might not have noticed leading up to Ziggy finding Mr. Garcia's body. I'd heard it said that Chinese people believed that if you saved a life, you were responsible for that life forever. I had a similar feeling about finding a body: my heart and mind would not be able to rest until I understood what had happened.

I took my laptop out to the deck with a cup of coffee topped with steamed milk and sat down to work. I was well into choosing the words to best describe our meals last night when my mother called.

"Good morning; I won't even ask if you're busy. But I have a request. My premonition was right. GG Garcia's wife, Andi, wants me to cater a memorial service reception at the Woman's Club on Friday. Any chance you could help me prepare Thursday and serve on Friday? This came up suddenly, and wouldn't you believe it, my most reliable worker is off the island for a week. I know Nathan's father is here and you have a ton of work to do, so I will understand if you can't fit us in."

But her assurances aside, I knew she wouldn't have asked me if she hadn't been pressed for help. And she probably knew my curiosity would get the better of any reservations. Finally, I doubted I'd be spending much time escorting Nathan's father around our island. He wasn't here to see the sights. "Yes, I can help both days. Would half the day be enough? I have to get some articles written too."

"Anything is great! You're a lifesaver. I'll ask Miss Gloria to help with serving, but I wasn't sure she'd be up for cooking."

I had to laugh there. The one and only dish she'd made for me involved tuna fish from a can. And spaghetti. And a can of some kind of gloppy soup.

"What are you working on today?" Mom asked.

"Mostly trying to manage my nervousness about meeting Nathan's dad," I admitted. "We have a lunch date at twelve thirty."

"Won't it be interesting to meet him, though?" my mother asked. "You ended up loving Nathan's sister, and even his mom."

This was all true. Nathan's mother, Helen, had visited unexpectedly last Christmas. She was tall and beautiful and emotionally self-contained, and she scared me half to death. But we did end up bonding over a murder and had developed a good relationship since then. Nathan's sister had been much easier to warm up to. "This is different," I said. "Nobody's giving me any warm-and-fuzzies about this guy."

My mother clucked sympathetically. "You know, my father-in-law, your grandfather Snow, was also a challenge. I don't think he ever really approved of me. Why would he? He never wanted his son to marry a girl who dropped out of college because she was pregnant. I was over-the-moon happy to be pregnant with you and even your father was thrilled, once he recovered from the shock. But his parents didn't see how this choice could do anything but hold him back on his best life path."

"I guess that would be hard for parents to swallow." I was trying to imagine how my own parents might have reacted to me coming home with that kind of news. Neither of them had been thrilled when I followed Chad Lutz to Key West on a whim. That had all worked out in the end, but there had been some painful moments along the way. Along with plenty of opportunities for a parent to tell their kid *I told you so*. Happily, they'd largely abstained from that.

"They were wrong, of course, about whether a child would ruin our lives. Even if they were maybe right about the two of us being too young to decide to be together. But you have always been a joy, Hayley; you were the precious gift that keeps on giving. I have not one whisker of regret."

"I know, Mom. You've told me that before, and I believe you. Thank you for bringing me into the world. Now, back to business. What kind of food are we making for the funeral reception?" I asked.

Sometimes mourners were very specific about what they wanted served. Occasionally they chose something the deceased would have enjoyed, though that seemed a little cruel, since death robbed a person of his or her appetite. Other mourners didn't care a bit about the menu because they were too sick with grief to think about food, or maybe they'd had a lousy relationship with the deceased and simply wanted everything over and done. In either case, most people understood that visitors paying their respects at a reception expected to be fed.

"She wants something old-fashioned," my mother said, "and lots of finger foods, so it's easy to stand and eat. Basically, the menu should blend in with the ethos of the Woman's Club. Nothing in the realm of fine dining."

"So, something bland like Nathan's father might eat?" I asked, adding a laugh. "I borrowed a cookbook from the library that was published by the women of that club in the 1940s. I'll look through it and see if there's anything we might want to use."

"You're the best," my mom said. "Also remember, you're the best wife Nathan could possibly have chosen. If Mr. Bransford refuses to see that, it's only his loss."

"Thanks. I'll let you know how it goes."

I hung up, wondering whether my paternal grandparents had ever truly welcomed me. Had they ever gotten over believing that my father had made the worst mistake of his life? That question made me wonder again why Nathan's parents had not stayed together. Was it really the crisis with Vera? Or had that event wedged open a small crack that already lay between them and turned it into a chasm? Or had the divorce been one parent's fault more than the other? Nathan's mother ran cool, but we'd begun to feel close. Did Nathan's dad have a personality flaw that did not allow him to grow into a warm person?

I supposed I would get a better idea of the answers soon. I had the sneaking feeling that there was more to our lunch than I understood just yet. Way more. Maybe he wanted to meet with me separately in order to pump me for information about Nathan's sister, Vera. Maybe I'd be able to offer him a bridge back into that relationship, but it wouldn't be simple. They'd been estranged for a good ten years, and my small, uninformed olive branches would be unlikely to change that.

To try to keep my nerves in check while waiting the last few minutes before lunch, I began to leaf through the Woman's Club cookbook. It was amazing how much tastes had changed over the years. For one thing, many of the instructions required a meat grinder, which most modern kitchens did not have. The recipes called for lots of unusual ingredients like pawpaws, crawdads, green turtles, old sour, papaya. I'd read a book recently about life in Key West in the seventies. It was wild and free and unspoiled, according to the authors. Everyone thought their own era was the best and that Key West had changed for the worse since then. Maybe the women who'd come of age in the forties felt the same about their time.

But didn't the dark current of human nature snake through every decade?

Chapter Seven

This is why the denouement of Ratatouille *has never quite hit me. I just cannot believe anyone, even a rat genius, could wow with an artful pile of zucchini.*

—Jaya Saxena,
"I Nearly Set My House on Fire Trying to Make the Lightning Mushroom From 'Ratatouille,'"
Eater, September 27, 2021

At eleven forty-five, I hopped on my scooter and headed down Truman Avenue toward Petronia Street. My heart felt as though it was beating so hard that bystanders could see it through my shirt. *Baboom, baboom, baboom.* I had been nervous meeting Nathan's mother for sure. Miss Gloria had reminded me of that this morning when she spotted me pacing up and down the dock, trying to tamp down my nerves. But at least for that visit, I had been able to channel my anxiety into figuring out what to cook and what sights to show her. In the end, with Helen's able assistance, we'd ended up solving a crime. This time, there had been no word about hosting

Mr. Bransford, either at our houseboat or at my mother's home. I had to manage the jitters inside my own head. My sister-in-law Vera's text earlier today had not helped one bit.

Heard you're expecting a courtesy visit from the paterfamilias.

I'd texted her back, asking what she thought was behind the sudden visit. Did her father feel guilty? Jealous that his ex-wife Helen had met and bonded with me and he'd not even come to meet me? What I didn't dare ask was who had told her. Probably Nathan, but maybe their mother?

I wouldn't try to poke too hard into his psyche, it's an abyss, a black hole, and ever so frightening down there! Don't take anything personally. He's a block of ice. Wait no, that's not quite it because ice melts eventually and he does not.

I arrived at Firefly way too early to be seated for our lunch reservation, so I parked the scooter in the rack outside the restaurant and walked the length of Petronia Street past Santiago's Bodega, another favorite restaurant in town, to the Truman Waterfront. The park was busy this morning with joggers, dog walkers, sunbathers, and a gaggle of shrieking children enjoying the water feature. Lots of locals had complained about the city's budget and plans for this property, but it had turned out to be a wonderful, well-used green space overlooking the Navy's harbor. This kind of relaxing space was hard to find on our little island. At 12:20, I returned to the restaurant and checked in with the hostess.

"I have a reservation for two upstairs on the porch? Hayley Snow."

She squinted, glanced at the iPad on the hostess station, and looked back up at me. "Oh, the food critic for *Key Zest*. Are you here to critique our lunch offerings?"

"No, a family outing this time." My smile felt thin and unconvincing. Before I'd landed my job, I'd read memoirs by Frank Bruni and Ruth Reichl, both food critics for the *New York Times*. They'd gone to great lengths to disguise their identities while working (aka eating out). They'd used costumes and elaborate fake names, all in the name of maintaining anonymity. I didn't love being recognized, because that placed extra pressure on the words I chose to describe the restaurant and its food. Those words needed to be fair but honest—nothing should change my opinions other than the taste and presentation of the food. On the other hand, this town was small enough that it had become difficult to hide.

She led me up a set of steep wooden stairs, through a small dining area, and out to the porch. I followed her to a table at the far side of the porch overlooking the street. A rat's nest of wires had been strung from the buildings on the other side to the pole next to the restaurant. Unfortunately, the unpaved lot full of cars across the way looked less than inviting. I decided to take the brown rattan chair facing the street just in case Nathan's father objected to urban blight. Which wasn't actually a fair description of what was happening here. The prices of real estate on this island had continued to shoot up, which meant many homes were being bought out, knocked down, and replaced with fancier replicas of old-time conch houses. This meant that the fancy new residences sometimes had dilapidated neighbors. Worst of all, longtime residents were often displaced from their homes.

A waitress came by to deliver mason jars filled with water and ice, setting them on the gray Formica table. Exactly at twelve thirty, the hostess reappeared with a tall man following her. He had the bearing of a military person: squared shoulders, clenched jaw, all in all physically intimidating. As he strode across the room behind the young woman, I could imagine what my husband would look like twenty or twenty-five years from now. Gray at the temples, lines at his eyes and lips, but an upright carriage and strong muscles. Like my Nathan, this was not a man who would let himself go. I tried to imagine him married to Helen, Nathan's mother. Physically, they would have been a stunning couple. Emotionally, from what I knew of my mother-in-law, maybe not.

"Hayley," he said, once they got to our table, "finally I get to meet the young woman who stole my son's heart."

"I like to think I won it rather than stealing it." I stood up and reached out my hand to shake his, wanting to avoid having an awkward hug or kiss attempt rebuffed.

He clasped it hard in both of his and gestured at my chair. "Please, take a seat." He sat at the same time and leaned back to study me. "You're not a whole lot like the other one."

I groaned inwardly. The "other one" was Nathan's first wife, Trudy, and it had taken me a while to unravel my complex about being his second choice. Had he brought her up to put me off balance? If so, his strategy was working.

"In this family, except for Vera," he continued, "we are not so good at selecting a spouse for the long haul. By all reports, Nathan learned his lesson this time."

"I hope so," I said, attempting to sound spritely and confident and wondering who would have given him reports. "I believe we're a good match. I do love him very much."

The waitress came to the table to take our lunch orders—a southern-fried chicken sandwich for him, hold the mustard and the barbecue sauce and the pickles, and a fried green tomato sandwich for me. I grinned at the waitress. "I'll take the pickles from his sandwich too." I added orders for pimento cheese and fried okra. Nathan's father's eyes widened.

"I can never order only one thing when I visit a restaurant," I explained. "I never know what I might want to use later for my restaurant review column. What if I ordered the wrong thing and there was something more delicious on the menu? As for avoiding weight gain, the trick is to taste everything but not feel obligated to finish anything. Anyway, Miss Gloria—that's my neighbor and good friend—always loves leftovers."

He nodded as if trying to absorb my rush of explanatory words, though his eyes had begun to look a bit glazed. "I understand that you've solved a few mysteries."

He didn't make actual air quotes with his fingers, but I could hear them in his voice.

"I did not realize you had police training."

It felt like he was testing me, but I wouldn't rise to his bait. I'd seen the woman sheriff's deputy brush off an annoying question, and I could do that too.

"No training," I said, "but I pay attention to people. People say I'm a good listener. And since I care about people in pain, I think about them and the problems they're facing. Sometimes the answers come clear."

"Nathan says you're very curious."

That felt like a challenge. "Are you sure he didn't say nosy?"

Nathan's father started to laugh, and I grinned right back. The waitress returned with our plates and wished us bon appétit. I loaded a big spoonful of the pimento cheese and another of okra on my plate. "Please feel free to try either of these."

He peeled off the top layer of his bun and looked with suspicion at the contents of the sandwich. Most of the territory underneath the bread was taken up by an enormous and beautifully browned piece of fried chicken that glistened with a sprinkle of salt. There was one slice of tomato and several lettuce leaves, which he removed from the sandwich and placed on his napkin. Then he picked up his knife and scraped the top of the bun, although it looked bare of any unwanted accoutrements to me. He noticed me watching.

"People think I'm strange and fussy, but I like to taste exactly the food I ordered. I don't want any chef's special secret sauce or secret attempts to force vegetables into my diet. I got enough of that during my years with Helen." He grinned.

My mother-in-law, his ex. It was hard to imagine her trying to force anything into this tree trunk of a man.

He shook his head, closed the sandwich up, and we began to eat. When he finished his lunch, he placed both of his utensils on the plate, moved the offending vegetables back, wiped his mouth with his napkin, and sat back in his chair.

"You might be wondering why I have called you here today." Then he chuckled, a graceless attempt at levity.

"Well," I said, thinking he was possibly the most awkward man I'd ever met, "I am curious. But I thought maybe you simply wanted the two of us to have a chance to get to know one another. Since Nathan is your son and I am his wife, that seemed logical to me."

"Correct," he said. "I understand that you met our Vera. How did she seem, in your view?"

This was beginning to make sense. It would add up that he was worried about his daughter but unable to ask her directly how she was doing and unable to ask much of his ex-wife. Plus, it appeared that an emotionally deep conversation would be difficult for him and Nathan. Heck, my husband hadn't even known his dad had moved to a new state and taken a new job. Would I be breaking Vera's confidence to give a report? I thought I could probably say enough to reassure her father without telling her secrets.

"I think she's doing well," I said, but I heard my words go up into a question mark. "When we were visiting her in Scotland, it was the anniversary of her kidnapping, and that brought back some unpleasant feelings. But she was able to begin to talk about that with her husband, who is a dear man, and even a little with us. She loves Scotland; she and William have a very nice relationship, from what I could tell. In addition, she has a few good friends, and she loves her work. All in all, positive."

The expression on his face was impassive. I had no idea what he was thinking—did he think I was fibbing? How did he feel about what I'd told him? How did he feel about the fact that his relationship with his daughter had virtually ended?

"I imagine that you must miss her. And surely she misses you as well."

The waitress stopped by our table to ask about dessert, and I looked inquiringly at Nathan's father. "The lime cake in a pool of raspberry coulis is supposed to be particularly good," I said. "But of course, key lime pie is iconic on this island."

He shook his head and looked at the waitress without consulting me directly. "We'll take the check, please. I'll take the check." He patted the table next to his place. "It's my treat," he said, as I opened my mouth to say I was planning to pay. "I insist. It's not so often that a man gets to meet his daughter-in-law for the first time."

Chapter Eight

When life lands a hammer blow in your face, do your best to respond to the hammer as if it had been a cream pie.
—Dean Koontz

I left the restaurant and drove downtown, feeling as though I needed to make an appearance in the office. Wally and Palamina were accustomed to my independent ways, as my job required a lot of "man on the street" activity. But it was good to show up and look busy once in a while and find out what the rest of the team was working on.

Danielle, the administrative assistant for *Key Zest*, was at her desk in the small vestibule.

"Hayley," she said, "I haven't seen you in ages. Is everything okay?"

This made me glad I'd made the decision to drop by. "Just busy," I said. "Nathan's father is in town on police business, and I've come from having lunch with him."

"My goodness, they don't give you much notice in that family when they're intending to visit. Is he staying with you?"

"Not a chance; he's not the kind of guy to couch surf. He's working on certification at the police department, and I think they're putting him up at the Casa Marina."

She shook her hand and ran her fingers through her blonde hair. "Very chichi."

I noticed the sparkle on her ring finger. "Do you have something you need to tell me?"

She leapt up out of her chair and came over to hug me. "I thought you'd never notice. I'm engaged. To a cop, no less!"

I hugged her back and gave her a big smooch on the cheek. "You didn't learn a darn thing from my experience, did you?"

"Nothing," she said, giggling, holding her hand out for me to inspect the ring.

"It's gorgeous, and you look radiant, and soon we must have drinks so I can hear every detail of how it happened and your plans for the wedding. But now I better get to work." I tipped my head at the office that our bosses shared. My space was beyond them, ten feet or so down the hall, very tiny but cozy and all mine. "I don't want to end up in the doghouse."

Palamina called out to me as I walked by. "Do you have time to check in with us for a few minutes?"

"Sure," I said. "Let me put my stuff down, and I'll be right there." I deposited my backpack on the desk, noticing a stack of messages that Danielle had taken and dropped in my in-box. She almost always remembered to text me as well as write out hard copies. I sorted through them quickly to be sure nothing super important had slipped through the cracks. One of them was from Davis Jager.

Confirming that I will be at happy hour tonight. The Fish Camp.

It seemed odd—and pushy and a little bit creepy—that he'd called my workplace to leave a message after already messaging my phone. He was desperate, obviously. I could only imagine Danielle bugging her eyes as she took his words down. She'd be curious for sure.

I tapped on my bosses' door and went in, carrying my usual folding chair to open alongside Wally's desk. Their space was just big enough for two desks and two chairs but crowded past cozy with a third. We had to work not to bump knees. "How is everyone?" I asked. "Sorry I haven't been around much—I've been doing a ton of research."

"What do you have planned for the restaurant roundup next week?" Wally asked. He crossed his arms over his chest with a stern face, as though he was suspecting I had nothing.

I took a deep breath, channeling my mother, Danielle, Miss Gloria, anyone with a chipper attitude whose ideas always sounded great.

"I had a brainstorm, and I think you'll like it. The piece would be called something like 'Eating Off the Rock.' I feel like I've plowed the ground around the restaurants here in Key West quite thoroughly, and everyone might like a change."

"Sounds intriguing. What kinds of places do you have in mind?" Palamina asked.

"Definitely I will do Matt's Stock Island Kitchen and also the Fish Camp at Geiger Key. I think people will enjoy hearing about that because it's funky and gives them the illusion that they discovered the keys long before everyone else, like the hippies who stumbled down here in the seventies and eighties. Plus, the food is fantastic."

"You'll need more than two." Wally again.

"For sure," I said. "Maybe Roostica, Hogfish, El Siboney, or the yacht club on Stock Island if I have time."

"You realize that fifty percent of the places you mentioned are owned by the same corporation," Wally said.

I paused, thinking over how to respond to that. Did he think I was a foodie fraud? Even if the same people owned several restaurants, each had a different chef at the helm. And a different physical vibe. Of course I knew that. But why try to argue with a grump?

"I do realize," I said, keeping my voice as sweet as simple syrup. "That's always an issue on this island, but we work around it. For a second piece, I'd love to do an article about old-fashioned food that reflects our island's history. I found a cookbook that was published by the Woman's Club in the late forties, and it has some amazing recipes. Those, along with food that we don't see much anymore, tie us to our Key West history. My mother and I are going to cook for an event with that cookbook later this week, maybe we could run a recipe or two with photos?"

Even Wally was nodding a little bit by the time I finished, and Palamina positively glowed.

"That sounds terrific," she said. "Our lead article will be an interview with Tom Hambright, the historian at the library, so this dovetails perfectly. Same deadline okay, Monday?"

That would be pushing things, but I could do it if I kept grinding and didn't try to reinvent the wheel with fancy reviews. Sure. Ridiculous amount of work, but sure.

Wally narrowed his eyes a little. "Now what about this body on Geiger Key? Unbelievable that you've been involved with another murder case."

I sat back in the folding chair, crossing *my* arms over my chest. It seemed like most everything he'd said to me lately was critical. I realized that might be why I spent less time at the office than I used to. Wally's aura was not much fun. A couple years ago, we'd broken up—though we'd hardly had much time together and never had been a great match. Almost zero chemistry, I'd finally had to admit. Then he'd watched me fall madly head over heels for Nathan, followed by our unscripted storybook wedding. And finally, his mom had died of cancer. Understanding all this, I usually tried to overlook his grumpiness and mixed feelings about me. I forced a smile.

"You can only pin this one on Nathan's dog, Ziggy. Eric and I drove out there yesterday for a picnic on the beach. I needed a break, and the dogs needed some fun. Ziggy was the culprit who discovered the body. If he hadn't been so excited about digging, I'd have passed the site right by and that guy still might be out there."

"Did you recognize the man right away?" Palamina asked.

"There were only bits and pieces of him showing," I said, grimacing as the memory of those bits hit my gut. "Because of the storm the night before, a lot of sand had been blown over the body."

"I'm sure Nathan has already warned you to stay out of police business," Wally said. "Even though you discovered the body and called it in."

"He has," I said in a neutral voice, even though Wally's scolding was totally annoying. "He didn't need to say it. Since the deceased was found outside the limits of Key West, it's not even his jurisdiction. And certainly not mine." I stood up, flashed a thin smile, and folded the chair. "I'll keep you posted if there are any problems; otherwise, expect the articles by Monday. Nathan's father is in town, so that's newsworthy too, right?"

I left their office and marched down to my nook to gather up my stuff. Why the heck had I felt it necessary to announce that Nathan's father was here? Somehow I had to let Wally know I had a life and a husband, no matter whether he resented it or envied it or not. Pathetic, but that's what our relationship had been reduced to.

Danielle stopped me on my way out. "Couldn't help overhearing all that. Wally is such a sourpuss these days," she whispered. "It's not only you. I think he's having a midlife crisis, and I wouldn't be surprised if he ends up leaving."

"Leaving *Key Zest*?" The magazine was his baby—he'd started it from nothing. I'd come on early, back in the days when we all wore matching yellow shirts dotted with palm trees. The shirt was exactly the wrong color for my pale skin and auburn hair, but I'd loved wearing the uniform that proclaimed I was part of the team. Next, Palamina had come on board, and the two of them had built the magazine into an online force that both locals and visitors depended on.

"I suspect he's considering leaving Key West too," she said. "He's not happy here anymore, so it might be for the best. If you want, I'll ask my sweetheart what he's hearing about the murder. I know Nathan is busy and also not the most communicative husband ever when it comes to top-secret police stuff. I have ways of getting information from my guy." She grinned mischievously and flashed her diamond.

"Sure, thanks. Keep me posted." I blew her a kiss and clattered down the stairs.

Chapter Nine

The sensory overload in this room made him feel suddenly ill, as if he'd overdosed on sugar, and besides, they shouldn't be having this conversation in front of a witness.
—Ann Cleeves, *The Long Call*

Back home on our boat, I spent an hour studying the recipes and notes in the Key West Woman's Club cookbook, searching for the angle I'd use in my article. Rather than being typeset, everything in the book had been written out in longhand and illustrated with drawings that ranged from stick figures to folk art. Then the pages had been copied and spiral-bound. I noticed that a good half of the women who had contributed recipes identified themselves only by their husbands' names: Mrs. Carl Johnson, Mrs. William R. Warren, Mrs. Gerald Garcia, Mrs. Cyril Marshall, Mrs. Frank E Bowser.

I could imagine the women, each at a desk or her kitchen table, laboriously copying the ingredients for her best recipe and then instructions for preparing it. They'd have their hair pinned up in knots and be wearing dresses with cinched waists covered by frilly aprons. Had there been infighting about which recipes would be chosen and who the artists might be? The recipes were a funny mixture of old and new, not shy about using canned goods or frozen vegetables and yet not squeamish about pounding conch until the cartilage released, cleaning feathers from a duck, or removing the bloodline from a piece of fresh tuna fish.

I glanced at my watch: four fifteen. If I was going back to Geiger Key, I should get there before sunset. That way I could drive to the end of the road first and see if there were details I hadn't noticed on the last trip that might relate to Garcia's murder. I wondered whether I should take Ziggy for company. Probably not. He'd gotten into enough trouble the first time we went.

Miss Gloria and her two cats emerged from her cabin onto her deck, blinking in the sharp afternoon light as though they were just up from a nap. I beckoned her over to say hello.

"How was Nathan's father?" she asked, once settled in a deck chair.

Ziggy snuffled T-Bone's butt until the kitten slapped him, then he retreated into the cabin of my boat. The little yellow tiger jumped onto my lap and began to knead my thighs and purr.

"Impenetrable," I said, adding a grimace. "He's handsome like Nathan but less accessible. And that's saying something, because as you know, Nathan's not the most touchy-feely guy ever," I added. "What are you fixing for supper?"

"We hadn't gotten that far." She patted her lap, and my Evinrude jumped up and rubbed her chin with his head. "Probably the leftovers from last night."

"I brought some pimento cheese from lunch, if you want that." I paused. "Or you could take a run up the keys with me to the Fish Camp. That man who was on the beach yesterday when I found the body thinks the cops are blaming him. He wants to talk. If you came, I could hear what he has to say but avoid having dinner with him."

She nodded. "It's probably not good for you to meet that man alone. Nathan would kill you. Then he'd blame me for not talking you out of it. We all know two heads are better than one. Furthermore, I am absolutely dying for a plate of their shrimp tacos. Plus a mojito if you're driving."

Which she knew I would be. No way was I going to allow her to get in the driver's seat of her big boat of a Buick when she could barely see over the steering wheel. She was fine to drive short distances—I hoped, anyway—but not eleven miles of a narrow road in the dark. "Can you be ready in fifteen minutes?"

"I'm ready now," she said, plucking at her sweatshirt. "I'll visit the loo and put the kitties away and be right out."

* * *

There was a fair amount of traffic heading north out of Key West, probably workers who'd completed their shifts at hotels or restaurants. One of the difficulties of our island was finding reasonably priced housing. Lots of people chose apartments or homes further up the keys, some as far as Miami. Driving that distance every day seemed mind-boggling to me, but people did what they had to do to survive. Along the way, I described again for Miss Gloria the sequence of what had happened only yesterday—the beach, the dog, the body, the sheriff's deputies.

"You're like a criminal, drawn to the crime scene," said Miss Gloria.

I laughed. "Maybe. I was thinking if I drove back this way, it might jog my memory. Maybe I'll see a car or truck I recognize from yesterday, something that didn't really register at the time because I was so shook up."

"Or maybe," she said, her voice getting excited, "maybe we'll see some witnesses we can interview. Or maybe we'll notice that someone has a security camera that could've caught the perpetrator early that morning. Maybe those sheriff's deputies aren't as sharp as our own Key West Police Department."

"You're not interviewing anyone," I said. "Your sons would kill me. After that, Nathan would finish me off."

Her sons lived in Michigan and were not altogether happy with their elderly mother living on a houseboat halfway across the country in a hurricane zone. But Miss Gloria refused to move back to the cold North. "I did my time up there," she would always say. Neither of her sons was in a position to relocate to our island. The compromise had been that I would move in as her roommate so I could keep a loose eye on her. Once Nathan and I had gotten married and our houseboat had been renovated, I'd moved out. But only next door, and with my police officer husband installed. That had mollified Miss Gloria's relatives for the time being. Still, getting her involved in detective work would be looked upon with great disfavor.

Eleven miles north of Key West, I took a right onto Boca Chica Road, known as Government Road to the locals. Instead of heading directly to the restaurant, I continued along the road toward the beach I'd visited with Eric only yesterday. As I had told Miss Gloria, I wasn't looking for anything in particular. Instead, I hoped to notice any detail I might have missed the day before. I drove the length of the road super slowly, both of us watching the scenery. She gave a running commentary on what she was seeing.

"Most of the homes are either stucco, painted in pink or green or white, or they are mobile homes or travel trailers," she said.

At a few points, the road was intersected by small canals, where boats of all sizes floated. This neighborhood would be a pleasant place to live if you wanted to be close to the water and you weren't big on nightlife or noisy crowded streets. Likely the home prices would reflect the distance from town as well as the closeness to sea level. One good storm could wipe out the whole neighborhood.

"Stop here for a minute," Miss Gloria said. She pointed to three people sitting on lawn chairs with two dogs under an awning next to their trailer. They had a security camera attached to the top of their metal home. "They look as though they spend a lot of time watching the road," she said. "It can't hurt to ask a couple questions."

"Like what?" I slowed down to consider her idea.

"Someone must've seen something. We could ask whether they'd heard anything about whether the man was killed on the beach or whether someone brought him here and dumped him. Maybe one of them was up very early and noticed an unfamiliar vehicle headed down to the end of the road and then driving back in a big hurry. Maybe they're the kind of people who watch the road night and day and that's their entertainment. Or maybe we can persuade them to give over their security tape? It's not like they have all that much to protect."

"I'm sure their home and the stuff inside feel as valuable to them as ours does to us," I said. "Living on a road that's the only route to the beach means a lot of people have eyes on them."

"Point taken," she said. "I, of all people, should be sympathetic."

That reminded me that twice over the past few years, Miss Gloria's houseboat had been ransacked. Nathan had been pleading with both of us to improve the security around our homes, but we hated feeling like we lived in a gated community—or a prison. Maybe it was time to take his advice. After all, Key West had grown a lot more crowded, busier than this little road could ever be. I pulled the big Buick over to the side of the road and turned to my friend. "I know there's no point in asking you to stay in the car. But please, let me ask the questions?"

She winked.

The two dogs, who'd been lazing in the dirt, scrambled to their paws and began to bark with excitement as soon as I opened my door. A blue-striped awning extended from the front of the mobile home, lending a bit of shade to two men and one woman who sat smoking in aluminum chairs. To the right of the drive was a boat trailer holding two kayaks: one yellow, one orange. A Jolly Roger pirate flag fluttered at the edge of the driveway above a NO TRESPASSING sign. Not altogether welcoming. If one of the dogs lunged at us, we'd hightail it back to the car.

Looking both ways, I approached the end of the driveway, stopping as the dark shepherd-looking dog let out a menacing growl. I grinned and called out to the people.

"Hello! I'm Hayley, and this is my friend Gloria." I put my arm around her shoulders. "Sorry to interrupt your happy hour. I was hoping to ask you a few questions. I was on the beach the other day when the body was found."

Miss Gloria interrupted. "She was not only there, she actually found the poor man. We wondered if you'd heard anything about whodunit?"

I groaned and squeezed her shoulder to remind her I was doing the asking. For all we knew, these people could have been involved in the death and would not welcome nosy strangers.

The woman stubbed out her cigarette in the dirt at her feet and scuffed the butt until it was covered with sand. "Nope. The sheriff's people came by to ask, but we hadn't seen anyone drop a corpse." The two men laughed.

"There's a fair amount of traffic running by during the daylight hours, so we've gotten used to tuning it out," she continued.

"Might you have noticed if someone drove by in the early morning?" I asked.

"Probably not," the smaller of the two men said. "We're not what you call early risers. Seems to me that the weather was terrible that night too." The other folks nodded in agreement.

I thanked them for talking with us, and we returned to the car and continued down the road to the cement blocks marking the beginning of the beach. A few cars and trucks were sprinkled along the water side, as there had been when Eric and I came. I'd hoped the drive would jog my memory about whom we might have seen along the parking area before we went onto the beach with the dogs. Had there been anyone in a big hurry rushing off the beach? But nothing leapt out at me.

"Maybe Nathan will have heard something when I get home. I think we've done enough out here. Anyway, I'm not noticing anything that stands out as important."

"Maybe this gentleman we're meeting for a drink has more information," she suggested. "Isn't that why we have a date?"

"First of all, *we* don't have a date, I do. And second of all, it isn't a date. I'm happily married and I want to keep it that way. This is a conversation."

She laughed, teasing me. "Whatever you want to call it is fine with me. But I say when a fellow phones to ask if you can meet at a bar for a drink, you might as well call it a date."

I hoped Nathan wouldn't see it that way. I turned the big Buick around, drove back down the road, and turned off onto the little spit of land that was home to the restaurant. To the right of the parking lot sat a motley collection of trailers with stellar views of the finger of water and the mangrove islands across from it. The entrance to the Geiger Key Marina—aka the Fish Camp—made visitors feel like they were approaching old Florida, Florida as it had been before it was "discovered" by hordes of tourists and built up almost beyond recognition. The dining area was constructed over a dock, and it was completely open to the air and elements, with only a tiki hut–style grass roof for cover. Diners sat at picnic tables overlooking the water and the mangroves. A short bar lined the left side of the approach to the dining area. The bottom of the bar was built of corrugated metal, with a rustic wooden serving surface. Behind the bar against the wall were hundreds of bottles of booze, a large-screen TV showing the weather report, old license plates, and a stuffed tarpon in full leap.

Davis Jager was seated on the last stool with a large glass of beer in front of him. His eyes brightened when he caught sight of us. "Thank god you came."

He appeared to have on the same clothes he'd worn on the beach yesterday, minus the bucket hat. Everything looked a little more wrinkled and soiled.

"I'm so glad to see you," he said. "I feel as though we are tethered together by this tragedy and incompetent police."

Oh no, absolutely not. I refused to believe we were tethered together by anything. "I am not so sure—" I started to say, but he cut me off.

"She thinks I murdered that man. Just because I know so much about what happens on that beach. And also because we've had a little scuffle about my bird column."

"You and the sheriff's deputy had a scuffle about your bird column?" I asked.

"Not her. I meant Garcia. I publish what I notice and observe in my blog. I intend my posts for true bird watchers, not drive-by bird tourists. He tried to use everything I wrote for his own nefarious purposes." He took a big swallow of beer. "If I see something rare, I want the dedicated bird people to see it too, not get a rush of idiots spooking the wildlife while trying to check a box on their life lists."

"How in the world could someone use bird information for nefarious purposes?' asked Miss Gloria.

He swiveled around on his stool and narrowed his eyes to take her in, all four-foot-something of her. "And you are?"

"I am Gloria Peterson, Hayley's best friend and next-door neighbor. I've solved a mystery or two myself. For the ones I haven't solved, I've served as support staff to Hayley here. She is the real expert."

I was beginning to regret bringing my friend. I didn't care for this man, and I certainly didn't want him to get the impression that we were interested in teaming up with him—for any purpose.

A willowy blonde waitress came over to alert us to an empty table by the water, where we could enjoy our dinner away from the crowd and revel in the changing light of the evening.

"My name's Amelia, and I'll be taking care of you tonight. I know you'll like this table," she said. "It's got the best view." As she stuck a pencil into her elaborately braided hair, I noticed the black wrist support on her left arm and hand. People sometimes didn't realize how hard the work of a server was.

"Do you mind if I join you?" asked Davis, picking up his beer as though it were all settled.

"We have some things to discuss privately," Miss Gloria said primly. "But why don't we have a drink with you, and then Hayley and I can tend to our business over dinner. Okay?" She glanced at me with her eyebrows raised.

"Sure." I didn't want to spend the whole night with this guy or get more chummy with him, but I kind of did want to know what he thought had happened on that beach. Wasn't that part of why we'd come?

We settled at the picnic table near the water, and Miss Gloria ordered a mojito and then the fried shrimp tacos.

"For the mojitos, do you prefer the dark rum or the light?" Amelia asked, pencil poised over her pad.

"Light," I said, at the same time she said, "Dark."

"No appetizers for the table?" Amelia asked.

I knew we should split up, not order the same thing, but I was starving, and also stressed by recent events. Sometimes taking care of myself had to come before the stomachs of the *Key Zest* readers. Anyway, I had eaten here recently and wouldn't have any trouble recommending the hogfish sandwich, the shrimp and grits, and several other dishes. I added an order of killer conch fritters just for the sake of authenticity. "Do you make your mojitos with simple syrup?" I asked.

"We do. They're amazing," she assured me.

Once she'd left with our orders, I turned back to Davis. "What do you think happened to GG Garcia?"

"If I knew that, I'd be the town hero, wouldn't I? He wasn't a nice guy, and I can imagine that some locals are celebrating his demise. Take the birding kerfuffle I had with him—he wanted to take a good thing for serious bird people and make it into fuel for his moneymaking machinery. That's always where his heart and his actions were—*What's in it for me?*" He rubbed a hand over his chin, and I could hear the rasp of his unshaven whiskers.

Davis seemed like a very different personality than the cocky man I had met on the beach. He was halfway to drunk, and that might explain some of it. Now he was beginning to repeat himself.

The waitress returned with two plastic cups of ice water and our mojitos. She took a couple of moments to wipe off the picnic table before arranging the drinks in front of us.

"They think I did it," Davis said, while she tidied up our area. "I swear I had nothing to do with it. I swear I was looking for ducks. But that sheriff woman did not like me, and she's assuming my presence on the scene was a sign of guilt."

I wondered if she suspected I was a culprit too. "Was there someone in particular who could be called Garcia's enemy?"

"Have you taken your animal to the Higgs Beach Dog Park?" he asked.

"Not seriously," I said. "Ziggy doesn't love to play with other dogs. He's more ball focused than dog focused." I narrowed my eyes, realizing he probably wasn't asking about Ziggy's personality. "Should I?"

"You might learn something," he said. "There's a little group of hard-core guys in the small dog park every afternoon around four thirty. I know that doesn't really fit, hard-core guys with small dogs. But Garcia owned a Jack Russell terrier that he adored. That animal was an awful bully, exactly like his owner. A friend told me that every time she took her dog, if the Jack Russell was there, it always ended in whimpers and tears. Garcia's mutt pinned her fluffy down and pulled hard on her ears until she screamed. You know what he said when she complained?"

"Get over it?" Miss Gloria suggested. "Suck it up?"

"Worse than that," said Davis. "Garcia told her that her dog needed to learn to manage bullying the way the women he'd dated had managed him. Some chick who was sitting across the circle from him asked if he was married to any of them, and he laughed and said, 'Not anymore.' Who would brag about that?" He wagged his head mournfully. "A mean son of a bitch, that's who." He got to his feet as Amelia returned to deliver the order of conch fritters. She winced a little as she set the plate down.

"Are you okay?" Miss Gloria asked.

Amelia smiled. "Repetitive stress injury, that's what the doc said. Ice and rest—not so easy when waitressing is your meal ticket." Miss Gloria murmured her sympathy.

"Anyway, talk to Entwistle," Davis said, ignoring the other conversation. "He's tall with white hair, and he comes with a black pug—go figure. Enjoy your food. Call me if you learn something?" He wandered back to the bar.

"Did that man have something to do with that murder?" Amelia the waitress asked, as she watched him go. "It's scary to think it happened right down the road."

"He was on the scene when the body was discovered," said Miss Gloria. "He's a piece of work for sure, but we doubt he's a murderer. These look amazing. Thank you."

She grabbed a fried conch fritter and popped it into her mouth, then waved her hand in a belated attempt to dissipate the heat so she could swallow. "I wonder who's going to take care of Garcia's terrier, now that he's gone. Did his wife love the dog too?"

I'd wondered the same thing. "Did you believe the story about the bird-watching argument? I'm having trouble believing anything that guy says. Though if he writes a blog, I suppose it would be easy enough to follow up."

"Those bird-watching people are intense," said Miss Gloria. "Before you moved to our pier, we had a neighbor who was obsessed with filling out his life list. He didn't want anyone on our dock making noise in the morning for fear it would chase off potential wildlife, not even regular sounds that come from the marina waking up each day. I do believe he would have murdered someone who got in the way of him seeing a rare bird."

Amelia returned with our dinners—huge platters of soft tacos smothered in salsa, cheese, and sour cream, with a side of rice and black beans and a handful of homemade chips. I knew the crunchy Key West pinks waited for me underneath the toppings. She set the tray down on the table so she could move our plates to our places using her good hand. "What else can I get for you? More drinks? Hot sauce? Napkins?"

"All set, thanks." I smiled at her and bit into the first taco with anticipation. Amelia moved to the table nearest us, where several teenagers were eating, talking loudly to be heard over the band playing at the far end of the tiki hut. Sliding onto the bench, she put her arm around the nearest girl, who had long dark hair, a white T-shirt, and a gloomy face. Amelia gave the girl a squeeze and leaned in to whisper something in her ear, then picked up her tray and returned to the kitchen. I was glad I was no longer a teenager, full of angst and drama.

"These are incredible," said Miss Gloria. We ate in silence for a few minutes, enjoying the view over the lagoon to the edge of the small trailer park. The cement retaining wall was lined with small motorboats. If you didn't mind the noise of the bar and the music coming from the Fish Camp, it would be an idyllic place for a camper. I wondered if the sheriff's department would have canvassed all the residents about the murdered man.

"What do we know so far?" I wondered aloud when we were done with dinner. Amelia returned to collect our empty plates, and once again we declined a second round of drinks and I asked for the bill. "Davis confirmed what we already knew from reading the news over the past couple of years: that Gerald Garcia was a bully. I will be interested to meet his wife and extended family, if he has one."

"How are you going to manage that?" Miss Gloria asked.

"I forgot to tell you, my mom and Sam want us to help with the funeral reception on Friday. It's at the Woman's Club."

"Put me down for that as well," she said. "People always say more than they ought to at a funeral reception. Emotions are raw and every slight feels fresh. And filters seem to switch off in the face of grief." Her expression grew distant and sad, as if she was remembering something in her past. She'd never talked much about the days and months following her own husband's death. I waited a few beats to see whether she wanted to say more, but she remained silent.

"I would imagine this event will be quite tense, since the guy was murdered and then left on the beach. It wasn't a death the family would have expected," I said. "I wonder how he was killed?" I could picture the dark splotch in the sand that might have been his blood. "I suppose it could have been accidental, but then why not report it? That makes me think it had to have been intentional. And what did they do, dig a big trench in advance because they planned to murder him? How the heck did the killer get the body to the beach? This person must have been strong, because Garcia was not a small man."

The vision of the two brightly colored kayaks that we'd seen next to the trailer down the road flashed to my mind. It wouldn't have been so hard if you'd brought the body under cover of darkness in a boat. Especially if you knew something about the tides, including what kind of evidence would be washed away in the storm by morning.

Chapter Ten

Robbing this dish of its heavy cream is like kissing through a screen door.

—Dino, a reader commenting on a recipe in the *New York Times*

Nathan came in about an hour after I had returned home with Miss Gloria. I was reading in bed in my nightgown, Ziggy curled up on one side and Evinrude on the other. After a busy day, it felt glorious to be here relaxing with my furry guys. Nathan came over to kiss me hello, smelling a bit of whiskey and cigar smoke. He looked rumpled, tired, and oh so handsome.

"You smell like a party," I said, cupping his cheek. "Did you have a good night?"

"Actually, I can't wait until this week is finished," he said as he crossed our bedroom, unbuttoned his dress shirt, and dropped it in the laundry basket. "The steaks were fine, and it was a beautiful night on the water. But I'd rather eat dinner with you than a bunch of cops sucking up to my father. He reported having a lovely lunch with you, though." He tipped his head, looking curious and a little irritated. Not with me, I hoped. "Did you figure out why he wanted to meet you alone?"

"Besides getting to know his only daughter-in-law?" I teased. Nathan smiled a little. "I think he's worried about how Vera is doing." I paused for a minute. "I even wonder if he wants to know about your mom and whether she's thriving on her own. But no one else in your family seems to be talking to him."

"With good reason," said Nathan, as he disappeared into the bathroom.

I heard the water rushing as he washed his face and brushed his teeth. He emerged, toweling himself off, and slid into bed next to me. "He pretty much destroyed his relationships with our family, and it won't be easy to repair the mess." As he tried to move the dog to the foot of the bed so he could get closer to me, Ziggy lifted his lips into a little snarl. "Sorry, Zig, you have to share the real estate. Even if you had an exciting week." He settled Ziggy on the other side of him and turned back to me, resting his head on his arm. "In fact, I'm not at all sure the relationships can be repaired. He's completely clueless. Tonight, he decided to give me tips for a happy marriage."

I snickered, though Nathan did not seem amused. "Do tell, what were the tips?"

"To be honest, I was too angry to absorb anything he said."

This made me sad but also made me wonder how well Nathan's dad could get along in his job, which was a big one, and touchy; juggling the egos of other cops would take a lot of finesse. And how was my own husband managing having his father in this temporary overlord position? I suspected it was taking a toll.

"I'm here, if you want to talk about it," I said. "Now that I've met both of your parents, it's easier to imagine that they might have had problems."

He lay back on his pillow and closed his eyes. "I think they would have limped along to the finish line had it not been for what happened with Vera. Neither one seemed particularly happy in that marriage, but they were stubborn people with high moral standards—or, at least in my father's case, a premium on the appearance of that. Under ordinary circumstances, they would have considered it a moral failure to dissolve the marriage and the family. But Mother never felt he handled Vera's case well—he was too angry and therefore unable to see the options clearly. Probably frightened as well. That resulted in him acting boorish with others in the police department as well as the press. People don't want to be scolded and badgered. That makes them less likely to help."

I could only nod; that seemed like common sense. To be honest, I could picture Nathan's father as angry and boorish—I'd want to get away as fast as possible. "Do you think your sister would have been found more quickly if he hadn't behaved as he did?"

After a pause, he blinked his eyes open and looked at me. "Truthfully, I think he did everything he could. But he did it with a complete lack of grace. Unfortunately, it appears that I may have inherited those qualities from him. Luckily, you saw through that."

Nathan flashed a wry smile, but he seemed tired, so I decided not ask any more hard questions. I snuggled up close to him with my head on his shoulder.

"What did you have for dinner?" he asked.

"Miss Gloria and I took a ride out to Geiger Key for shrimp tacos at the Fish Camp," I said. "One of the most delicious meals on the keys."

"Geiger Key?" he asked. I could feel the muscles in his body tensing.

Ruh-roh. Best to fill him in on everything before he blew his cool, which tended to happen when he was tired and frustrated. And worried about me.

"I needed details of the shrimp tacos for the piece I'm writing this week. Plus, Palamina wanted photos showing the restaurant's setup."

I was about to confess my conversation with Davis Jager when his cell phone buzzed, saving me from further investigation. "This is Nathan," he said, then listened for a few minutes. It sounded like the baritone voice of the other fellow up for captain, Lieutenant Smith.

"I think that's a terrible idea," he said, and then listened some more. "She would have told me." More listening.

"Hold on a minute. She's right here, so I'll find out."

He pulled the phone away from his ear. "They identified a parking ticket in Garcia's pocket as coming from the Opal Key garage. That means we're now working with the sheriff's department on the case. Second, Davis Jager was attacked in the parking lot of the Fish Camp. He's been taken to the hospital, critical condition, unclear outcome."

I gulped, feeling a surge of fear. "When did that happen?"

"Maybe an hour ago? They want you in for more questions. What's your schedule tomorrow?"

"I'm helping Mom and Sam with food prep for Garcia's memorial reception in the morning. By noonish I could be free."

Nathan reported that to his colleague. "Okay," he said, "have a good night." He put the phone on his nightstand and turned back to me.

"We'll let you know tomorrow morning where and when to meet," he said, his eyes full of worry.

"I'll certainly be there, whenever," I said. The police department was close to Mom's industrial kitchen, so not out of the way. I'd be able to get over there quickly.

"I can't believe you and Gloria were at the Fish Camp right before this happened. That's a horrendous coincidence." But his voice turned up in a question mark, and I absolutely could not lie to him.

"We did see Jager at the bar," I said. "It wasn't complete coincidence. He wanted to talk to me, and I needed to nail down the article I was writing. Miss Gloria was happy to come along for company. By the time we got there, Jager was on his way to loaded, I'd say. He seemed very worried about how much of a suspect he is in GG Garcia's death. Other than that, he was in one piece when we left. However, if he was attacked, I guess that takes him off the list of suspects."

"Not necessarily," Nathan said grimly. "Before you come over tomorrow, it would be a good idea to write some notes about exactly what you saw and heard while having dinner on Geiger Key. Who was he talking with? Was there anyone else in the background that you recognized, as you look back on things? The sheriff's deputy will be there for the interview as well—the woman. She isn't going to be happy to hear that you were on the scene of another violent incident."

"Nathan," I said, putting my hand on his arm. "I didn't go looking for trouble. I went looking for dinner. If I had the chance to talk to this man with whom I was bonded by nature of a shared bone-chilling discovery, you know I would take it. I didn't think it would hurt anything. He seemed fine when we left. I'm sorry if you think it was deliberately reckless. Or if it embarrasses you in front of your peers. Or is it your father?"

He practically sputtered with indignation. "That's hardly fair. Do you really think that little of me?"

I rolled away from him a few inches so I could meet his gaze. "I don't know what to think. But I'm sure we shouldn't discuss this anymore tonight. I'm getting upset and so are you, and we're liable to say things we don't mean. Besides, neither one of us will be able to sleep a wink. Things always look brighter in the morning."

"Do they?" he asked. "There will still be one dead man and one near death when we wake up. And my wife whom I adore was practically on the scene of both." He hugged me quickly, then pulled the covers up to his chin and turned away to face the wall. Amazingly enough, he dropped off to sleep within minutes.

It took a long time for me to let my worries go. What did Jager really want from me? If he didn't survive, I would never know. I tried desperately to review all the people we'd seen at the Fish Camp. I replayed my memories like a reel of film, visualizing the drinkers sitting at the bar, the diners seated at picnic tables around us, the waitstaff, even the people we had seen at a distance across the lagoon, relaxing outside their campers, enjoying the evening air and the live music from the restaurant.

Maybe Miss Gloria would remember something I hadn't noticed. Though she was older and prone to forgetfulness, she had a quirky ability to pull important details out of her hat.

Chapter Eleven

Mrs. Quince was sipping the stock. "Taste this, Nell." She beckoned her over. "Your sadness, my dear child—you've let it affect your cooking."

—Jennifer Ryan, *The Kitchen Front*

Nathan was up and out before I awoke and, as usual, left a pot of coffee for me in the kitchen, along with a note. *Be very careful today*, he said. *There's a dangerous person on the loose, and you and Miss Gloria are now in a vulnerable position. Meet us for lunch around noon? I'll text the details.*

This gave me an extra frisson of fear, as if I weren't anxious enough already. I dressed quickly and went over to Miss Gloria's boat carrying two steaming cups of coffee topped off with frothed milk. She was just emerging from her cabin, hair awry and cats in tow. She gave me a sunny grin. "If you and your coffee aren't a sight for sore eyes, I can't imagine what would be."

"Prince Charming?" I suggested, forcing a chuckle. Once we'd settled into her lounge chairs, I told her the news. "In a nutshell, Nathan thinks someone might have tried to silence

Jager Davis with an attack at the Fish Camp last night, and he worries one of us could be next. He asked if we could try to remember as many details as possible about who we talked to and who else might have seen us talking with Davis."

"Oh dear," she said, stroking T-Bone the tiger, who'd landed on her lap, tawny, lanky, and sleek. "I assume you told him about the people at the end of the road?"

I paused. "Actually, not. We were both so tired and we started squabbling, and then one of his cop buddies called. I have to meet them at noon somewhere. And then I'll spill my guts."

Miss Gloria nodded. "Best to tell everything you can think of."

I knew that was almost always the best tack to take with Nathan, but it wasn't always easy. "Back to the restaurant—can you tell me what you remember? I was so annoyed with Davis pushing his way into our dinner that I kind of forgot why we went. Maybe I didn't focus enough on my surroundings." My voice had begun to wobble.

"You had no way of knowing he'd be attacked," said Miss G. She reached over to stroke my hand. "This wasn't your fault." She waited a beat until I nodded, then closed her eyes and continued. "From the parking lot, we entered the restaurant through the bar area. That's where we saw your man, Davis Jager. Seems like there were five or six wooden barstools with backs. Maybe a couple was sitting at the end? I remember them both wearing flip-flops, and he had a pretty green gingham shirt that the wife had to have chosen, right?"

"Yup." I laughed. "Keep going, you're doing great."

"There was an empty stool and next to that, two guys talking with Jager. Did you recognize any of those people?"

I tilted my head back against the deck chair. "The problem is, I wasn't thinking about observations, I was thinking about what Davis Jager wanted. And how we could hear the facts so I could pass them on to Nathan without getting overly involved."

She nodded. "That's why we're such a good team—you keep your focus on the big target, and I'm interested in everything else. I'd say they were all middle-age or above, and a little bit scruffy."

"Yes!" I added, "One of them had a dog at his feet, a small black animal. Who looked kind of elderly because of the white on his snout."

"Then we were taken to our table near the water by the waitress with the blonde braids. Remember, she had a brace on the one arm? Had you seen her before?" Miss Gloria asked.

I closed my eyes again, trying to picture the scene. For some reason, she had looked familiar, though it hadn't registered in the moment. I waited for the memory to float in so I could grab it. My eyes snapped open.

"The other day, when I went to the beach with Eric and the dogs, there was a whole lineup of people along the left side of the road before you hit the Jersey barriers. After that, you can't go any further in your car, remember? Some were fishing, a few people were in the water. Anyway, I did see a couple barbecuing. I wasn't really paying attention because they had a big dog on a frayed leash who was lunging at Ziggy. I had wanted to hurry him along so Nathan's dog wouldn't get into an unpleasant tussle in which he'd be clearly outmatched. That leash looked like it could snap and set the dog loose at any moment."

"What breed of dog was it?" Miss Gloria asked. "Did it match the dog at the bar? Or maybe those two dogs who barked at us when we stopped by that trailer?"

I shrugged. "Turns out I'm a lousy witness this week. Is it possible that the woman cooking hot dogs was our waitress? Would you spend your time off up the road from where you worked, grilling?"

"I suppose it depends where you live. If you live in a house without a water view and you love the ocean, why wouldn't you go to that beach? It's a lovely spot and not overcrowded, so why not? And everybody has to eat—if they're like us, three squares and a few snacks." Miss Gloria finished her coffee. "So maybe this woman you saw looked a little bit like the waitress and maybe she didn't. Had you seen that man before?"

"I can't say for sure. I could mainly describe the dog."

"What else do you remember about our waitress at the Fish Camp?" my friend asked.

"For as busy as the place was, she seemed very attentive. She came by four or five times at least before she delivered our dinner to check on us, see if we needed more drinks or anything else. Was it possible she was listening in? If so, she would've overheard our conversation with Davis Jager."

"But what did he say that might have gotten him beat up?" Miss Gloria asked. "Why would she care?"

"Seems like he mostly wanted to get the authorities off his back and direct me to the dog park." I shrugged. "I'm going to help Mom with some food prep this morning." I collected the empty mugs and stood up. "Would you please be extra careful today? Maybe take one of your pals if you have to go out?"

"I'll try," she said, flashing me a grin that wasn't altogether reassuring.

* * *

I pulled into the strip mall along North Roosevelt and parked my scooter in front of the industrial kitchen where my mother and Sam would prepare food for Gerald Garcia's funeral reception. A small amount of work could be done in the tiny kitchen in their van, and sometimes the venue where the event would take place offered a kitchen. But for most jobs, the caterer did the lion's share of the work ahead of time and kept the food in warming ovens, ready to plate it on-site. I spotted the two of them unloading their vehicle in front of the building and went over to help. I picked up a heavy box of vegetables and carried it into the kitchen.

The counters and appliances were all stainless steel. Dozens of large pots and cooking implements hung from the ceiling, and more were stacked on the shelf underneath the island. The only decor on the pale-blue walls was a large calendar with the caterers' schedules marked off. Nothing fancy or sexy about this space, but it was practical and easy to keep immaculately clean. Several caterers in Key West shared this kitchen, and my mother was on the committee to ensure the highest standards of cleanliness prevailed. Nobody wanted a Health Department citation to shut down their business. Nothing was kept in the two refrigerators or the walk-in unless it was related to the food being prepared that week.

"Can you imagine accidentally using someone else's mayonnaise or sour cream well past its sell-by date for your special wedding curried chicken salad, and then half the guests fall ill?" my mother had asked when one of the caterers complained about having to bring in fresh staples for each event. "There is no room for mistakes in this business."

"What's on the menu?" I asked as I unloaded mangoes and avocados from the box. My mother was quite creative in designing food for her parties. She always offered the old standbys that some people loved, dishes such as Key West pink cocktails, fish dip, key lime pie, and so on. But if the party had a theme or the bride had favorites, my mother was famous for accommodating. For a wedding last New Year's Eve, she'd even agreed to produce hundreds of corsages made of croissants, a disaster from start to finish.

"Mrs. Garcia wanted old-time recipes," Mom said. "She gave me a copy of their Woman's Club cookbook so I could prepare a few of those recipes, along with the updated 1988 version. I heard the most amazing thing from the president of the club yesterday. Remember Martha Hubbard?"

Of course I remembered her. I had helped solve a poisoning several years ago that had just about finished off her business as well as the business of another old friend, Analise, who gave culinary tours of the island. "Yup."

"Turns out Martha's a member of the club, serving on the hospitality committee. She loves preparing historic dishes from the olden days in Key West, and she offered to bring some specialties like mango fritters and papaya squares. She'll bring pies, too, to supplement our cookies."

"Does old-time recipes mean head cheese, and Spam, and vegetables out of a can mixed with Miracle Whip?" asked Sam. He seemed to love serving as my mother's first assistant, but he loved teasing her most of all.

"Let's hope not," my mother said cheerfully. "We'll focus on finger foods, since most people won't be sitting." She clipped the list of recipes to a stand on the counter. "I asked Cole's Peace Bakery to slice some loaves of bread lengthwise." She pulled four loaves of sliced bread out of the brown paper bags on the counter. "My mother used to make little three-decker sandwiches when her friends were coming to lunch," she explained to Sam. "The fillings were always different, like egg salad in one layer and tuna fish or cream cheese with olives in another.

"At Christmas time she had her bakery dye some of the bread loaves red and some green, so the layers of the sandwiches were multicolored. Do you remember, Hayley?" Her face looked a little melancholy, and her voice was wistful. We'd both deeply mourned the loss of my sweet grandmother. Sam crossed the room to fold her into a hug, then came over to hug me.

"I wish I could have met her. She must have been something special to have produced and raised you two," he said.

"She was." Mom smiled at him and dashed a tear away. "We'd best get busy."

She pulled a copy of the Key West Woman's Club cookbook from her bag. I leafed through it. This was the newer edition, printed in 1988. The recipes written in longhand in the older book were now typeset, and the drawings at the beginning of each chapter were much more uniform and professional.

"On the list this morning, we'll make the sandwiches with egg salad, pimento cheese, and watercress and cream cheese. They'll keep well if we wrap them in damp cheesecloth, and then plastic wrap. We'll also bake the choux pastry puffs that we'll stuff with chocolate pudding and lime-scented cream tomorrow."

Once we had the food laid out or stowed in the refrigerator, I began to work on the pimento cheese, chopping jarred red pimento peppers in oil into small pieces, slicing scallions, and grating cheese. Sam started on the egg salad, and my mother began making the choux pastry.

"Tell us what's new about that awful murder case," said my mother.

So far this morning, I'd done pretty well at suppressing the details so I could work without ruminating. But since my mother had asked, I would tell them something. "The plot gets thicker," I said. "Apparently Davis Jager—who was on the beach yesterday when I found the dead man—was beaten and left for dead last night." I paused, wondering whether it would worry them too much if I told them more. *Keep it factual*, I told myself. Well, almost factual. "Miss Gloria and I ran into him last night at the Geiger Key Fish Camp, so this is doubly scary. He thought the sheriff's department was trying to frame him for the murder. But this puts a different perspective on things, because maybe he saw something or knew something he didn't reveal to the authorities. And maybe the murderer realized this and went after him."

"I'll say," Sam said. "This brings the murderer closer to you. And we don't like that one bit."

I nodded slowly. "In fact, the cops found a parking ticket from Key West in his pocket and now apparently are wondering whether Garcia was killed in the city and then taken out to Geiger Key. One of Nathan's pals called last night, late. They want me to come by at lunchtime to answer more questions."

As I'd suspected would happen, a cloud of worry scudded over my mother's face and settled into her eyes.

Sam asked, "Are you saying this Jager was the main suspect in the murder, but now he's been attacked? Where does that leave the case?"

"I actually have no idea. I am hoping they'll share something with me at lunch, not only ask what I know and remember. Because even though I found the guy, my memories of that event don't seem to amount to much. I think I've already told them everything I know."

I scraped the scallions and pimentos into a large bowl, along with blocks of softened cream cheese, and began to shred a massive block of cheddar. I glanced at the clock ticking on the wall—a knife and fork served as minute and second hands—and realized I needed to leave in forty-five minutes. "I feel badly that I can't stay all day. Do you have a lot left to do?"

"We'll manage," she said. "We have cookies to bake, and we'll assemble and wrap the sandwiches. I'll make Pat Kennedy's dough for the pigs in a blanket, and then we'll wrap the dogs tomorrow and bake on-site so they're warm."

My mouth had begun to water. Those pigs weren't fancy finger food, but when they were served at a party along with grainy mustard for dipping, they were often the first snacks to be scarfed up. "Remember at dinner the other night when you were recalling the anniversary party for the Garcias?" I asked my mother. "Will you tell me more about that? One of them said something odd in their toast that you were trying to recall?"

"I remember that clearly," said Sam, "because I was taking a turn manning the bar, which was next to the stage." He began to crack open hard-boiled eggs and drop them into a large, stainless-steel bowl. "First of all, they stood at least two feet apart. No holding of hands, no palm resting lovingly on his bride's back, no tender kiss, not even any eye contact." He walked over to my mother, gave her a one-armed hug, and kissed her on the lips.

"I realize they were married much longer than we've been, but if their relationship had any magic at the beginning, it looked like it was long gone. They didn't even pretend for the onlookers, which I found heartbreaking. I wondered why they'd even throw an anniversary party if they were practically estranged." He returned to his station to resume peeling eggs. "She said the usual, how life with GG had been a roller coaster of adventure. She had imagined they would leave Key West and travel the world, but she'd soon realized that, being married to him, she would have all the adventures she'd ever need right here in town."

"Hmmm," I said, as I stirred the minced vegetables into the big bowl of cheeses. "That could mean anything."

"Right," Sam said. "And I took it at face value, that he was a lively man who didn't shy away from conflict. But then his turn came. He said that when he'd gone to meet her family for the first time, he realized she wasn't the pick of the litter. But over time, her depths had been revealed."

"Not the pick of the litter? That's so insulting," I said. "What does that even mean—that she had sisters who were smarter or prettier?"

My mother shrugged. "People laughed," she said, "but it was uncomfortable. She looked of two minds—on the one hand, she wanted to drop through the floor. On the other, she wanted to pick up the nearest heavy object and bash his head in with it."

The three of us looked at each other. Was this how GG Garcia had been dispatched?

"Don't the shrinks say that if you have a complicated relationship with the deceased, the mourning is more complicated as well? It's going to be a most interesting memorial gathering," Sam said.

Chapter Twelve

She moved through the crowd, a needle and thread weaving herself into the fabric of it all: the town, the people, the mingled fragrance of fries and pizza and hot cast iron.
—Ellen Airgood, *Tin Camp Road*

A text came in from Nathan at eleven forty-five.

We're headed out to the sub precinct now. Whenever you can get here is fine. Sooner better than later. Deputy Rogers will be here too.

I said good-bye to my mother and Sam, gathered up my stuff, and went out to my scooter. Every Monday, Nathan had lunch at the Sister Noodle House with Chief Brandenburg, Lieutenant Smith, Steve Torrence, and various other officers, depending on who was on duty and who could get away. They called this restaurant the Key West Police Department sub precinct. The shop was located in a strip mall off North Roosevelt Avenue, in the same block as Starbucks and Gordon Food Service. A Cantonese restaurant seemed like an odd choice for a police hangout to me, but Nathan had shrugged when I asked about it.

"Something for everyone," he said. "We like the free refills and huge portions and the no-fuss atmosphere. Nobody in this crowd is interested in fine dining. And the owners take good care of us. Plus, they give us the table at the back of the restaurant so we can discuss official business without worrying about being overheard."

I took a deep breath on the sidewalk outside the restaurant. Of course, I adored Nathan and Steve Torrence, and I liked the chief, or what I knew of him so far. But I was still nervous in the company of a group of police officers. This was probably a vestige of my life BN—before Nathan—when seeing a police officer meant I was getting a traffic ticket or had committed some other minor infraction. Besides, the sheriff's deputy was a wild card. When she'd come to the beach to investigate Garcia's murder, she'd struck me as businesslike, competent, and not particularly friendly. Davis Jager had obviously been upset about her suspicions of his being involved in the murder. Now that he'd been attacked and hospitalized, I hoped her laser focus would not shift to me.

Eight officers were seated at a rectangular table at the far end of the narrow restaurant, past the kitchen with its pass-through window on the right. Nathan had explained that the officers took turns deciding who would sit facing the entrance. By training, police were always watching for trouble, never wanting to be taken by surprise. Today Nathan had his back to the door and didn't see me come in. Watching his face brighten would have made things a little easier. *Get over it, Hayley,* I coached myself. *You've married into it, so you might as well relax.*

I approached the table, which was already covered with huge plates of Chinese noodles, barbecued pork, dumplings, and fried rice. At first glance, they'd chosen mostly carbs, with only small bits of vegetables making an appearance. Colored paper parasols hung upside down from the ceiling, which struck me as a funny contrast to the tableful of strong men and one strong woman. I had never wanted to be the kind of wife who dropped in to check on her husband while he was bonding with the guys, but this was a command performance, not a neighborly hello.

I was shocked to see Nathan's father at the far end. Had he been invited to join them, or had he asked to come? Would this interview change his opinion of me? I knew it shouldn't matter so much, if at all, but I began to move from being a little anxious to feeling almost desperate.

"Hayley Snow!" the chief called out, then got to his feet to gesture at an empty seat across from Deputy Rogers. "Join us." Nathan stood up too and gave me a peck on the cheek as I passed by.

"I think you know everyone, right?" the chief asked. "I understand you and Darcy Rogers have also met."

"Unfortunately, it's true," I said, sliding into the empty seat. Oh lord, that had come out all wrong. We nodded at each other, and I flashed a weak smile. She didn't look quite so commanding seated in front of a platter of spring rolls and tempura something or other, but she was clearly a serious person.

Steve Torrence asked, "Is it also true that your husband's dog found the body? Maybe we should put him on the payroll." He winked and smiled. He would know I was anxious and want to help me relax.

"Unfortunately yes on that too," I said, "but Nathan's got him pretty well trained. I managed to lure him away before he did any real damage to the crime scene. By the time I got there, he'd shaken loose fingers from the sand." I shuddered. "To be honest, it was horrifying."

The chief spoke up. "At least he didn't eat anything, right? I answered a call years ago from a woman who had been using a band saw and lost control of her tool. She accidentally cut off three fingers. We got there quickly, but before we could do anything about it, one of her three dogs snatched up a finger and swallowed it."

The other officers burst out laughing. "Leave it to the chief to talk about severed fingers over lunch," said Lieutenant Smith.

"I never did find out if they managed to attach the two fingers that were saved," said the chief. More laughter.

A small Asian man approached the table to ask if I would like to order something. I declined, saying I had snacked while I was helping my mother. Which was true, but I felt so nervous right now that I doubted I could swallow. "A glass of water, please?"

Deputy Rogers said, "Your husband mentioned that you had a conversation with Davis Jager last night. I'd like to hear about that. Did he seem particularly worried about anything?"

"Yes. For one thing, he thought you had identified him as the killer." I took a deep breath and told them everything I could remember about the meeting, including Miss Gloria's observations on who was sitting at the bar. I added a few sentences about what we'd done leading up to our time at the Fish Camp. "Before we ate, Miss Gloria and I drove down to the end of the road—you know, where it peters out into concrete blocks? We chatted with three people who were enjoying the evening alongside their trailer. They claimed not to have seen anything unusual the morning when Ziggy and I found GG Garcia."

The deputy's face had grown sterner. "Let's go back to the restaurant, if you don't mind. Did Davis Jager seem concerned about his own safety or possibly yours?" she asked. She had dark-brown eyes with a lighter ring around them, which made her seem softer than her questioning suggested.

"As far as I could tell, he wasn't worried about someone coming after him, but he was very worried that you believed he was the murderer. That's why he wanted to talk to me, I think. Miss Gloria and I both noticed he'd been drinking quite a bit before we arrived, so he wasn't one hundred percent coherent." I wondered if they would tell me exactly what had happened to him in the parking lot and also about his condition at the hospital. I decided I would ask those questions after they finished with theirs.

"Back to the morning where you discovered the body. Have you remembered anything else about people who might have been on the beach that same day?"

I told them about our waitress at the Fish Camp, how she'd bordered on overly solicitous and how I wondered if I had seen her grilling hot dogs on the waterfront the day before.

"Did she seem to recognize you?"

"I can't say for sure. Now I wonder whether she was trying to listen in on our conversation. The restaurant is usually mobbed, and last night was no exception. The staff are always running their legs off to keep up—and no one wants to wait for their food or their drinks, of course. But she came back to check on us multiple times."

"But she wasn't one of the people you talked with before dinner?"

"No," I said, "she was working when we arrived at the Fish Camp."

"Where was Davis Jager when you and Miss Gloria left the restaurant?" she asked.

I paused a few seconds to try to visualize the scene accurately. "I believe he was back at the bar, but I couldn't swear to that. We didn't have any further conversation."

"Is it your impression that Mr. Garcia knew Mr. Jager?" Deputy Rogers asked.

"I don't know about a personal connection, but certainly Jager knew of Mr. Garcia. Everyone who pays attention to the local radio station or Facebook would know him. He's been all over the news. Davis did mention something about a conflict between the two of them over rare birds—something to do with his blog. I believe that happened online, not in person, but I haven't had time to follow up." Two of the cops exchanged glances, as if to wonder why this was my job at all. From the tense expression on Nathan's face, I could imagine he was thinking the same thing.

"Oh, and there's one other thing. I forgot to mention the dog park."

"What about the dog park?" Nathan asked.

"He said that GG Garcia took his Jack Russell there most evenings and hung out with a bunch of guys who knew him well, so it was possible one of them had some information about what happened."

"Does Davis Jager own a dog?" Darcy Rogers asked.

"I don't know; it didn't come up. I would think he would have mentioned it, because of course I had Ziggy with me when I found the body," I said. "Dog people usually fawn over your dog if he's cute—which Ziggy is—and then start talking about their own dog. He told me to look for a white-haired guy named Entwistle. He seemed to think Ziggy and I would hear more about the murder if we went than if he did."

"We?" Nathan asked, his face creasing with a deeper frown.

"Actually, Nathan," said Darcy Rogers, tapping her slender fingers on the table, "it's not a bad idea. She goes over there with the dog and sits in that circle and listens."

"Absolutely not," said Nathan, glowering at her.

Darcy kept talking as if he hadn't said anything. "You could send one or two undercover guys with their dogs to hang around the outskirts in case there's any trouble. She could even be wired. I would go myself, but I never look like a civilian no matter what I'm wearing."

Looking at her formal bearing and minimalist hairstyle, I thought she was probably right.

"Listen," Nathan said. I could see the vein in his temple pulsing with tension. "No offense intended, but in the Key West Police Department, we do not send civilians out to do police work. Send the undercover guy with his dog; it's a lot safer."

"I really wouldn't mind hearing more—" I started to say.

"Here's why that wouldn't work," said the chief. He passed around his phone with photos of two undercover officers with their canine partners. The men looked rough and scary, the German shepherds even scarier. "You infiltrate a small dog park with a guy like this and a big mean dog, and the whole place would be cleared out in minutes. They'd probably call the police to top it off."

"It's true," I said. "One of the cardinal rules in the small-dog park is no big dogs allowed. That rule comes right after pick up your poop. Or maybe even before. Every dog has its place. The big-dog park adjoins the small-dog area, so the little guys sometimes stand at the fence and bark their heads off, pretending they could take any one of those monsters on." I'd thought I'd lighten the mood with my dog park lore, but Darcy Rogers's face remained completely serious.

"In other words," said Darcy, "it would be easy enough for the undercover guys to be stationed in the big-dog area. I could go into the small-dog park at the same time as Hayley—I'd borrow my neighbor's Yorkie. She's very timid, so I'd be hanging around outside the group with her, not in the thick of things."

"I'd be happy to hear more about it," I said.

At the same time, Nathan said to Darcy, "If you're going to be there, I can't see why you need my wife at all."

"You need her because Darcy here looks and talks like a cop. They'll button up tighter than a too-small shirt collar on a fat guy," said Chief Brandenburg.

It was beginning to sink in how seriously they were taking this arrangement. I thought they must be expecting a lot more trouble than a simple conversation.

"I'm not comfortable going in as a decoy if you haven't told me what's happening," I said. "I know something is happening. Why put undercover resources on the scene if it isn't?"

"That sounds fair to me," said Nathan's father. "You owe her that."

All the eyes at the table turned to stare at him.

Then Darcy Rogers shifted her gaze back to the chief, and he finally nodded.

"Entwistle is one of our murder suspects," she said. "We don't have enough on him to make an arrest, and if we brought him in for questioning, he'd lawyer up before we finished reading his rights. He's a former partner of GG Garcia, also his cousin, and a very wily and ruthless man. However, he tends to boast at times when his silence might do him more good. In other words, the dog park is exactly the kind of place where he might talk too much."

"Am I supposed to be asking these people something?" I asked. "About the murder? Try to stir up conversation, or what?"

There was a beat of silence.

Darcy Rogers looked at each of the men and finally back at me. "If it comes up and there's a natural way to ask more about who they think killed Garcia, go ahead. I'd say the best approach is act clueless, like you're a tourist and curious about everything to do with the town," said Darcy.

"Dress up a little bit so they can see your legs," added one of the cops I didn't know well. He waggled his eyebrows suggestively.

Nathan frowned at him. "She's already going in as a sitting duck, and now you want her to attract sexual predators?"

"Maybe it would be good if someone could explain the dressing-up bit?" I asked, trying to sound like I was one of the team, not a scared, tentative female.

"The only reason," said the chief, "is that Entwistle won't talk unless it's to a cute woman. You should only do what you're comfortable with. Okay?"

I nodded.

"Mostly you're listening," said Darcy Rogers again, directing her comments at me. "If there's a lull in the conversation, you could ask what happened. Say something about how you're worried about crime in town, is it safe to walk on the beaches at night, and so on. Got it?"

"Okay. What does he look like?"

"You can't miss him. He's over six feet with white hair and a black pug dog." That matched what Jager had told me.

After more heated back-and-forth about the wisdom of sending a civilian to follow up on Davis Jager's tip, Nathan finally grudgingly agreed with the plan. "If anything happens to her . . ."

"She'll be fine, I promise. But we should do this today, because Garcia's murder will be fresh on their minds," Darcy said. "If we wait another day or two, the discussion could be over. If a new girl comes into the park sniffing around, asking questions about old news, they're going to be suspicious."

I agreed to meet the undercover officers at the police department at three forty-five. We would go over the plan in more detail, and I would see all of them in disguise so I would know who to call on to get help if I needed it.

The lunch group broke up, and I followed Nathan out to the sidewalk.

"Are you certain you want to do this?"

I nodded slowly and swallowed. "If it can help solve the murder, I'm happy to do it. You know Ziggy as well as I do; who knows if he'll cooperate. But you know I'm good at listening, and it sounds like I'll be perfectly safe. Probably safer than I'd be at the dog park on an ordinary day."

Nathan's dad emerged from the noodle house and walked over to where we were talking. "Son, you've got yourself a feisty one here." He laughed and clapped Nathan on the back. "I think she'll be just fine in that dog park. And I'll dress up in my loud tourist shorts and sit across the road by the beach in case there's any trouble."

I gave my husband a good squeeze and a kiss and drove the scooter back to Houseboat Row. Somehow I had to pound out the drafts of the articles I had promised to send my bosses on Monday before three o'clock. But first, I'd find my undercover outfit.

I sorted through my drawers for my shortest shorts and also found a T-shirt that I rarely wore because it was a little too tight and a little too thin, with an uncomfortably deep V neck. Finally, at the bottom of the lingerie drawer, I found the push-up brassiere Danielle had given me as a gag gift for my bridal shower. It was black lace, which would show as a suggestive shadow through the thin T-shirt. I also found a flowered visor, on loan from my mother, that I had deemed too silly to wear around town. But a tourist would wear such a thing, especially one dressing like I was planning. Suddenly I was beginning to lose my nerve. I needed to focus on my work.

I began to shape the notes I had taken on the Stock Island and Geiger Key restaurants into the words of a column. Stock Island, I told my readers, had a different vibe than Key West—partly funky and partly upscale marinas, but definitely worth sampling. I described the meal I'd shared with my mother and Miss Gloria and Mrs. Dubisson, and also recommended a burger or fish sandwich at the bar on the far side of the pool. I mentioned the other popular eateries on the island, including Roostica for their Sunday gravy; El Siboney for the same Cuban dishes you could get at their branch in Key West, but usually with less of a wait; and Hogfish for classic fried-fish dinners with music on the dock. I spent more time on the ambience of Geiger Key. It wasn't my most brilliant writing, but it was serviceable and informative. I could tweak it this weekend when my mind was fresh.

Then I laid out the two Woman's Club cookbooks—the old version I'd found in the library and the newer edition I'd borrowed from my mom—and began to summarize the essence of vintage Key West Food. Fish was featured on most menus, of course, because we lived on an island, so it was always available and always fresh. Many recipes featured conch fritters, conch steaks, conch chowder. The tough bivalve was very popular in the 1940s, if conclusions could be drawn by studying the older cookbook.

A text came in from Nathan. *Still okay about the dog park plan?*

All good, I texted back. *Would it be okay if I messaged Davis Jager in the hospital? I have his phone number from the other day. Only to check in on him. I'm not going to interfere with the case, only see how the poor guy is feeling.*

There was a longish pause, and then the dots indicating that he was typing. *Okay*, he said, *but please stick to inquiring about his health?*

Sometimes I got annoyed with my husband for acting overprotective, but in this case, I thought he was right to be cautious. The timing of the attack on Jager was too much of a coincidence for me to assume it had nothing to do with Miss Gloria and me and our appearance at the Fish Camp last night. On the other hand, Jager might tell me something he wouldn't tell the cops. He wouldn't want to draw police suspicion in his direction. I sent a text off, inquiring about his health, but heard nothing back. Feeling too antsy to concentrate on work, I did a Google search for Davis Jager's blog.

The top entry had the title *Spotted a Rare Bird? Keep Your Beak Shut!* He had written that as a bird lover, he believed his first responsibility should lie with protecting the birds, not inviting masses of ignorant amateurs to rush in with their cameras and life lists. *If the bird appears in a strange habitat, likely he or she has been blown off course and is confused and quite possibly stressed and worn down by that experience. A flush of bird watchers could only make his experience worse.*

After taking a few notes to share with Nathan later, I pulled a chicken I'd been defrosting out of the fridge, painted it with olive oil, salt, and fresh rosemary, and slid it into the oven at a lowish temperature. It should be perfectly crispy and cooked through by the time I got home. At the last minute, I added a handful of garlic cloves to the pan, and some squares of butter. I would use this to make a quick roasted-garlic gravy later. I peeled and cubed potatoes and left them on the stovetop in a pot of water. In my experience, it was always best to be ready for dinner ahead of time, not scrambling around for ideas when starving. That often led to omnivorous snacking, unhealthy takeout, and late-night indigestion.

At three thirty, as planned, I got on my scooter and buzzed over to the police department nearby. With all the changes in our world, it was no longer possible to walk in the front door without getting vetted. A visitor was required to pick up the phone and explain her business. I told the woman answering the phone that I was meeting Nathan and several other police officers for a powwow. She buzzed me in. Steve Torrence emerged from his office at the end of the hall to usher me to a conference room. He paused midway down the hall and began to snicker.

"Good god, woman," he said, waving me to follow, "where in the world did you come up with that outfit? I think you're going to fit right in with our team."

I swatted him on the back and followed him into the conference room. I watched recognition and then shock cross Nathan's face.

"Is it that bad?" I asked.

"It's quite perfect," said the chief, trying to hide his grin. "These are our undercover officers, Byrd and Mancuso. You fit right in."

Neither looked as though they'd had a haircut or a shave in many weeks, possibly months. They wore cut-off jeans and faded T-shirts and ball caps with logos from two different baseball teams. One had a tattoo of New Jersey on his calf and a sleeve of fuzzy-colored images on each arm. The other had an obvious tear under his shirt's armpit where dark hair poked through.

"Even more important to our team, please meet Schatzi and Wolf." He pointed to the two large black dogs seated attentively next to their handlers.

The men reviewed the plan, with the chief ticking off individual items. "Byrd and Mancuso will be staked out in the big-dog park with their shepherds. Your father-in-law will be at Higgs Beach, either on the beach or perusing the names on the AIDS Memorial. The rest of us will be a block away in a van with a flower shop logo so as not to attract attention. But all you have to do is shout," he said, his eyes boring into mine, "and we will be there instantly."

As if he could read my mind, Nathan said, "Yes, it may look like it's overreacting, but we have one man murdered and another clinging to life in the hospital. It's possible the person responsible for both will be in the dog park circle. We're not taking any chances with you."

Chapter Thirteen

Mr. Tucci recalled that he found her in the kitchen the morning after, in her bathrobe, using her bare hands to tear cold flesh from the piglet for a platter of leftover pork.

"How can you not fall in love with a woman like that?" he asked.

"It was the way the light hit the carcass," Ms. Blunt said.

—Frank Bruni, "Hollywood Ending,
With Meatballs,"
The New York Times, October 2, 2012

I swung back by the houseboat to pick up Ziggy, who danced with excitement when he saw me heading to the closet where we stored his carry bag. I tucked him into the bag, fit it into the back basket of my scooter, and drove across town on White Street to Higgs Beach. The dog park was part of the Clarence Higgs Memorial Park, directly across the street from the Atlantic Ocean and the White Street Pier. I parked the scooter on White Street, around the corner from the entrance to the small-dog park. I could hear Ziggy whining from his basket in response to the yaps and yips behind the fence.

My heart was beginning to beat faster, and my face felt hot. I took off my helmet and replaced it with the flowered visor, then extracted Ziggy from his bag. He looked around, his sleek little body vibrating with excitement. As soon as I clipped on the leash and set him on the sidewalk, he began to pull me toward the dog park entrance. Inside the chain-link fence, ten or twelve small dogs cavorted around a circle of people in white plastic chairs.

"Here we go," I told Ziggy. "Let's not do anything too dumb. A bunch of your father's police buddies are watching."

Once I'd fumbled through the double gates set up to prevent doggy escapes, I unsnapped Ziggy's leash and watched him charge into the knot of dogs. I sidled toward the circle of owners, noticing that there was an unoccupied chair near the water spigot. I picked it up and moved it to the shade outside the group, pretending to nonchalantly scroll through email on my phone. I was determined not to scan the adjoining big-dog park for my undercover guardians. I also wanted to avoid studying the beach across the road where my father-in-law had promised to station himself. Once I felt I could breathe and act more normally, I looked around the faces in the circle and smiled at a man who met my eyes.

"New here?" he asked. He pushed the blue cap with a leaping fish logo back from his forehead and swiped at a patch of damp.

"New to the dog park, not the island," I said. "Ziggy is my boyfriend's dog, and I promised I would take care of him this week while he's visiting his mother in Miami."

"There are a few rules you should know about." He laughed. "Pick up your poop, don't give the other dogs treats without asking, and bring gossip."

This prompted a laugh from the other people in the group, and I snickered like it was the funniest thing I'd heard all day.

"I didn't bring anything for you today," I said in a breezy voice. "Next time."

I settled back in the chair and fixed my gaze on my phone, determined to step out of the spotlight and listen.

The dog owners chatted about an electricity outage that had occurred briefly yesterday after a sailboat hit a power line on the Seven Mile Bridge. "They oughta have their boating license suspended," said a big, white-haired man across the circle with a pug on his lap. I assumed it was Mr. Entwistle, tall with white hair and the right kind of dog.

The group of dogs, including my Ziggy, burst into the circle, panting wildly. Entwistle distributed treats, and a second dog, a white-and-brown terrier, jumped onto his lap, knocking the black pug to the ground. The new dog licked Entwistle's chin and then took off with the gang again, the pug puffing along at the rear. Could a man who dogs loved also be a murderer?

"What do you suppose his wife will do with Rocky?" This question came from the woman to my left, who wore psychedelic pink-and-green leggings and a crop top, none of which left much to the imagination. As my paternal grandmother would have surely said.

"From what GG said in the past," said Entwistle, scowling, "she won't keep him. The dog bit her a couple of months ago when she was trying to snap his leash on. She was perfectly happy to have me pick him up today and said I could keep him as long as I wanted." He broke into a grin. "She didn't appreciate GG taking Rocky's side about the bite. He said the dog couldn't help it: he doesn't care much for women."

"We women aren't big fans of his either," said the leggings lady. This brought another big laugh from the group.

"Which dog is Rocky?" I asked. "And why does something have to be done with him?"

"You may have read in the papers about GG Garcia's murder?" Another man pointed to a handsome Jack Russell terrier that had pinned down a white poodle and was chewing on her neck. "The one on top is Rocky. He was a lot like his owner."

"It was all in good fun," said Mr. Entwistle. He swiveled his head and looked me over from crown to feet. I felt as though I were getting peeled.

The woman in the loud tights pushed her sunglasses up to the top of her head. "One lady brought her little Havanese to the park a couple months ago. The dog was timid to begin with. Rocky bullied that poor thing to pieces, and it was all she could do to wrestle her dog away from him." She blew out a breath of air and shook her head with disgust. "Do you remember what GG said when he realized the lady was mad?"

The men in the circle nodded, Entwistle with a smirk on his face. The woman turned to me.

"He said, 'Your dog will have to learn to push back the way the women in my life have with me.' He was a little bit of a jerk," she added, using air quotes as she said *little bit* and looking over at me.

"A jerk who got things done," said Entwistle, listening from across the circle. "Half the projects in this town have been accomplished thanks to him. Do you think Stock Island would be anything other than a cesspool complete with trailer trash if it wasn't for his big ideas for their marinas?"

Which was a super-harsh assessment. It encapsulated one of the hardest struggles on our island: Were we pricing ourselves out of the housing market for the nonrich folks who needed shelter? If so, where were the worker bees—on whom our tourism-driven economy depended—going to live? I pulled my phone out again so I could pretend to text while I listened without showing too much on my face.

Entwistle snapped his fingers. "The trouble with GG was he had no loyalty and no limits to his greed either."

"Have they arrested anyone for his murder?" the woman in the tights asked. "I'm guessing they'll come up with a lot of suspects."

"Why is that?" I couldn't help asking. "Was he unpopular?" I tried to keep my voice level and barely interested, remembering how tense the police officers had been in our meeting. I focused on remembering everything anyone said: that GG Garcia had been a womanizer, a civic visionary, a destroyer of homes and small businesses, a thorn in the side of the city commissioners. I didn't dare ask any other clarifying questions for fear I'd appear suspiciously nosy.

Ziggy came running up to me, panting heavily around the dirty tennis ball clenched in his mouth. He dropped it at my feet. "Good boy, Zig," I said, pitching it back into the open space. Two of the terriers chased after it, but Ziggy was too fast, scooping it up before they arrived. To my left, what looked a black Lab puppy splashed into the kiddy pool near the spigot and flopped into the water.

"Is there to be a wake for Garcia?" the man next to Mr. Entwistle asked.

Entwistle grimaced. “Fancy Woman’s Club thing. As if Garcia ever set foot in that building without getting dragged by his wife or his mother.”

At that moment, Rocky, the Jack Russell, noticed the German shepherd patrolling the fence in the adjoining big-dog park. Barking shrilly, he rushed over, the other dogs in tow, and began to fling himself, snarling, at the big black dog behind the chain-link fence. One of the undercover cops, who’d been slouching on a bench, ran over to collect his dog, releasing a stream of swear words under his breath. So much for undercover.

“Control your animals,” he snapped at our circle.

I snatched up Ziggy and clipped on his leash. Entwistle collected Rocky and followed me to the gate.

“Do come back,” he said, brushing a strand of hair off my forehead. “We hardly had the chance to talk.”

I gritted out a fake smile and made my way out of the park, noticing the man across the street wearing baggy pink plaid shorts and a battered, wide-brimmed straw hat. He was seated on a bench next to the AIDS Memorial reading a paperback. Good lord, this was my father-in-law. Did he travel with that outfit in his suitcase? I kept my head down and hurried to my scooter so as not to make eye contact or burst out laughing and give either of us away.

The woman in tights seriously disliked GG Garcia, I was pretty sure of that. And several others weren’t that fond of him either. Only Entwistle had stood up for him, and wasn’t he supposed to be a major suspect? Well, sort of stuck up for him, in a backhanded way. He creeped me out, especially with the hair brushing bit, but that didn’t mean he’d killed Garcia.

Unless he was a very good actor. I fastened Ziggy into his carrier and drove home.

Almost from the parking lot, I could smell the glorious scent of roasting chicken coming from our boat. That always made me happy. Today it sent the message that things were normal, though I was not at all sure this was true. Once inside, I stripped off the silly outfit right away, changed into jean shorts and a T-shirt that read *Home is where the cat is*, and messaged my notes to Nathan. Then I called him.

"Is it okay to put you on speakerphone?" he asked. "The chief and my father want to hear your report."

I repeated the snippets of conversation I'd heard and my reactions to the various characters. I summed it up by saying that while GG Garcia wasn't well liked, he seemed to be admired for his ruthlessness, adding that I couldn't be sure I'd gotten a murderous vibe from Mr. Entwistle. "I didn't like him, though, even though some of the dogs did. And he did say GG lacked loyalty."

"Thanks for helping us out," said the chief. "Let Nathan know if you remember anything else."

Nathan came back on the line. "You did great," he said, then dropped his voice. "Did that asshat hit on you?"

"He did, but I handled it. I don't know what I found out, but maybe you'll find something useful in those notes."

"My father was very impressed with your cool," he said.

"And I was impressed with his undercover outfit." I snickered. "Seems like a lot of effort went into that dog park thing and not much came back . . ."

"He wants to see our place." Nathan interrupted me, his voice loaded with resignation. "He wonders about coming over for dinner. I told him you were extremely busy this week and it was too short notice."

"How long is he going to be in town?" I asked, thinking madly about when we could shoehorn him in. It would be so rude not to invite him after he'd asked, even though a normal relative would have given us notice. And probably a son with a warm relationship would have invited his father long before this. I glanced at the calendar on my phone. Definitely not tomorrow, when I was due to help my mother with her memorial reception at the Woman's Club. That would be an all-day affair, and I was certain to be bushed by the end—in no shape to host a dinner party. Maybe a day on the weekend.

"He's leaving Saturday morning on an early flight to Miami," Nathan said. "He'll be done with his mock accreditation work tomorrow night. But not to worry: I told him this was a crazy week for all of us, and he didn't warn us he was coming."

I heaved a big sigh.

"Is he free tonight? I put an organic chicken in the oven and set it on slow roast before I left for the dog park. I think he would eat that, right?"

"Are you sure you can manage this? I know you're very busy. Mashed potatoes?" Nathan asked.

"Of course, and roasted garlic gravy that he can take or leave."

"I hate to make you scramble," he said, his voice holding a mixture of gratitude and reluctance.

"It's fine, really. Should I ask Miss Gloria? She would love to meet him and would definitely bring a spark to the conversation. I know my mother is swamped, or I would invite them too." In truth, for once I was glad they were swamped, because six people constituted a serious dinner party with its accompanying pressure. I might adore all the attendees except the guest of honor—I didn't know him well enough to have formed an opinion—but I wasn't up for that tonight. Even if I had done a lot of the prep work before leaving for the dog park.

"Miss Gloria would be perfect. I'll extend your gracious offer to my father and let him know what we're eating," said my husband. "Something like seven o'clock?"

I glanced at my phone. That gave me about an hour to pull things together. "Sounds about right."

"You're a gem among wives, you know that, right?"

"Actually, I do know that," I said. I figured he could hear the grin in my voice. "It's nice to be appreciated."

Chapter Fourteen

If I give you all of my recipes, you won't have any reason to come home," my mother used to joke. It was a self-deprecating observation with a grain of truth. Food is home is family.

—Nicole Zhu, "Chinese Cooking Helps Me Connect With My Mother—And Helps Me Prepare to Lose Her," *Electric Lit*, April 8, 2021

Over the next hour, I cooked the big pot of potatoes and mashed them with salt and pepper, a large square of butter, and a few dollops of sour cream. Then I whisked more butter along with flour and stock into the chicken drippings for gravy and, when it had thickened, finally whirled that together with the garlic cloves that had roasted to a rich softness alongside the chicken.

As I was sliding the prepared food into the oven to keep warm, Miss Gloria arrived on our deck with Sparky and T-Bone, who settled into one of the lounge chairs with Evinrude.

"It smells divine in here," she said, coming into the kitchen. "I can't believe that man is showing up for dinner with no notice. Who else but you would be able to pull such a thing off?"

"My mother and grandmother, of course." I grinned, feeling a lot better now that everything was ready and she was here. "What do you think for a green vegetable—green beans almondine? Brussels sprouts? Or plain old peas?"

"If he's a fussbudget, hardly anyone objects to plain old peas," she said. "How can I help?"

I moved a few dishes of ingredients for predinner snacks from the counter to the table. She perched in a wicker chair facing our little built-in banquette with its sea-blue cushions and began to stuff pimento cheese into short lengths of celery.

"Okay," I said, more to myself than to her. "I'll cut up the chicken in half an hour. The potatoes are warming in the oven. The peas I'll heat up last minute. Cookies and ice cream in the freezer. I'd love to make a key lime pie, but we've run out of time. If he'd given me a tiny bit of notice, I could have picked up a pie at Key West Cakes."

"Everyone loves cookies and ice cream," my friend said. She looked up from her work and frowned at my cat T-shirt and cutoff shorts. "Are you wearing that to dinner?"

"I guess not." I laughed and went into the bedroom to change into a pink sundress that skimmed my body without feeling tight or show-off-y. Nathan always said it brought out the reddish glints in my hair and the bloom in my cheeks.

At five minutes after seven, I heard the men's voices and felt the slight rock of the boat as they stepped from the dock to our deck. I carried a tray of hors d'oeuvres out to the deck, where two bottles of wine were waiting. "Welcome to our home," I told Nathan's father. I set the food on the table and gave him a peck on the cheek. "This is my dear friend and neighbor, Miss Gloria Peterson. And these are our feline residents, Evinrude, Sparky, and T-Bone. You've already seen Mr. Ziggy, or at least, you've seen him in action. And this is Nathan's father, Chester Bransford," I added for Miss Gloria's sake, even though it was obvious from looking at the two men that they had to be blood relations.

"A pleasure," said Nathan's dad. "I'm delighted to make your acquaintance. My friends call me Skip." Miss Gloria's tiny hand was swallowed up in his big one. "Your place is very cozy," he said, looking around the deck. In truth, our home felt small with two big men and all the animals added to the mix. I was relieved that it was cool enough to eat out on the deck. Nathan poured glasses of wine while we explained the nuts and bolts of living on Houseboat Row and how I, and then Nathan, had come to live here.

"He wasn't especially keen on the idea of living on a houseboat with neighbors close by, but he fell in love with this gal and was smart enough to act on it," said Miss Gloria.

Fifteen minutes of small talk later, Miss Gloria helped me ferry serving dishes to the deck—a steaming bowl of mashed potatoes, a platter of crispy-skinned chicken, a small bowl of peas, and the gravy.

"This looks delicious," said Skip. He loaded his plate with food, even serving himself a spoonful of roasted-garlic gravy, though he was careful not to contaminate his mashed potatoes.

"Is there any progress on the case of the body on the beach?" Miss Gloria asked.

I hadn't had time to tell her about my visit to the dog park, so I described the various characters I'd met and summarized what the people had said about GG Garcia. "Apparently he was a womanizer, and he steamrolled objections to his projects in town. Even his dog is a bully," I said. "He tried to take on a German shepherd through the fence between the two dog park sections and whipped all the other little dogs into a frenzy. Including our Ziggy."

"Why was the dead man's dog at the park?" Miss Gloria asked.

"A friend brought him," I said. I glanced at Nathan to see if he minded me adding my comments about Entwistle. He gave a small shake of his head. "Apparently Garcia's wife was not fond of him."

"Not fond of the dog or her husband?" Miss Gloria asked.

Everyone laughed. "It might have been both," I said.

"Poor dog is probably mourning his father and wondering why he didn't come home last night," Miss Gloria said. "That's why he behaved badly."

"You see why we love her?" I said to Nathan's father. "She can find a bright side in any situation and a good streak in even the worst character."

Miss Gloria beamed, then turned to Nathan's dad. "Speaking of characters . . . we've met your ex-wife, Helen, and in fact, after a somewhat rocky beginning, we've grown very fond of her. And now meeting you—if I may be so bold—I can't help feeling curious about why the marriage ended."

Skip looked a little stunned, as did my husband. "She cuts right to the bone, doesn't she?" Skip asked, looking around the table. I could only shrug and grin.

"But I don't mind telling you. We were all having a hard time because of what happened to Vera. Helen blamed me and

I blamed her. I thought she should've kept a closer rein on Vera—she should never have been allowed to hang out with those wild kids. Helen thought I was wrong to assume she was solely responsible for guiding Vera. She also thought I did lousy police work—if I'd done a good job, she would've been recovered sooner. Finally, I never have been a good communicator, or so I was told." His smile was a little grim. "Things grew very frosty between us. In the end, I looked outside for what I couldn't get in my marriage. And that didn't go over well."

"And why would it, sir?" asked Miss Gloria. "I hope you've learned your lesson in case there's a next time."

"You're a very blunt lady," Skip said, softening the words with a stiff smile.

"Once you pass that eighty-year-old landmark," said Miss Gloria, "it seems silly to hold back, don't you think? And besides, we want to know what our Nathan's future has in store for him. And what we might have to watch out for. Hayley is my best friend in the world, so I feel a duty to look out for her."

I could tell Nathan was dying inside, but he was also laughing. Miss Gloria was a pip through and through.

"How in the world did a lady like you end up living on a houseboat in Key West?" Skip asked Miss Gloria.

She launched into the story I'd heard so many times: she and her husband Frank had been living in Michigan when neighbors invited them down to the keys on vacation, and they'd fallen in love with Key West. As she talked, my mind wandered a bit and I mulled over what I had discovered at the dog park. It didn't seem like enough to justify all the attention from the police—the vehicle disguised as a flower delivery van, the canine officers posing like big dog park regulars, Nathan's father in that ridiculous outfit. I had tried to report everything I'd noticed in detail, but it didn't add up to much. I hadn't much liked Entwistle, but I hadn't been able to confirm their suspicions about him.

When Miss Gloria had finished relating her Key West story, I asked Nathan, "What were you hoping to learn at the dog park? I feel like I've disappointed you guys. I can't quite understand why so many police were involved."

"Here's the thing," Nathan said. "The attack on Garcia looks like a vicious crime perpetrated on what's essentially a public beach. Then a fellow who begins to nose around a little bit about the murder ends up unconscious in the hospital. And no one from the public is talking to us. Whether they're afraid of someone or really don't know anything or are trying to protect themselves or someone else, no one's coming forward. We're not getting the leads we need from the community."

"You can't solve cases without community help," said Nathan's father. "I learned that the hard way back when I was a cop on a beat. It's important to cultivate relationships with the people so they trust us. Obviously, we can't be everywhere, and civilians see things we might miss. If they're afraid to come to us, we don't get their information and we don't solve the crime.

"But the bottom line is, we were hoping you might hear something damning from Entwistle, or about him. Or recognize someone at the dog park who'd been at Geiger Key the night before."

I reviewed my memories again in case I'd overlooked someone, but the dog park inhabitants were unfamiliar to me. "Sorry, if there was overlap, I missed it. I think I told you about every word Entwistle said."

"Don't worry about it, sweetheart; the case doesn't hinge on you. What are you two ladies getting up to tomorrow?" Nathan asked as I served ice cream and cookies.

"There's a funeral reception for Mr. Garcia at the Woman's Club tomorrow late afternoon. We're helping my mother and Sam with the serving. Actually, I'll be there all day finishing up with cooking."

"It's going to be a feast, from what Hayley tells me," said Miss Gloria. "Plus, we'll have a front-row seat to any family drama. Will the police be in attendance?"

"We'll definitely be in the back of the room for the memorial service, but cops stick out like sore thumbs at a party," Nathan said. "As usual, listen as much as you can, but please leave the action to the professionals."

"You know we're good at that," said Miss Gloria, winking at Skip. "Both Hayley and I can talk a dog off a meat wagon, but we can listen just as well."

I caught Nathan and his father exchanging a knowing look and a smile. I didn't like the idea that they shared the notion that we women couldn't be good listeners, but I did like the possibility of Nathan bonding with his dad.

Once our company had departed, Nathan helped me stash the dishes in the dishwasher and put away the leftover chicken. The potatoes and gravy were gone.

"This was amazing," said Nathan, kissing me on top of the head. "Thanks for coming up with such a feast on short notice."

"You're welcome. I'm glad to see you enjoying your father," I said to Nathan, as we retired to the bedroom.

"I wouldn't have chosen the word *enjoying*," he said.

"Oh? What word would you use?" I sat on the bed and patted the spot beside me. Ziggy and Evinrude jumped up and began to jockey for position between our pillows. "While you're explaining, I never did quite understand how he ended up here."

Nathan heaved a big sigh and dropped his polo shirt and socks in the laundry basket. "I told you that he's here in Key West on the mock accreditation team, right? It's their job to go over every square inch of our paperwork to make sure all our policies have been followed and documented. He can't do the real accreditation because it would be a conflict of interest, obviously." He ran his fingers through his hair and wiped his eyes. "According to the chief, he asked to be on this team. He's got so much seniority and experience that no one was going to turn that request down. Unfortunately, he's finding some discrepancies in some of our documents and acting like a bit of a dick about it. It's completely embarrassing—a grown man having his father find fault with the work he's done for years, including the work of my colleagues and the work of the chief. Ridiculous."

He stomped into the bathroom to get washed up for bed. I wondered if I'd ever understand what had gone so wrong between them. I also couldn't help wondering whether my pal Miss Gloria was losing her marbles in a small way. That might explain her asking questions that were blunt to the point of rude.

Chapter Fifteen

Make your appetizers small, pretty, zippy, and easy to handle—for it is very very hard to greet an admiral with decorum when involved with a limp piece of celery overstuffed with soft cheese, and practically impossible to exchange witticisms with the suave novelist when one's whole being is concentrated on the problem of what to do with olive pits!

—*The Key West Cookbook* by the Members of the Key West Woman's Club, 1949

The Woman's Club was housed in a stunning two-story home on Duval Street, right in the middle of the downtown party action. The Hard Rock Café sat a stone's throw to the right. To the left, visitors could grab a fast bite at Wendy's. A row of touristy craft booths was located across the street. My tarot-card-reading friend Lorenzo took a second shift there after his nightly appearance at Mallory Square until he determined that alcohol-infused tourists and tarot were not a good mix.

Wide white porches and tall columns against the red brick set this building apart from other structures in the neighborhood. Welcoming wicker benches were placed on the front porch, and it was easy to imagine wiling away an afternoon watching the Duval Street shenanigans while feeling comfortably removed from the madness. The inside was equally beautiful, with wooden floors, old-fashioned wallpaper, wicker seating, and balloon window treatments. Chandeliers, large mirrors, and stained-glass windows reminded visitors of more elegant, more formal days.

My mother and Sam had parked their van in the yard behind the home and were busy unloading coolers and boxes. I stashed my scooter and plunged into the work, ferrying food from their truck into the kitchen.

Martha Hubbard arrived shortly after we did, and I helped her transport her goodies into the kitchen as well. She seemed much more relaxed than she had the last time I saw her, when she was deeply afraid that her food had caused a poisoning death. Fortunately, we had been able to help find the real killer. I gave her a quick hug. Her cheeks were rosy, and she looked thin, fit, and happy. She wore a white T-shirt, revealing colorful tattoos on her arms, and had tied her sun-streaked hair back into a stylish knot.

"This is going to be quite a feast," I said, looking over the sea of hors d'oeuvres.

"Andi Garcia has been a member of this club forever," said my mom, "and besides, her family is old Key West, with roots that reach way down below the water table. The ladies wanted us to do something special for her in this terrible time."

"Your mother's right. Even though it may sound harsh, this event has a lot more to do with supporting Mrs. Garcia than mourning her husband." Martha tied a crisp blue apron over her cutoffs and handed another one to me.

I could hardly imagine how Mr. Garcia had behaved over the years to create this kind of rancor in the wake of his death. "Mom said that you belong to the Woman's Club as well?" I asked, now super curious about what she knew about the Garcias.

"I love the history here," she said, a grin on her face, "and I love making recipes from their old cookbook. At most of the meetings, I make a few vintage dishes and give brief talks to the women about how ingredients and cooking have changed over time." Her eyes lit up as she described several of her favorites. My mother bustled over to me with a platter of three-tiered rectangles wrapped in damp cheesecloth.

"If you could cut these into finger-sized sandwiches and arrange them on platters, Sam and I will work on the shrimp puffs and the pigs in blankets."

"Absolutely," I told her, then washed my hands and began to cut up the first miniature sandwiches. They looked adorable once sliced, with stripes of wheat and white bread enveloping the layers of pimento cheese and egg salad.

"I've never been in this building before. It's gorgeous," I said. "I've seen the bleachers set up in the front yard for the Fantasy Fest and other parades but never thought about coming inside."

"It really feels like old-time Key West, doesn't it? You lose that sense out on Duval Street," Sam said. "This house has a fascinating history. Did you know that the first Key West library was established right here in this building? The books were stored here, and the Woman's Club paid for librarian salaries and all the other expenses until 1948, when the land on Fleming Street was donated to build a real library."

Martha added, "This house is one of the few brick homes on the island, built by Captain Martin and Eleanor Hellings for one of their daughters in 1892, shortly after the terrible fire that wiped out half of Key West. It has been owned by the Key West Woman's Club since 1940. And the members are very dedicated to taking care of it—in fact, restoring it to its former glory."

I'd have more time to look around when we were cleaning up after the reception. We spent the next hour arranging sandwiches on platters and filling choux pastry shells with lime-scented vanilla and chocolate pastry cream. My mother cut up fruit and tossed it artistically into baskets carved from whole watermelon rinds while Sam peeled pink shrimp. And then we unloaded and arranged cookies, hundreds and hundreds of them, along with key lime squares, Bess Truman's Ozark pudding containing black walnuts and a dash of rum in the whipped cream, and guava duff, all prepared by Martha from the recipes in the Woman's Club cookbook.

"We'll heat up the conch chowder when we get back," my mother said. "Tiny cups of soup will be one of our passed hors d'oeuvres, along with the hot cheese puffs filled with shrimp salad and Pat Kennedy's pigs in a blanket. I tripled that recipe because, silly as it may sound, they always go first. And trust me, it's not only kids who scoop them up. We'll pop those in the oven right before the guests show up."

She was beginning to sound a little manic.

"Did you make every recipe in the cookbook and then some?" I teased. "I hope we're not serving turtle soup." The idea of harvesting the green fat under a turtle's shell to make one of the recipes I'd seen in the cookbook made me queasy. I was overall an adventurous eater, but here I drew a line.

"It looks that way, doesn't it? It feels a little like that too. But we eschewed the spiced tongue and sweetbreads supreme," Sam said, putting a comforting hand on my mother's back and adding a wink. I was instantly grateful (again) for the way he kept her grounded. "And no turtle soup."

"We'll see you and Gloria back here at four. Please remind her to wear a collared white shirt and black pants and leave off as many sequins as she can manage."

"Will do," I said. "We pressed our outfits yesterday so we'd be presentable, humble, and respectful, as good servers should be." I paused, torn over whether I should tell them about the dinner the night before and Miss Gloria's worrisome comments. "I'm wondering," I said, "whether her age is starting to show."

"What do you mean?" my mother asked, her face alert with concern. "Does she seem tired?"

Sam came over to stand beside her. They loved Miss Gloria almost as much as I did.

"Not exactly," I said. "She knows how to pace herself with naps. When she's awake, she has as much energy as I do. But we had her and Nathan's father over for dinner, and she asked some pretty rude questions. About why his relationship with Helen failed and so on."

Sam snorted with relieved laughter. "That's our Gloria. She doesn't suffer fools gladly, and from what we've heard about Nathan's dad, he might be one." He straightened his shoulders. "Sorry, I shouldn't talk that way about your father-in-law."

We'd all heard a little too much about him from both Nathan's mother and his sister. Nathan barely spoke of him.

"We'll help you keep an eye on her tonight," my mom said, still looking concerned. "We don't want to stress her out with too much work. Speaking of trouble, have you heard any more about the murder?" she asked.

"Nobody's been arrested," I said, "and I'm not sure they even have solid suspects." I took a deep breath, wondering if it would be a mistake to share more worries with my mother. But I'd hate for her to hear this from someone other than me. "Davis Jager was attacked the other night, and he's in the hospital."

My mother's eyes popped wide open. "Do they think this is connected to Garcia's murder? Are you in danger too?"

"I can't imagine why I would be. Besides, I didn't see anything; I only found the body." But of course, her questions had the instant effect of churning up my insides.

"Have you heard anything?" I asked Martha. "You know the Woman's Club crowd as well as anyone. Everyone in the club probably knows the Garcias."

She wrinkled her nose. "I've been pretty busy with other jobs, but I'll certainly keep my ears open tonight." She washed her hands and wiped them on her apron. "Have you considered going to visit your friend Jager at the hospital? Maybe he's remembered something about what happened."

I shook my head. "No. I did plan to text him again later and I told Nathan that, but I wouldn't call him a friend. I met him briefly standing over the body, and we talked a bit the other night when I saw him at the Fish Camp. I wasn't all that fond of him after those interactions either."

"Besides," said Sam in a stern voice, "it's not really her business at all to go off investigating. That's asking for trouble, as we've seen in the past."

My mother was nodding vigorously. "That's not Hayley's job."

"Point taken," said Martha, "but remember how I didn't want to talk to the police when I was in some trouble? Hayley was the one who encouraged me, reminding me that trying to keep the secret would only make things worse. I never would have come forward without that encouragement. This guy may have similar reasons to keep quiet, who knows?" She looked at me again. "But he seems to have connected with you."

"Ask Nathan first," my mother suggested, her forehead furrowed. She picked up the overstuffed bag containing her planner and menus and who knew what else. "We need to get going. If you could help Martha set up the tables and locate tablecloths, I will owe you forever. Everything else looks good." Her gaze swept the kitchen. "After that, go home and put up your feet for fifteen minutes. We'll see you in a couple of hours."

As Martha and I wrestled the tables out to the covered porch, I asked, "What can you tell me about GG Garcia's wife? I'm getting the feeling their marriage was not made in heaven."

"I don't think she liked him much by the end," Martha said. "I've catered dinners many times in their home, which is, by the way, spectacular. But you know how you can tell at a party when a couple is still in love? They circle around to touch base with each other, and smile across the room even if they're talking to other people. There was none of that." She snapped the leg of the table we were working on into place and started back inside the building.

"If you don't mind, while I get the chairs, please bring the white tablecloths out? You'll find them in one of the hallway drawers. Most of the time, caterers use their own stuff when they have events here, but since we're doing this for Mrs. Garcia, we have permission to use anything we find."

I hurried back to the hallway, admiring the built-in cupboards filled with linen and old-fashioned china and flatware. The drawers were painted white, with glassed-in shelves above them displaying the club's collection of china and serving dishes. After opening several drawers, I finally found one containing the tablecloths that Martha had requested in a smaller cupboard built in the corner. But the drawer balked just inches out, sticking on the one underneath. I was able to wiggle my fingers in and extract the linens. I carried them out to the porch and helped Martha spread them out.

"Do you think she disliked him enough to actually murder him?" I asked as we finished the last table. "And then leave his body at the beach during a storm?"

There was a long silence while she unstacked chairs from the dolly she'd rolled outside. "I couldn't say. You'll have to talk with her yourself."

Did her silence mean she knew more than she was willing to share? Possibly, I thought. Maybe a caterer was like a therapist, reluctant to share a client's secrets. This made some sense to me, as I could imagine that a gossip wouldn't earn repeat business in a small town.

Chapter Sixteen

I've long believed that good food, good eating, is all about risk. Whether we're talking about unpasteurized Stilton, raw oysters or working for organized crime "associates," food, for me, has always been an adventure.

—Anthony Bourdain, *Kitchen Confidential: Adventures in the Culinary Underbelly*

Even though it had been an insane week and I hadn't stopped running for what felt like forever, I judged that I had enough time to blast up to Stock Island and try to talk with Davis Jager. I thought I'd have a better chance of getting some important information about the murder and the attack on him in person, rather than through trying to call. Despite my mother's concerns, I thought Martha had a good point. Jager had tried to contact me, which suggested he'd tell me more than he might tell someone in uniform. Assuming he was still alive. For now, I ignored Mom's advice about asking Nathan for permission; he'd already agreed that it made sense for me to talk with Jager—to inquire about his health, at the very least. I'd tell him everything else when I saw him tonight.

I drove into the parking lot of the hospital and headed inside, wondering how best to weasel my way into seeing Davis Jager. If he was in the ICU, probably nothing I could say would make a difference. I had to hope he was doing better than that.

But I was in luck, even if he hadn't been. Without questioning my motives for visiting, the receptionist gave me a visitor sticker and directions to his room—good signs, I thought. His door had been left ajar, and I tapped lightly. "Mr. Jager?" I pushed the door open, bracing for what I'd see. "It's Hayley Snow. I am so sorry for what happened to you."

The head of the man in the bed was swathed in bandages, though his face was mostly clear. His skin looked sallow, mirroring the pale green of the hospital walls, and under his eyes were sunken half circles of gray. Given that, and the absence of his trademark bucket hat, I wondered if I had the right room.

His eyes blinked open, and he croaked, "Come in." Definitely Jager.

I perched on the edge of the chair next to the bed. "I wouldn't have bothered you here in the hospital, but the police are very worried about why you were attacked. I am too!"

He cleared the rasp from his throat and struggled to speak. "Somebody doesn't want me to tell secrets. They probably think that I saw too much. That's plain as the nose on your face."

"Then the question that follows must be, what secrets? Do you know who did this to you? Do you think it's related to Mr. Garcia's death?"

"I have no idea who attacked me. But what else?" he asked. "The coincidence is too great."

"Okay." I sat back in the garish orange plastic bedside chair. "I'm sure the police have asked you this already, but did you notice anyone at the bar who looked familiar? Maybe someone you saw on the beach that morning? Or someone who appeared to be watching you?"

He looked sheepish. "I'm there fairly often, so I know a lot of people. You noticed, I'm certain, that I'd had a few pops. That explains two things. First, I wasn't watching my environment for possible trouble. Any wild bird would have been more careful about his potential predators than I was. Second, I overheard the doctor in the emergency room tell the paramedic that had I not been so drunk, the assault might have killed me. As it was, I was clocked hard on the head and flopped to the ground unconscious before they had a chance to finish the job."

"So you think it was more than one person?" I asked.

He started to nod but winced partway through and palmed the back of his head gingerly.

"Yes. Because I felt more than one blow at the same time. The person who kicked my leg couldn't have been the same one who hit my head."

I tried to think about how to access details that he might not have realized he noticed. "It kind of looked like you're a regular at the Geiger Key bar," I said. "Do you have buddies who show up and hang out with you?"

"It's a rotating cast," he said, "but I especially like the bartender. He's entertaining but he doesn't get in your face. Best of all, he pours strong drinks and tall beers. I live just up the road, so I don't have far to go to drive home."

"How about that night? Who was there?" I asked.

"Entwistle, and Al, who lives across Route 1 from Government Road. We call him Pizza Al because he's the manager at Pizza Hut." He chuckled, but that appeared to hurt his lips.

"Those guys I've known forever, so I can't picture why they'd want to beat me up."

"Tell me about Entwistle," I said. His name and face had come up too many times in the past days for me not to pay attention. How was it that I hadn't even noticed him there?

"He was a friend of GG Garcia's. Or maybe not a friend; maybe a colleague would be the better word."

"A colleague in what kind of business?" I asked.

"Development," Jager said. "He has the same scorched-earth mentality that Garcia did."

"Was he also involved with birds?"

"I doubt that. We certainly never talked about birding. Sometimes he brings his dog to the bar, but it's one of those unpleasant little pugs, old and crabby. The thing growls at anyone who walks by so the waitresses aren't that thrilled to see them coming. Bringing that thing to the beach would definitely hamper his ability to spot birds."

I vaguely remembered the black pug at the dog park. He had been overshadowed by Garcia's Jack Russell, so I couldn't speak to his personality.

"What about some of Garcia's other projects, like new development up this way? Was Entwistle one of his business partners? Was Entwistle angry with him about something?" I could picture Jager blabbing at the bar about what he'd seen on the beach, thus making the killer very worried.

Jager pushed himself up in the bed, but it appeared difficult and painful. "Honestly, I don't know him well enough to say. You should call Pizza Al. He knows everything about everyone. You wouldn't believe how much time that guy spends on the phone. He's everybody's pal. He means that, too; it isn't an act.

He'd drive you to Miami in a heartbeat for a doctor's appointment or to have lunch with your mother if that's what you needed." A small light came to his eyes. "He lives in the condos directly across from the turn in the road, so he may have seen something the morning of the murder. His dog Romeo spends a lot of time out on the deck." He reached for his phone on the table beside the bed and, after some awkward flicking, managed to come up with Al's number and read it off.

I dutifully tapped it into my notes, even though it felt like another dead end. Did he think the dog would have spotted the murderer? "I'll let you rest, but one more question. When we were chatting at the table by the water, can you picture who was at the surrounding tables? Anyone who might have overheard us talking?"

He pressed his hand to his forehead. "My ex always said I drank too much, and maybe for once she was right. Wasn't there a table of kids near us? I remember our waitress was friendly with them, and I was thinking if they were old enough to drink, it wasn't by much. A couple boys and three really cute girls. One was a blonde, and the other two had dark hair. It wasn't like my teenage years. I never scored with cute chicks."

His eyes fluttered shut. I said good-bye, exited the hospital, and started home. As the traffic from Stock Island to our pier ebbed and flowed, I puzzled over Davis Jager. Unless someone had fingered and beaten up the wrong guy, he must have stepped hard on someone's toes. Yet he seemed to have no clue about his possible enemies.

Chapter Seventeen

Sympathy is nice and necessary when it's fresh. But if you leave it out too long, it curdles like old milk.
—Laura Hankin, *A Special Place for Women*

By the time I reached Houseboat Row, I was on the verge of running late. Not cool when working a funeral reception. Not cool ever in the catering business. I texted Miss Gloria as soon as I parked to tell her we should leave in ten minutes flat. Then I dashed to my boat to splash water on my face and slap on more deodorant, brush and tie my hair back, and pull on the white shirt and black pants that I had fortunately hung up out of reach this morning. Not a pet hair on them.

"Ziggy," I told Nathan's little dog, who was watching me with a distressed expression, "we're going to run out to the parking lot for a pee, and I promise something so much better later."

I snapped his leash on and trotted down the finger of the dock so he could relieve himself. "You'll be in charge tonight," I said. "But that doesn't mean throwing the cat overboard."

Back in the houseboat, I ruffled the short, shiny fur on the top of his head and kissed him in the same place. Evinrude raised his head from his perch on my pillow and blinked. I crossed the room and whispered to him, "You're really in charge, but sometimes I have to pretend so he doesn't feel left out." Then I kissed his head and dashed outside to meet my friend.

On the way to the funeral event, I caught Miss Gloria up on the murder case, including my visit to Jager. "If you happen to overhear anything that you think might be related to the murder, please let me know. I'm sure Darcy Rogers and probably several of our Key West police are going to be there and we can pass the information along rather than handling it ourselves."

She giggled. "Are you telling me to butt out?"

I began to laugh with her. "I've been told that more times than I can count, and I'm simply sharing it with you. Seriously, though, somebody at this party must know what happened on that beach. Who would be better at listening than unobtrusive servers too busy with delivering food to seem like a threat?"

She held up her palm for me to slap. "Gotcha."

By the time we had woven through the usual Key West afternoon traffic and parked in the back of the building near the Red Barn Theatre, the Woman's Club was bustling with activity. Though my mother had gently questioned the decision, the widow Mrs. Garcia had insisted that mourners be served flutes of champagne as soon as they entered. I took up my station at the front door with its red stained-glass inserts, smiling a greeting, directing guests to the ballroom, and offering the drinks. I wondered whether this was something Mrs. Garcia herself needed—and who wouldn't?—and whether she thought it would look better if everyone was drinking along with her. Most people wandered about the front rooms with glasses in their hands, chatting and laughing. That, along with the more casual funeral attire that was common in Key West, made the gathering look more like a party than a memorial service. A few women had dressed in skirts and high heels, and a smattering of men were attired in suits, but most came as though they lived on a tropical island—flowered shirts, linen pants, and flip-flops.

My tray empty, I left Miss Gloria to finish distributing her drinks and hurried to the kitchen to help my mother get the food platters ready. There was to be a short memorial service in the main space before food would be served. I hoped to get my part of the prep work done quickly so I could stand in the doorway on the side of the room and listen to the speakers. I'd seen no better way to get a sense of a person's humanity than to tune into what was said after they died. Quite naturally, there would be some exaggeration of the deceased's fine qualities, but underneath that window dressing, the real personality shone through.

Fifteen minutes later, the president of the Woman's Club, a distinguished-looking woman with gray hair, silver hoops in her ears, and a flowered headband, took the microphone at the front of the ballroom and asked the guests to be seated. Those of us in the kitchen moved to the doorway to avoid clattering around during the talks and to listen. The room had been set up with a hundred or so folding chairs facing the lectern, and now every one of them was filled. An enormous chandelier glittered over the guests, and beyond that, I could see tourists streaming by on the sidewalk along Duval Street. They would have no idea what was happening inside the handsome redbrick building they were passing. That was one of the strange things about this island—partying visitors looked in at the residents' lives like people peering into a fishbowl.

"We welcome you all to our home today," said the president, "where we share the Garcia family's grief and share stories remembering GG Garcia." She glanced at the occupants of the front row, where the widow was seated. Other front row inhabitants included two gray-haired women—one seated at each end—and a young man who had his arm around Mrs. Garcia. I assumed he was her son. He looked to be in his early twenties, with a thick head of dark hair, a strong nose, and a gold chain around his neck. She held herself stiffly, not melting into his arm as I might have expected. One of the older women was dressed all in black with a black lace scarf draped over her head, as if she was an old-world Italian *nonna*.

"I did not know GG well, but I count Mrs. Andi Garcia as one of my closest friends," said the president. "She is the dearest, funniest, most thoughtful friend a woman could ask for, and a stalwart in our organization. And that is exactly why we all wanted to hold the celebration right here." She smiled warmly at the family. "Today there will be speakers and music from members of the Southernmost Chamber Music Society. After that, we welcome you to the porch for some delicious snacks from the kitchen of our own Martha Hubbard and from our town's favorite caterer, Janet Snow."

I glanced at my mother to make sure she'd heard that she had been tagged as the town favorite. She was smiling.

"After the service," the president continued, "please feel free to walk around the rooms downstairs. We've almost completed our renovations, and we all agree they have turned out beautifully. With no further ado, I will introduce the Reverend Steve Torrence to lead the service."

My friend Steve moved forward to take her place, wearing his white robe and a golden stole—a big change from the police uniform I'd seen him in yesterday.

"It is always a sad honor to be part of a celebration of life. But the service reminds us not only of the sadness left by death, but the joy generated by life. As it is said in Romans, 'And I am convinced that nothing can ever separate us from God's love. Neither death nor life, neither angels nor demons, neither our fears for today nor our worries about tomorrow—not even the powers of hell can separate us from God's love.'"

He led us through prayers and read several more verses from the Bible that I recognized from other funerals. "Now a few of Mr. Garcia's friends and family have been invited to share stories about GG, as he was known."

The first to approach the podium was the tall, white-haired man I'd seen at the dog park, who by Davis Jager's account had also been at the Fish Camp the other night. Mr. Entwistle was popping up everywhere. Would he have the guts to speak at someone's funeral if he'd killed him only days earlier? Actually, it sounded like the perfect cover—if the man was completely cold-blooded and brazen.

"My condolences to the family," he said, nodding at the first row. His gaze lingered on Mrs. Garcia. "Gerald 'GG' Garcia was one of a kind. That's saying something on this island full of quirky personalities and flat out nuts."

There was a ripple of laughter from the audience, but Andi Garcia's face remained stony.

"He tended to hurtle right to the edge of any precipice, because he craved excitement and danger. Sometimes he jumped. And sometimes he lost his balance and fell. But almost always, he survived." He paused for a moment, looking pensive.

Was he honestly sad, or was this a performance? At this point, I suspected every show of emotion.

"He wanted to claim the world, even though not all the world agreed with being claimed. He cared very little for elected authorities, generally believing he knew better than they did. And to be honest, he was often right about the shape of Key West's future. He loved his memberships in the most exclusive clubs, but he was also generous, and I admired him for that. He loved beautiful women"—I, along with the rest of the mourners, waited for some embarrassing, horrifying disclosure—"witness his wife and mother."

He grinned at the row of family and pointed up at the ceiling like a football player who'd scored a touchdown and wanted to give God his due.

"We will miss you, buddy," he added, and then returned to his seat, stopping to speak softly to the widow on his way. She stiffened, shrinking away from his touch as he reached across her to shake her son's hand.

Something was going on there for sure. I wished Mr. Entwistle had explained more about these precipices—was it this tendency that had gotten Garcia killed? I would try to approach him later in the party and hope he didn't recognize me from the dog park.

A small man with a deep baritone voice, accompanied by a woman playing a violin, began to sing a rendition of "You

Raise Me Up" that reminded me of my grandmother's funeral and brought tears to my eyes. To keep my composure, I studied the mourners in the first few rows. On the left side, opposite the Garcias but farther back, another old woman had watched Entwistle return to his seat. Now she glared at the back of GG's son's head with a look of pure venom on her face. She was flanked on either side by lovely teenage girls who appeared frozen with—what? Sadness? Fear? I couldn't be sure, except I knew from my own experience that it was hard for someone in the bloom of youth to absorb an unexpected death.

We listened to a few more speakers, but no immediate family members spoke. I heard nothing that might shed light on the man's murder. The club president took the podium again and repeated her invitation to the reception.

The next hour elapsed in a blur as we ferried platters of food to the tables on the porch, cleaned up debris, and offered hors d'oeuvres to the guests. The woman who'd been playing the violin had moved out to the garden and was accompanied by a second woman with a flute. They played soft classical music in the background that clashed with the sound of drumming that floated in from Duval Street. I knew this would be coming from the fellow who set up every night on the sidewalk and beat drums fashioned from industrial plastic buckets. Tourists loved his vigorous performance and tipped him well.

I carried a platter of piping-hot pigs in blankets to the corner of the room where Mrs. Garcia was chatting with some friends. My mother had told me that Andi Garcia was fifty-two, but she looked both younger and older. She had the kind of dark hair and olive complexion that tended to age slowly, and I was sure she'd had access over the years to expensive beauty treatments and fitness specialists that kept her looking young. The tragedy of her husband's violent death, however, was etched in her face.

"I'm Janet Snow's daughter, and we are so sorry about the loss of your husband," I said. I didn't give my first name, hoping she wouldn't recognize me as the person who'd found the body. But why would she? Fortunately, my face hadn't appeared in any of the local papers. It wasn't as if she'd blame me for the murder, but seeing me might bring up feelings so raw that she'd lose her composure. Or refuse to talk to me. Or worst of all, pepper me with questions about the details of how I'd found him and the shape he'd been left in.

"You're doing a lovely job with the party," she said, adding an automatic smile. "Exactly what I asked for."

"Thank you. We have loved cooking recipes from the Woman's Club collection. Have you tried one of Pat Kennedy's pigs in blankets?" I offered her the plate and a napkin. She accepted a napkin, then took one piece and dipped it into the bowl of mustard. She nibbled, then rolled the hot dog into the napkin and handed it back to me.

"I'm sorry, it was delicious. I've been having trouble eating anything lately."

"Of course," I said. "This week's events must have been a terrible shock. You've arranged for a lovely way to see him off." I mentally pinched myself for sounding awkward and tucked her trash into the pocket of my apron. Perhaps I could ask one more question before I moved on.

"Was your husband a birder?" I asked. The more I thought about it, how many reasons could there be to appear on that strip of beach other than dog walking, bird watching, nude sunbathing, communing with nature, or something nefarious? My guess for this man would be nefarious. Maybe he'd been involved with trafficking drugs; that wasn't unheard of in the Keys. Or even worse, humans.

"Sort of. Not really. What he loved was posting about random rare birds so he could bask in the glow of having discovered them. That was one of the precipices that Mr. Entwistle referred to, and quite unpopular with the true birding set." She began to look upset, and across the room I spotted Darcy Rogers, dressed in a mourner's dark clothing rather than her uniform, glaring at me. If I was going to get any more information from Mrs. Garcia, it would not be today in this setting with these onlookers. Out on the side patio, we both heard raised voices.

"Again, my deep condolences on your loss." I said that to her back, as she'd already headed toward the disturbance. I followed in her wake. The young man I'd assumed was her son appeared to be drunk. Very. He was yelling at the elderly woman who'd been sitting with the two teenage girls—one blonde, one brunette. The two girls cowered behind the woman.

"Get the hell out!" he shouted, his face contorted into an ugly mask. "You have no right to be here." He started toward the brunette with his fists clenched, and all three backed away and hurried down the sidewalk that led to Duval Street. I feared he would follow them, but his mother grabbed his arm roughly and pulled him toward the back garden.

Darcy Rogers startled me as I stood in the doorway, wondering what the heck I'd seen. I offered her the plate of hot dogs. "They're especially good with the grainy mustard," I said, grinning foolishly.

She gave a tight smile and took one. "Be careful not to get overly involved in this murder case," she said, "or you'll be in danger of flushing out an angry predator who could be way more than you could handle. Or even worse, pushing him back into his burrow. Best to leave the detective work to the professionals."

Which I'd heard from other law enforcement types before, but all of them had been men. Her warnings irked me—maybe even a bit more because I might have expected her to applaud my contributions. "I did find the body. And that means I started out closer to the situation than any of us are comfortable with, including me. Aside from that, you did ask me to get involved with that ridiculous dog park stunt. Today, we both find ourselves at a service for the murdered man. I'm listening to conversations while I work. Period. You can count on me sharing anything I hear with Nathan."

She gave me a brief nod. "I suppose I deserved that scolding." She ate the little hot dog. "These are amazing," she said, and took a second.

I smiled, took a deep breath to try to settle the jackhammer in my heart, and turned away to distribute the hot dogs to other mourners. A few minutes later, I returned to the kitchen to reload my platter with shrimp puffs, and Miss Gloria followed me in. "What was that about?"

"I have no idea," I said. "That kid was nasty drunk."

"For sure," she said, picking up the last plate of hot dogs. "If you have a minute, I have someone you'll want to meet—Mr. Garcia's mother. She may be eighty-nine, but she's a holy terror."

"Absolutely," I said, now curious about my friend's description. "I'll follow you." I trailed her through the chatting crowd to a smaller room at the front of the house with dark-wood floors, a red oriental rug, and tall windows that reached almost floor to ceiling. Martha had described it as the former men's lounge. The old woman with the black lace headpiece was seated in a white damask upholstered chair. I couldn't help wondering whether that same upholstery had been in residence when mostly men used this space. The chairs seemed like magnets for spills and stains.

I turned my attention to Mrs. Garcia. It sounded harsh to my own mind, and I would never say it aloud, but she was wrinkly and dour, with a dowager's hump and an unfriendly scowl. She reminded me of a witch in a fairy tale. Hansel and Gretel, maybe.

"This is my friend and neighbor, Hayley Snow," Miss Gloria said, gesturing at me and then pulling me a little closer to the old woman. "This is GG's mother, a mover and shaker in this town. She has been a stalwart member of this club forever. She was telling me about the early days and how much things have changed."

"I am so sick to death of hearing about how things are much better now than they were back then. If we wanted green turtle soup back in the day," the old woman said, emphasizing her words by rapping her cane on the wood floor, "we ordered it. We didn't give one moment's thought as to whether it was politically correct. We knew it was delicious, and it was tinted that gorgeous pale green that reflected whatever the turtles had eaten. How is that different from free-range chickens or grass-fed beef that all the food police recommend now, I ask you?"

I smiled weakly; her green turtle description was making me feel a bit queasy. I wasn't about to voice my position that the turtles were endangered, whereas chickens were not. A dim lightbulb flickered in the back of my mind. If her son was like her, I could begin to see why some people hated Garcia. Maybe it was hardwired into this family, the sense that the world belonged to them and they were free to trample over its soft spots. The question remained: Which of the people he'd crushed might have hated him enough to do him in?

"I am so very sorry for your loss," I said, a bit nonplussed by her comments and not sure what direction to take them in. I stashed the appetizer plate on a nearby end table, took her hand, and gently squeezed the mottled skin of her fingers.

"Everyone is telling me that, everyone's sorry. But obviously not *everyone* can be sorry, because he was murdered by *someone*. Possibly more than one someone." She grimaced and pulled her hand from mine.

Standing to the side and back of Mrs. Garcia, Miss Gloria raised her eyebrows and fluttered her lashes, signaling me to ask questions. I kept talking.

"You're right, and what a shock this must have been for you. Do you have a theory about what happened to him?" I asked.

A funny look crossed GG's mother's face. "I know what you're thinking. He wasn't the easiest man to get along with. Just ask his wife."

She tipped her chin across the dining room, where we could see her daughter-in-law Andi accepting condolences from two older women. Her son was no longer in view. "In the old days," the elder Mrs. Garcia said, focusing on Miss Gloria, "we might have disagreed with our husbands, but we kept our complaints between us ladies. We figured out ways to work around those silly men. And we kept a smile on our faces on the home front. It made things go more smoothly. Men are weak, and they can't bear to hear any kind of criticism from their wives. They want to hear that they're strong and handsome and virile."

Yikes. Nathan would be disgusted with that description.

"But surely you don't think Andi murdered her husband?" Miss Gloria asked.

Mrs. Garcia squinted. "Probably not herself. But she had the means to hire it done."

"Were they that unhappy?" I asked, which was probably more than she'd be willing to say. Before she could answer, I spotted my mother waving furiously from the hallway. "Will you excuse me? I need to get back to work, it seems. Again, I'm so very sorry for your loss." Mrs. Garcia inclined her head like a queen, and I hurried off to help my mother.

The rest of the late afternoon event passed by in a flurry as we first served desserts, then collected empty glasses, crumpled napkins, and small plates of rejected or partially eaten hors d'oeuvres. It was close to seven when Martha and I made a final sweep around the downstairs rooms to clean up anything we might have forgotten. All the attendees had left by then. In the kitchen, my mother and Sam and Miss Gloria were busy packing up the leftover food and dividing it into plastic containers.

"I thought you might want to take some of this home," she said to me. "I can't imagine that you feel much like cooking tonight. Or even going out. Nathan wasn't here for the party, so he won't be sick of our goodies." She grinned.

"I did see him on the front porch listening during the memorial service," said Sam. "I wonder if they've figured things out?"

"My sense is they're flummoxed by the murder," I said. "Darcy Rogers from the sheriff's department was quite rude, telling me to mind my own business. That was after I was chatting with Andi Garcia and right before her son went off on several of the guests."

"You've heard that old saw before." Miss Gloria snickered, took off her apron, and folded it up on the counter. "We've gathered plenty of clues, though," she said. She told the others about meeting the dead man's mother and how she'd suggested that Andi Garcia might have been unhappy enough in the marriage to hire a hit man.

"I find that hard to believe," said Martha, shaking her head. "I've known her for a long time, and she's a decent person. She's quite capable of taking him to the cleaners in a divorce, but not murder."

"What did you think of that Entwistle fellow?" I asked, realizing I hadn't gotten around to chatting with him at the reception. "The police seem very interested in him, and he certainly had a complicated history with GG Garcia."

"I'm no detective," Sam said, "but my mind keeps going back to the body left in a storm to be discovered the next day. Would either a serious hit man or a big strapping man leave him like that? Wouldn't they have buried the body or at least dumped him out at sea? Unless the point was to send a message. And to whom, about what?"

His comment brought the picture of the dead body to mind. The sand blown over it had been shallow enough that Ziggy could easily uncover it, exposing more bits of Mr. Garcia's body to passersby. Yes, in fact, I could imagine Mr. Entwistle leaving him there to send a message that he wasn't to be trifled with.

I tried to remember whether there had been other markings in the sand, but my brain was fried from the last few days. I looked around the kitchen. Most of the food had been packed up, but there were many dishes soaking in the sink, plus clean platters and pitchers and silverware that needed to be returned to their proper places. The tables and chairs also needed to be folded up and stashed in their respective closets. The prospect of all that work made me slump with exhaustion, and my mother and Miss Gloria looked exactly the same way I was feeling.

"I have a suggestion," I said to Martha. "I would love to help you finish cleaning up and putting everything away, but I'd love for it not to be tonight. If you're willing to leave it, I could meet you here early in the morning to wrap up. If I don't go home and spend a little time with my husband, he may forget he has a wife."

She grinned. "Smart lady. I would love to have your help. Since you're interested in the history of this place, I can tell you more while we work."

"Are you sure you don't want to do this tonight?" my mother asked. She looked worried and tired. "We have another event tomorrow—what was I thinking? I can't be here in the morning. But I feel awful leaving it for you girls."

"Go on," Martha said, shooing her and Sam out. "It won't take more than an hour."

After stashing our containers of food in the basket on the back of my scooter, Miss Gloria and I motored home to the pier. "I'll be asleep within the hour," she said. "Thanks for including me in the fun. Let me know what you find out tomorrow."

I kissed her on the cheek, grateful as ever to have such an interesting, loving friend. How many women in their eighties would be thrilled to work their tails off at a funeral reception?

"Will do."

I found Nathan and the animals on the living room couch, watching a basketball game on TV. "You guys look cozy," I said, dropping my stuff on the counter. "Are you hungry? I come bearing leftovers."

"Always," he said, coming over to kiss me, then added a hug and nuzzled the top of my head with his chin. "Evinrude wanted to watch Cat TV, but I voted him down. How was the party?"

"Interesting," I said. I put a half dozen pigs in blankets in the toaster oven to heat up and grabbed a couple of yellow gingham plates from the shelves above the stove. I arranged a bit of everything on those—sandwiches and shrimp puffs on one, desserts on the other—while Nathan poured us each a glass of wine. "Deck?" I asked.

"Sure," he said, ferrying the dishes outside. The sun had just set, so the light was soft and pink, and the quickly dropping temperatures promised welcome winter weather ahead. I grabbed a sweater and switched on our outdoor fairy lights, which hung in sparking swoops over the deck and made our home feel even more magical.

We began to eat. "Tell me what you learned," he said.

"Me? I was working the party," I said, fluttering my eyelashes to look innocent.

"I'm sure you were." He waited.

I needed to tell him everything I could remember, beginning with my visit to Davis Jager at the hospital. "That reminds me that I meant to send you the link to his birding blog." I did a quick Google search and came up with the blog, then passed him the iPad so he could scan the post. "The bottom line is that he thinks bird watchers have an ethical responsibility to wildlife. He doesn't post whereabouts of unusual birds because he's afraid that would cause a stampede of amateurs. GG Garcia was the opposite. If he could use that info to sell one of his products or properties, he was all in."

Next, I told him about the hospital visit, explaining why I had judged it important to speak with Jager in person. Nathan's expression turned worried, but he didn't scold me, so I continued.

"He doesn't remember much about the night before he was attacked—too drunk. He remembers seeing Entwistle there at the bar with his black pug, and he remembers a tableful of teenagers because they were annoyingly loud, but not much else. The parking lot was dark, so he didn't see whoever clocked him. He was guessing it might have been more than one person. He might come up with more if you interviewed him."

"He was released earlier this evening," Nathan said, his voice flat with resignation.

"He was?" I was shocked, given how bad he'd looked in the hospital.

Nathan said, "He threatened to sign himself out, and the doctor agreed he could go. Claims he felt like a sitting duck in there, and he'd felt worse days with only a hangover."

"Do you have someone watching him?"

Nathan looked glum. "We don't have the manpower."

Then I told him about my conversations with Andi Garcia and, later, her mother-in-law. "Neither one of them could be called warm and fuzzy, but probably not murderers either. The person I had really hoped to chat with, Mr. Entwistle, was gone before I could get to him." I also mentioned Garcia's son drunk and yelling at the guests. "Mom said she'd seen you lurking on the porch during the memorial service. Did you collect any new information?"

"I'm afraid not as much as you flushed out." Nathan put the key lime cream puff he'd picked up back on his plate. "I'd really rather you stayed away from Entwistle. He's a nasty man and a leading suspect. Okay? I'm not trying to control you, honest." He leaned in and took my hand. "If anything happened to you, I don't know how I could stand it."

Chapter Eighteen

Food offers not only fuel for the body but also a connection—between the people who have joined you at the table, between the generations who have shared a recipe, between the terroir (the earth) and the culture and cuisine that have sprung from it.

—Ann Mah, *Mastering the Art of French Eating*

I met Martha Hubbard back at the Woman's Club at eight AM. The building was quiet, and so were the streets outside. Nobody much was up and about in downtown Key West on a Saturday morning.

"Good morning," Martha called from the kitchen, her arms already up to the elbows in soap bubbles in the big double sink in the center island.

"Oh no, I didn't want you to start without me!" I hurried in and deposited my backpack on the chair nearest the door.

"I only just arrived. If you don't mind bringing over the dirty dishes, we'll soak them for a bit before we try to wash. Then while I'm washing, if you could empty the dishwasher and just put all the clean stuff over on the counter, I'll know where to put it away. Once we have that in shape, we can stack the chairs and tables, and everything will be back in order."

"Sounds like you've done this before," I said with a grin. As we worked, we chatted about the memorial event the day before.

"Have you heard anything new about the murder?" she asked.

"Not a peep. The police are perplexed. And it's not as if they aren't working on it."

"I don't know if this is related to anything, but I guarantee you there were at least two women at the party last night who'd taken turns as GG's girl on the side," Martha said. "I've heard there were others as well."

"Good lord," I said, "how does someone like that have the nerve to show up at his funeral? Does his wife know about this?"

She wrinkled her nose. "Yes. It must've been terribly embarrassing for her, because I'm sure she recognized both. It's almost impossible to keep a secret in this town. He tended to end his girlfriend relationships in an ugly way, so none of them was probably in the mood to protect his marriage, or his wife's feelings. Or his reputation."

"That seems a little mean-spirited," I said.

She nodded. "Once he dumped them, several came whimpering back to the club here to tell their girlfriends how awful he was."

"How dreadful for his wife," I said, thanking God that Nathan didn't have it in him to become a cheating bastard. In my mind, I backed away from that thought for a minute to see if it really rang true. I was quite sure it did. Shortly after we'd first met, I'd realized he was attracted to me, and I felt the same about him. He told me the romance with his ex-wife had been filed in the morgue. But she'd persisted, returning to Key West, desperate to try again. He hadn't even wanted to go on a coffee date with me until he was absolutely certain his first marriage was lifeless.

"Was one of those women particularly angry with him?"

"Honestly, I didn't pay that much attention to the drama," Martha said. She chuckled, but then her face grew grim. "It's not really funny, and I shouldn't make light of it. He was the kind of man who could make a woman feel special—and make her believe that the reason the other relationships and his marriage failed was that he didn't have the right woman. I suspect that each of his lovers was devastated to find out that was baloney." She paused for a moment. "I'm not telling you this to gossip; I'm saying it so you'll understand. One of the women he got involved with was old enough to be legal, but barely. She wasn't at the reception. And there have always been rumors about girls even younger than that."

This man was sounding worse and worse. I had to wonder why Andi, his wife, had put up with him so long. It could have been the money and the lifestyle he provided. By all reports, they were very well off and had a beautiful home. But there also could've been a lot more to their marriage than what he'd disclosed to the women with whom he had affairs. Over the past several years, I'd seen well-known politicians show a similar weakness in public. Once an affair blew up in a man's face, it wasn't unusual to learn that the woman he relied on most was actually his wife. The very one he'd cheated on. But what must a wife feel after discovering that her marriage was not what she'd thought it was, and neither was her husband? What if she felt obligated to stand by him after having been publicly humiliated? What might she feel? A great rage, I imagined.

I found Martha's descriptions of Garcia's shenanigans both astonishing and horrifying. "I'm having trouble wrapping my head around the idea that any woman who'd been with him had the guts to come to the memorial service."

"It is kind of unbelievable, isn't it? I don't know how to explain it, or even why so many women found him that attractive and were willing to breach normal boundaries. He was handsome, of course." She laughed, watching the expression on my face. "No, not my type."

The image of the sandy bits of his clothing and body revealed by Ziggy's digging flashed to my mind again. "I can't speak to that, because I didn't know him when he was alive," I said.

"He was bursting with energy, as you could guess by his involvement in so many activities in our town. Plus he had enough confidence and chutzpah that he didn't mind running against the tide. Most of the time, I might add. He held many unpopular opinions, but he didn't seem to tire of the fight. Some women find that kind of vigor irresistible." She rinsed the suds from her hands and turned to face me. "One of the women was Andi's best friend, Theresa Martin. I should underline *was*. There's been a hard frost between them ever since. Andi Garcia was not forgiving."

"Why would she be?" I asked, trying to keep the picture of a woman attempting to steal my husband and then wanting to reconnect with me out of my mind. "With his other women, wouldn't you think his reputation would proceed him? If you knew he'd had several affairs and that they'd all ended with him dumping the woman involved, why would you think your relationship with him would end up any different?" I picked up a clean dish towel and began to dry a china platter with delicate daisies sprinkled around the rim.

"Be careful with that one," Martha said, with a quick wink. "It's a vintage Homer Laughlin."

"Yikes," I said, setting the plate gently on the counter. "That could give me the dropsies."

"A couple of our members have been on the hunt for vintage china to stock our shelves. It's special, isn't it?"

Martha began to carry a stack of serving plates from the kitchen to the hallway, where they were to be stashed back in the cupboards. "It is mind-boggling, but GG Garcia had that kind of intensity about him. And once he was focused on you, you began to feel that you were the only one in the world that mattered. Or that's what I observed. The chosen woman felt beautiful inside and out once he selected them."

I followed her into the hallway and began to sort the serving spoons and forks into the drawers as she instructed me. "Tell me the women you know about and a general trajectory of their involvement with GG."

"I mentioned Theresa," she said, easing a sticky drawer back into its slot. "I think she was sorry as soon as she got mixed up with him. I can't speak to why she did it, but Andi certainly felt betrayed. She wasn't going to get over it anytime soon. You may have seen Theresa at the back of the room, a bottle blonde with a narrow face and a nice figure. I think she wanted to be there for Andi even if Andi wanted no part of her support."

"I'm not getting the sense that you thought she would have killed GG Garcia?" I asked.

"Not at all," said Martha, returning to the kitchen for another load of dishes. "She was pissed at him for dragging her into the situation, but she understood that she could have said no. He spent a lot of time at the dog park, and I think she flirted with him there and it went too far. I don't believe it could have been Sylvie either. Too young."

"How young?" I asked, feeling a little sick to my stomach. I was almost beginning to feel that this man had gotten exactly what he deserved.

"I'd say she was nineteen or twenty, maybe old enough to know better, maybe not. But not enough sense to restrain herself. I suspect he would have convinced her that she was the most beautiful of all because she was young and untouched."

"But she wasn't at the service?" I asked.

"No."

"Do you think her family might have known that Garcia seduced her?" I asked. Even if she wasn't the killer, I could imagine an enraged father or brother dispatching him.

"That's certainly possible."

We returned to the kitchen to get more stuff.

"I'll get the glassware, if you don't mind putting the tablecloths back where you found them yesterday."

I carried an armful of linens to the corner cabinet. Today, the weather being more humid and the outside doors having been open for the event, the wood seemed more swollen. I pulled gently, not wanting to damage the old drawer. No luck. Obviously, I couldn't jam the carefully ironed tablecloths through the small opening. I set the linens down, squatted, and gave the drawer underneath a good tug. The whole thing popped out, knocking me back on my butt. Now the drawer above slid out easily so I could replace the linens. I then tried to return the bottom drawer to its space. Something blocked its path. I couldn't leave the mess here for members to stumble over.

On hands and knees now, I used my phone's flashlight to see what was causing the jam. A brown box, discolored by age, had been pushed into the back corner of the hutch. It must have dislodged from its hidden corner during the party preparations and moved enough to jam the drawer. I eased the box out and opened the lid. It was full of papers, and at first glance they looked to be related to the earliest version of the Woman's Club cookbook.

I had a flash of memory about the cardboard box my mother and I had uncovered in my grandmother's kitchen pantry after she died—the only space in her home that hadn't been organized to within an inch of its life. The box had been crammed to overflowing with handwritten cards containing recipes and notes about cooking in addition to articles torn from magazines and newspapers. After my grandmother passed, we'd managed to transfer its contents to a sturdier box. My mother had shared a sheaf of the recipes that she'd thought I'd enjoy, if only for nostalgia. She'd put the rest away to sort through later, and I suspected they still resided wherever she'd stashed them.

Buried in the middle of this box, I found the loosely bound pages of a diary. I opened it to the first page.

Dear Diary,

How many years have I heard mother and auntie and grandmother talk about the events at the club and the renovations of the gorgeous home, and planning for the cookbook that will celebrate all of it? So many! I can't believe I'm going to be part of it. I'm going to keep a record of every minute!

Mother says I'm going to help cook some of the easy dishes, and Mrs. Griswold was so excited when she saw me doodling on a scrap of paper. She told mother that I was as good as any artist working on the project and probably better than most of them. She said she'll insist that they include some of my drawings too. She loved the sketch of the flamenco dancers and she's promised to show it to everybody. Maybe I'll get to be an artist after all!

And then she told mother, your daughter is very pretty, too, and has such good manners. We should hire her to help at some of our events.

Can you see why I'm so excited?

Love,

CC

The next few pages consisted of illustrations, including several that I'd seen in the cookbook. In the same childish looping hand, the author had included the names of the recipes that would accompany each of the drawings. Mrs. Felton's conch chowder had a conch shell, then there was a swimming turtle for Mrs. Harris's turtle soup, and a tree loaded with ripe mangoes for Mrs. Blair's fruit salad.

I called Martha over.

"You won't believe what I found." I explained about the stuck drawer.

She knelt down beside me and begin to leaf through the papers. There were pages and pages of line drawings, recipes written in spidery handwriting, and several faded blue mimeographs of pages of the cookbook.

"Let's take the whole thing out and bring it into the kitchen where the light's better." We each picked up an end and carried the box to the adjoining room. It wasn't bulky or heavy, but it felt fragile.

"There could be some treasures in here," I said. "I'm writing an article for *Key Zest* about food in the olden days of Key West. Maybe I could take photographs of some of the handwritten recipes and illustrations and use a few of them in my piece, if you think that's okay. But who packed the box up, and why was it hidden?"

"I don't have time to look through this now; I'm due at Williams Hall for a cooking class at noon. But this is so cool," Martha said, her voice brimming with excitement. "When I get a little time, I'll scan some of them for my next food presentation for the members."

"I wonder if this stuff is valuable," I said. "Probably more for its historical significance than anything else. I could take a few pages over to Tom Hambright in the Florida history room at the library. If you have any time tomorrow, we could work together and get it sorted out. Come for lunch, and we can work outside on the deck."

The words were out of my mouth before I could consider the pressure of serving a meal to a talented chef.

"Sunday lunch is free," she said, smiling, "if you promise to make something easy. Nobody ever asks if they can cook for me."

That made me feel good. For some reason, I felt that looking through the box shouldn't wait. When my grandmother had passed away, there hadn't been any urgency to sorting things out, as she'd died of perfectly natural causes. Her life was straightforward—if she'd carried secrets, she hadn't shared them. There wasn't one thing mysterious about her. Maybe this box wasn't connected to GG Garcia's murder, but there were secrets to be uncovered in this club's history for sure. I wanted to know what they were.

Chapter Nineteen

With that technique, a wok imparts wok hei, which translates to "the breath of a wok" and tastes like a thrill.
—Genevieve Ko, "Kitchen Shortcuts That Mimic a Wok,"
The New York Times, October 20, 2021

On the way home, the busyness of the week finally hit me. I swore to myself that I would take the afternoon off to concentrate on me and Nathan. Maybe I wouldn't even cook; maybe we'd go out for a change—though he had spent a lot of time at restaurants with his colleagues and his father this week. That thought reminded me that I had promised to make something for Martha Hubbard. Which meant frantically paging through blogs and cookbooks until I found the right recipe, then shopping for ingredients if I didn't have everything on hand. Chances were, I wouldn't.

I parked in the lot at Houseboat Row and trotted down the finger of the dock to our home. A few of our neighbors were sunning themselves on their boats, and I called out quick hellos as I passed. Nathan was sitting on our deck with the animals, looking anything but relaxed.

"Did you get everything finished?" he asked, once I'd hopped aboard and kissed him.

"Spic-and-span, and a mysterious discovery besides." I went inside the boat to wash up, dispense treats to Evinrude and Ziggy, and grab a cool drink for each of us. Once I was settled in the lounge chair next to him with a purring cat on my lap, I told him about finding the box. "Martha's coming over tomorrow for lunch, and we'll look through it together."

"I have a golf date tomorrow morning," he said, "if that's okay?"

"Absolutely, it's your day off. You don't need to spend it looking at old recipes. Did you get your father off okay?"

He sighed. "As if it was that easy—nothing ever has been with him. He finished his work but then changed his flight so he can stay for the weekend. I couldn't say anything about it because he isn't really our guest, so I don't have any control about when he goes."

I didn't say anything either, imagining that his father probably wanted to connect with his only son outside of police business. I wondered if he'd told his father he was playing golf tomorrow. My husband had grown up with the game but abandoned it when he and his father had become estranged. During our so-called honeymoon to Scotland, he'd rekindled his enthusiasm for playing. But I wasn't sure he was ready to spend five hours in a golf cart with his father, even though Skip would probably love to be invited. I reached over for Nathan's hand and squeezed to show my wifely sympathy—for whatever Nathan was feeling.

"Anyway, he had a suggestion." His expression grew stern. "You do not have to go along with this; you don't owe him anything."

Now I was super curious, and even a little nervous.

"He wants the three of us to take a ride up to Geiger Key. He's convinced that you'll remember something more. He thinks that since a few days have elapsed, that will have given your subconscious some time to percolate." He heaved another big sigh. "Worst that can happen is we get a drink and come home."

I could feel warring reactions building up inside. On the one hand, I was tired and would like nothing more than to stay home and do nothing. On the other, all those questions about the murdered man were circulating in the back of my mind. Nathan's father was a highly trained police officer who'd solved a lot of difficult cases over his career. If he had a sense that looking at the scene again might produce something new, he was very likely right.

"Obviously, if we find something new, we turn it over to Deputy Rogers, right?"

Nathan nodded.

"I'm game," I said. "We can grab dinner there too. It's a win-win."

We drove across town to pick up Nathan's father at the Casa Marina Hotel, a gorgeous resort that overlooked the Atlantic Ocean. He was waiting outside near the parking lot, chatting with the uniformed valet. I opened the passenger door to move to the back seat of Nathan's SUV.

"Thanks for humoring me. I am quite capable of sitting in the back seat," Skip said as he slid in, looking over his shoulder at me.

I shrugged. "My legs are shorter than yours, so I don't mind a bit."

As we drove up the keys, I gave the usual running commentary for guests about the highlights of Stock Island, pointing out the golf course and the road leading to the sheriff's department, Mount Trashmore, a homeless shelter, and the hospital.

"Hurricane Irma came across the strip of land ten miles north a couple of years ago and destroyed a number of homes," Nathan added. "It veered away from Key West at the last minute. It could have caused catastrophic damage if it had hit our more populous town rather than up the keys. Even so, Route 1 was lined with ruined mattresses and appliances. It's taken residents a long time to recover."

As we drove, I began to shape the opening of my article for Key West. *Sometimes living on an island might begin to feel claustrophobic*, I could say. *Even fabulously gorgeous and always fascinating Key West can close in on a person from time to time. Especially in the high season, when the streets and restaurants are crowded, a field trip to the next keys north might be welcome.*

As I typed this into my phone, I felt the flicker of homesickness that I'd experienced when I first moved to the island. I had come at the invitation of Chad Lutz, a man with a lot of surface charm, whom I didn't know well. Certainly not well enough to relocate down the length of the country and move in with him. The bloom of our rose quickly faded, and he booted me and Evinrude to the curb. At that moment in my life, so lonely and embarrassed, I couldn't imagine that I'd last on this island. But I had lasted, and I'd found the man of my dreams and, equally important, work and friends that I adored.

"What's the plan?" I asked as we approached the turnoff to Geiger Key.

Skip looked over his shoulder again. "Nothing too structured. As I was saying to Nathan earlier, I have found over the years that returning to the scene of a crime after a day or two can jog loose a memory that you didn't know you had. Even if that doesn't happen, having two fresh sets of eyes to look over the same scenery may produce some new information."

"I suggest we walk the beach first," said my husband, "then we'll go to the bar."

At that moment, a text came to his phone, followed very quickly by one to mine. I glanced at my screen. Danielle.

Her note said that her police officer boyfriend had learned from the autopsy that the manner of death for GG Garcia was indeed a blow to his head, but this had not happened the way it had seemed on first glance. *Interestingly*, she continued, *the bump on his forehead was not enough to kill him. Either he fell back and struck his head on a rock, or someone hit him from behind and then he fell. The blow caused massive bleeding inside his brain because he was taking a heavy-duty blood thinner—that's why he had bruises on his legs too. Being a long-time drinker apparently didn't help. Plus he'd consumed a small quantity of opioids, so he may have been unsteady. The coroner called it an acute subdural hematoma. They think he died quickly, but likely not instantly, like Natasha Richardson or Maya Deren.*

I texted a quick thanks and then read the note aloud to Nathan and Skip.

Nathan picked up his phone and glanced at the message he'd received. "I have the same information, only without the Hollywood comparisons," he said.

"None of it quite makes sense, because wouldn't the killer want to hide what he did? Why leave the body there? You'll see when we get to the place where Ziggy found the guy. If we hadn't discovered him, someone else would have eventually. I don't understand why he was left for dead unless the killer intended for things to end that way. I only saw bits of his face and hand because so much sand had blown over him in the night. I didn't linger to watch them clean the rest of him up." Which I was grateful for—deeply grateful. Though they didn't need to know I was wimpish in that way. Although Nathan could probably tell from the way I was blathering.

"Maybe it was a warning—to someone else," said Skip, as we turned off Route 1 onto the smaller street leading to Geiger Key.

"I assume they searched the area for possible weapons," Nathan said.

I kept quiet as we drove past the wider part of the spit of land where Miss Gloria and I had interviewed the trio of beer drinkers. The men would be turning over the possibilities, and I didn't want to distract them. The drinkers weren't out, but there was a trash can brimming with empty beer bottles, and one of the dogs emerged from the shade thrown by the trailer and barked with alarm as we passed.

This being a Saturday afternoon, the beach along the road was busier than it had been the day Eric and I visited. People floated in brightly colored tubes in the shallow water, sunned themselves on the beach, and ate picnic lunches. A gaggle of raucous teenagers shared a big float that was tethered to a rock on the beach. The scent of grilling meat wafted in our direction on a puff of air. I scanned the area carefully to see whether I recognized any repeat visitors.

"This place sees a lot of action," said Skip. "It's hard to imagine that nobody saw anything. Do you feel sure the officers called to the scene canvassed everyone?"

Nathan stared at him. "It's not my people, so no, I wouldn't swear to it. In general, the sheriff's department is very good."

Skip offered a curt nod.

"Keep in mind that we were here earlier in the day," I said, scrambling to ease the tension between them. "This area gets more crowded as the heat builds up. Likely it was dark when Garcia was either killed or dragged here."

Nathan parked the SUV at the end of the road nearest the concrete block barrier. The two men followed me along the beach for fifteen minutes.

"Let's walk down to the point where the little inlet crosses this spit, then work our way backward." Nathan turned to look at his father. "If you're up to it."

My father-in-law sputtered with disgust. "We can sprint it if you'd rather." He strode ahead of us, his shoulders tense.

"You're baiting him," I said to Nathan in a low voice.

Nathan said nothing in response, and I didn't push it. He walked ahead of me, either annoyed with my comment or wanting to catch up with his father. I hoped it was the latter.

This time, as we walked along the beach, I tried to pay attention to things I might not have noticed on my other visit. The sky was perfectly blue but spotted with puffy clouds that were edged with pale tangerine and the promise of sunset. Again, I noticed the cairns constructed of beach stones. By the time I reached the end of the beach and caught up with Nathan and his dad, his father had sunk up to one ankle in gray-brown mud. His shoe made a sucking sound as he pulled it out, looking disgusted. He shook his foot and then dabbed at it with a white handkerchief.

"This is what the bird watcher told the sheriff's department people," I said, pointing to his leg. "No one could get through this way easily because of the muck. And I can't believe they'd drag a body over the chain-link fence. Surely the Navy would have better security than that."

"Supposing they left a small boat on the other side of this creek?" Nathan's father asked, squinting at the mangroves off in the distance.

"But drag the dead weight all that way?" It seemed preposterous to me, though anything was possible. "Even with the heavy rain the night before, you'd think they'd have left some evidence on the beach."

They poked around a little more, and then we walked back the way we'd come.

"What's with all these rock piles?" Skip asked as we passed three cairns in succession.

"They can have lots of meanings," I said. "Monuments, directional aids, burial sites. Since there's only one way in and out on this beach, they probably aren't meant to give directions. If you're willing to think spiritually, Lorenzo tells me that people create the piles as a spiritual exercise in patience, balance, and gratitude."

"Fascinating," said Skip, though I couldn't tell whether he actually meant that or was teasing. Or scornful.

Once we reached the driftwood structure, I paused to explain how I'd found Garcia. My gaze caught on a short length of yellow crime scene tape that flapped in the breeze.

"Eric and I had set up our chairs and were having lunch when I noticed that Ziggy had disappeared. I followed the barking and found him here." I gestured at the area behind the wood hut. "That is where Garcia was."

Nathan and Skip squatted down to look at the trough in the sand. Any finger marks were gone, and of course the body, but I could make out a darker patch that might have been blood. There were dozens of footprints around the ditch. That made me doubt we were going to find anything new. Nathan's father straightened up and looked in the direction of the sea. His gaze ran over the driftwood hut as he took in the found objects arranged in fishing nets as decorations—shoes, paintings on pieces of tin and wood, beer bottles.

"This place isn't busy like one of your Key West beaches, but it's busy enough," Skip said. "I imagine this structure might be a destination for a certain kind of tourist. And maybe a magnet for kids? That leads me to this question: Why leave him here? And why do such a lousy job of covering him up? The killer had to have known that the body would be discovered fairly soon."

Nathan looked up at him, squinting in the sharp afternoon light. "My guess is the killer was an amateur, a panicked amateur. Or else, as Hayley said, someone wanted him to be found that way."

To my mind, that eliminated no one. "Possibly both?" I suggested. "Maybe Garcia was killed accidentally on the beach and the killer panicked and ran. Suppose, for example, he came here that night with his wife and they got into an argument and she got angry enough to lash out and clock him with something—I don't know what exactly. Once she realized what she'd done, she freaked out and thought about digging a hole but did a lousy job." A detail that I hadn't remembered floated to mind—his feet and legs had been covered in more sand than his upper body.

"But clocking him in the head with a heavy object and leaving him here? That's cold-blooded." Nathan shook his head and stood up. "It's a stretch. Why haven't they found a murder weapon? What about the alcohol and drugs?"

"He was a big womanizer," I reminded them. "Andi Garcia would have been embarrassed and humiliated and angry because he had more than one affair. Each time he swore he'd never cheat on her again, but each time he did. I can't quite picture her killing him on this beach, but she definitely had motive." I felt guilty imagining that decent-seeming woman as a murderer. Wouldn't it have been a lot easier to file for divorce?

"But she wasn't the only one with a motive," Nathan said. "I'm going to drop in on Entwistle after golf tomorrow."

"Count me in," said Skip. "Both the golf and Entwistle." Nathan looked at him, then quirked a smile. I was almost certain he hadn't invited his father to play golf, but he didn't look unhappy about it, maybe more surprised.

We walked back the way we'd come, then got back into the car and began to drive slowly until we reached the trailer where Miss Gloria and I had talked with the residents. Nathan and Skip studied the home after I pointed it out.

"This is definitely the closest place to the beach," Nathan said. "If anyone saw something, it should have been them."

"Then why not tell me and Miss Gloria when we asked the other day?"

"Because people always keep secrets. The secrets may not turn out to be the exact information you came in looking for but something they don't want the world to know. Why should they spill those dirty secrets to a couple of nosy ladies who didn't ask the right questions?" Nathan's dad grinned, showing he meant no offense. Though, in truth, I was a little offended.

Nathan nodded, looking at his dad. "What they don't seem to understand is that holding back on their own stuff makes them look guilty as hell. Let's go have a chat."

The two men got out of the car and marched toward the trailer. I followed a few steps behind, interested to listen in on father and son working together, both of them competitive and definitely testy. Nathan rapped on the trailer door, and the woman I'd seen the other day answered. She wore capri tights and an oversized T-shirt and had her hair pulled back into a sloppy ponytail.

"Yes?"

Nathan held out his badge, and my father-in-law did the same. "We're with the police department, working on the murder on the beach."

The woman grimaced. "I've already talked to two sets of sheriff's deputies." She tipped her head in the direction of the beach. "I've said everything I knew, which obviously can't be what you're looking for."

"If you don't mind," said Nathan, in a pleasant voice that I barely recognized, as though he'd instantly slipped into "good cop" mode in the presence of his father, "we'd like to ask a few more questions. We have an open murder investigation going on, and we'd like to nail the responsible party. That way the neighborhood can feel safe again."

The woman shifted her weight to lean against the door, drew a pack of cigarettes out of her waistband, and lit one up. "My husband and his brother don't think much of talking with police. But I'm nervous about living so close to where it happened, and I'd like to get this cleared up."

Nathan nodded. "That's exactly what we're after. I know people have asked you this before, but do you remember hearing any unusual sounds the night the murder took place? Anything like a car engine passing? Or the motor of a boat? Any shouts of distress?"

"I don't sleep too good—chronic pain," the woman said, fitting a hand to the small of her back. "I'm often up in the night to try to stretch it out. Sometimes I take a drink out to the porch"—she gestured to the lawn chairs set up under the tent—"and stay until I get sleepy."

"And last Monday was one of those nights when you couldn't sleep?" asked Skip, his voice smooth as melted caramel.

"Yup. It was early, say, midnight or eleven? An hour or so before the rain blew through. There was a scooter that drove by, maybe two people on it?"

"Could you describe the people or the scooter?" Nathan asked. "Male? Female? The bike's color? Anything like that?"

She smoothed a stray hank of hair back into her ponytail. "Sorry, not really. I had those shooting pains, like someone's stabbing me in the low back. I'd taken a pain pill, and a sleeping pill, and a hit of Scotch. Anything to knock it back." She flashed a regretful smile. "I figured it was some kids looking for action. We get a lot of that down here. We let them have their fun unless they're bothering us or out of control with a party. Like I said, my husband isn't big on cops, so we don't call unless we absolutely have to. No offense." She gave Nathan a side-eyed glance.

"None taken," said Skip, reaching out as if to touch the woman on the shoulder. "Were you still outside when the scooter came back through?"

"Nope," she said. "Right after that I went to bed, slept like the dead myself."

Which didn't surprise me a bit, given what she'd reported swallowing.

"One more question," Nathan said. "Did you know the man who was murdered, GG Garcia?"

"Unfortunately." She grimaced. "We couldn't stand that guy; nobody could. Most of us have lived here for years—it's our little square of paradise, the only one we'll ever have." Her face had tightened up like a piece of dried fruit. "He wanted to buy everyone out at a rock-bottom price so he could build another resort. What about the people who live here, who can't afford anything else? And hasn't he ever heard of sea level rise?" She shook her head. "We could tell he was going to push until we gave in. I don't wish anyone murdered, but at least this way his project's dead."

But was it? I wondered. What if Entwistle had been his partner in this development idea?

"Do you think that's why Mr. Garcia died?" Skip asked, sliding the question in like it had no more weight than *What did you have for lunch?* "Because he was pushing people out?"

Suddenly the woman startled as she focused on my face. "Don't I know you from somewhere?" Then her eyes got wide. "You were here the other day with an old lady."

How Miss Gloria would hate that description. "I found Mr. Garcia's body, and so I understand how spooky it is not to have this case solved."

She nodded, but her lips were set in a way that made me believe we'd reached the end of the interview. Nathan saw it too and handed her one of his official cards.

"In case you think of anything else. Thanks for talking with us," Nathan said, and we trooped back to the car.

"We got more out of her than the sheriff's department did," Nathan said as he slid into the driver's seat.

"She's scared," I said. "Her husband didn't want her to talk to the authorities, but she doesn't like the idea of a dead man right up the road."

"I think you're right," Skip said. "We wouldn't have gotten a word from her if her relatives had been there. Do you think one of them did it?"

"The motive is there, and they had access, and would know the time when the beach would be deserted. But why would he meet them at night?" Nathan rubbed his chin. "Though from the sounds of it, the men could have done him in when she was dead asleep."

I directed Nathan to drive to the Fish Camp, less than a half mile up the road. The Saturday night party there was in full swing, which made it hard to find a parking place.

"We may have to wait for a table," I cautioned them.

"That's okay," said Skip. "That gives us time to look around. Maybe talk to a couple patrons."

"What did you think of the woman in the trailer?" I asked the men while we waited in line to speak to the receptionist.

"I think she still knows more than she was saying," Nathan repeated. "I suspect it has to do with her roommates and possibly drug running."

It didn't surprise me that drugs might be involved with Garcia's death. Key West was right on the path for deliveries from South America in particular. At least once every couple of months, the newspaper reported square groupers—aka bales of marijuana—washing up on the beaches. Steve Torrence had told me more than once that the number-one problem on this string of islands was opiate use and addiction. Really no different than anywhere else.

"Do you think Garcia was drug running? Dealing? Feeding his own habits?" Skip asked.

"Can I help you?" the hostess asked.

"Table for three?" I asked.

"Fifteen to twenty minutes' wait, but you're welcome to have a drink and stand near the bar."

I recited my last name because *Snow* was easier than spelling out *Bransford*.

We each ordered a local beer and retired to the porch railing to wait. The band had kicked into action at the far end of the dining area and was playing a loud and clashing rendition of Billy Ray Cyrus's "Achy Breaky Heart." It seemed that half the diners had gotten up to dance. But even over the noise of chattering people and music, I heard a familiar voice.

"What the hell is he doing here?" I asked, not exactly realizing I had said it aloud.

Nathan stiffened, looking around the restaurant. "Who?"

"Davis Jager. Twenty-four hours from the hospital to the bar." I pointed across the crowded waiting area to the bar, where Jager was talking with another guy with dark hair and a muscular square shape.

"Let's go talk to him," said Nathan.

"Maybe better she talks to him alone first and tells him we're here, if he sounds agreeable?" asked Nathan's dad.

I watched my husband's face morph from annoyed to wary. "Possibly. Are you okay with that?" he asked me.

"Of course. If he's willing to talk to you, I'll wave."

I wove through the crowd to the bar. "Mr. Jager, how are you feeling?" Honestly, he looked pale, his eyes watery, and a bandage peeking out from under the back of the bucket hat. The hat itself had a new stain that I suspected was his blood. "Never in a million years would I have expected to find you here. Not today, anyway."

"It's my home away from home," he said, breaking into a wide grin. "I feel a whole lot better here than I did in that johnny coat." He snickered and took a pull on his beer. "Hey, I want you to meet my pal, Pizza Al, the guy I was telling you about." He clapped the back of the sturdy dark-haired man standing next to him.

"Very nice to meet you, Al," I said, smiling.

"This is Hayley. She's the one who found that body on the beach." Jager pointed across the water in the direction of the trailers on the other side of the finger that bordered the Fish Camp. "I was telling her that you might have some insight into what happened that night."

"No actual facts," Pizza Al said. "But I have had insomnia this week, and so Romeo the dog and I were out on the porch that night until around three."

"And from your porch you can see people coming and going on Government Road?" I asked.

"Pretty much you see it all," he said. "Davis here said the man was killed after midnight before the rain came in, so that helps narrow things down. From what I saw, there was a blue pickup truck, a scooter with a couple of people on it, and a white Prius."

"Any that you hadn't seen before that night?"

"The truck and the scooter," he said, nodding confidently. Then he frowned. "I can't swear to the truck, because lots of residents on this spit own one."

"Men or women on the scooter?" I asked. "Could you tell?"

He paused to think, tapping his fingers on the bar. "A smaller person driving, bigger in back. But other than that, it was too dark to see. Truth is, I didn't know there was going to be a quiz or I would have studied harder." He laughed, white teeth sparkling against his dark skin.

I smiled politely. "Did you know Mr. Garcia?"

"Who didn't?" he asked, a scowl replacing the grin. "He had his sights set on this little strip of land, which made no sense to most of us. Except the folks in Key West and Stock Island were sick to death of him and had shut him out lately. I think he believed the people living here would be easy targets. That he could buy them out for cheap and then develop something ridiculous. At least we're safe from one knucklehead's dumb ideas for a while."

"I'll drink to that," said Davis Jager, holding up his beer bottle.

I touched the back of his shoulder, gently, in case this was where he'd been whacked. "Be careful out there," I said.

"Maybe go easy on the alcohol tonight? And get your friend to walk you out to your car?"

It wasn't like I felt we'd bonded over Garcia's death as he seemed to think, but he was endearing in a bumbling sort of way.

"I'll look after him," Pizza Al said. "We all love him, even though he's a pain in the butt." Jager laughed and tapped his fist on Al's shoulder. I could sense that the affection between them was real.

I got back to the guys at the same time a waitress appeared to lead us to our table. We ordered, then returned to the conversation.

"You were there a while," said Nathan, watching me intently. "You must've had quite a chat."

I took a sip of my beer. "The other guy I was talking with is his friend Pizza Al. He was awake the night of the murder, and he lives in those condos on stilts on the other side of Route 1. He remembered seeing a big pickup truck and a scooter carrying two people, one smaller than the other. He thinks Garcia was murdered because of his aggressive development business."

"There was a pickup truck parked alongside that trailer," said Skip. "If nothing else breaks loose, maybe we make another visit."

Nathan shrugged as if discouraged. "Unfortunately, the scooter description leaves about half the population of the keys in the running. I'll talk with Deputy Rogers and see if she can get her people out here to canvass the neighbors again."

"What you have here is basically nothing," his father said. "Possibly that bird watcher did him in. Did you think of that?"

"Then what, knocked himself out to give himself an alibi?" Nathan asked.

Skip ignored that. "Or someone who lives along Government Road? Someone must have seen something, but they are unwilling to come forward."

They sounded crabby and discouraged, but that often happened to Nathan at this stage of a case. "You can't force a solution," he'd said in the past. "Or you hang the wrong guy."

The waitress arrived with our dinners, plain grilled burger and fries for Skip, shrimp and grits for Nathan and me. "I don't know how you don't end up in the coronary unit with your diet," Nathan told his father.

"What, like shrimp and grits isn't a heart attack on a plate?" Skip asked, a smile creeping over his face. "Besides, I'm too mean to die," he added. "Isn't that what your mother always said?"

Chapter Twenty

No, I wasn't going to be one of those people who just offers themselves up to jealousy like an all-you-can-eat buffet. I was going to figure something out.

—Laura Hankin, *A Special Place for Women*

By the time I got up the next morning, Nathan had already left for the golf course. He'd left me a note saying he'd taken the dog out and that he'd seen Evinrude slip into Miss Gloria's place through the cat door. Sitting at our little kitchen banquette, I sipped a cup of coffee and skimmed through the news in the local paper. The Citizens' Voice was full of complaints and kudos in equal measure about the Fantasy Fest event that had concluded last weekend. Honestly, most of the locals I knew breathed a deep sigh of relief when that set of body-painted, sexual-adventure-seeking, charged-up tourists departed the island. This week would be more relaxed—Jimmy Buffett's Parrothead fan club was coming to town, but those folks came for the music and the weather and were mostly decent human beings.

As soon as I stuck my head outside to check the weather, I felt the humidity and heat that had rolled back into Key West overnight. I was feeling uninspired about baking—the heat of the oven would fill up our cabin like a coal-fired furnace, even with the air conditioner running. Instead, I poured a second cup of coffee and carried it and the original Key West cookbook out to the deck. My plan was to skim through the introduction and look at some of the illustrations to make notes for my article, before choosing a recipe to prepare for lunch with Martha.

The foreword was delightful. Written in very neat script, it described breakfast and lunch on the patio of someone's home, and then the most incredible dinner served by an imaginary cook, Lily Rose. I could almost smell the flowers the author was describing, and the scents of the food put on the table. As I read, I felt myself sinking into old Key West.

When I reached the appetizer section of the book, the handwriting had changed to a dark and sloping style. The drawings that accompanied the recipes spanned the gamut from professional to amateur and cartoonish. About halfway through, I saw the first art that I recognized, several beautiful block prints of iconic Key West buildings done by Martha Watson Sauer, a name I knew from perusing the Key West Art Center. She was known for her artwork decorating the Key West Aquarium along with other local sites and had been employed by the Works Progress Administration. She would have been in her mid to late thirties when this book was being developed. If she had been alive, I would have loved to ask her about the process of pulling the cookbook together. Would she have remembered the young artist who'd been thrilled about having her artwork included?

As I read through the recipes and introductions, I thought I could get a small sense of what life was like during these years for women in Key West, fondly referred to as the "Old Rock" by the woman who wrote the foreword and connecting essays. Many of them didn't appear to work outside the home. At least on the surface, I suspected they had more time than today's women—enough to pluck feathers from ducks and tenderize mollusks and extract meat and milk from fresh coconuts. In contrast, they also concocted soups from cans of Campbell's—chicken and clam, tomato and pea—combinations that sounded odd to the modern ear and palate. I couldn't wait to sort through the box of letters and drawings with Martha to get her insights.

With that thought, I realized I'd spent an hour reading through the cookbook. Now I had no time to cook. Plan B needed to be hatched pronto. A plate of crudités and good cheese with one of Old Town Bakery's baguettes might check all the boxes: easy, fast, delicious, low stress. I always kept a stash of cookies in the freezer, and I could cut up fruit for a salad. I hurried inside to make our bed, move dirty clothes to the laundry basket, and straighten up the kitchen so the place would be fit for visitors.

Ziggy seemed antsy, running back and forth from the kitchen to the deck and barking at everything that moved. I hadn't taken him on a decent outing since the incident at the beach. Our undercover visit to the dog park had been truncated and wouldn't count for much in his book.

"What do you say we take another run to the dog park?" I proposed. "We didn't stay very long last time, did we?" The dog's little ears perked up, his narrow tail whipped, and he looked like he was smiling. I didn't tell him that the main reason for the trip would be the stop at Old Town Bakery.

"Maybe we'll get a chance to chat with Theresa or Entwistle. But please, let me do the talking."

He wagged his tail again and grinned a slobbery, doggy smile. I grabbed my helmet and a soft cooler with a cold pack, and we trotted up the dock to my scooter. I fastened him into his dog carrier and started the engine.

The humidity was living up to the newspaper's prediction, with a heavy promise of more heat and possibly a thunderstorm later in the day. I drove over the Palm Avenue bridge and took a left on Grinnell Street. I popped into the small bakery and emerged with the bread, two kinds of cheese I hadn't tried before, a homemade dog biscuit, one of their life-changing cinnamon rolls, and a latte to go. The morning had taken a big step up. I tucked the cheese into the cooler, then put everything else except the coffee into my backpack.

"Maybe we'll get lucky and you'll find good company," I said to Ziggy as we drove off. "Probably lots of doggy people had the same good idea to get here early and beat the heat."

I parked in the scooter lot across the street from the park and snapped on Ziggy's leash. He stiffened with excitement as we drew closer, noticing five or six other small dogs chasing balls and each other. I let him go as soon as we got through the second gate.

"Have fun and be careful!" I called as he roared off, the same thing my mother would always say when I was old enough to go out by myself as a teenager.

I settled at one of the concrete picnic tables in the shade and begin to peel away and nibble the concentric rings of caramelized dough. I closed my eyes to savor each bite of the sticky bun—maybe I'd find the resolve to save some of it for Miss

Gloria if I ate slowly enough. Nathan wouldn't care about it one way or the other.

Halfway through the pastry and my coffee, I noticed Theresa Martin, the woman Martha said Mrs. Garcia hadn't spoken to since finding out about her affair with her husband. Wearing slim denim shorts and an oversized pair of sunglasses, her white blonde hair fastened up in a neat twist, she was standing apart from the other owners, watching her little brown terrier play and glancing at her phone. Ziggy came roaring up to her, and she fed him a treat and told him he was handsome. He glanced at me as if to say he thought she was all right.

I walked closer to her, my brain scrambling for how to approach a conversation. Straightforward, I thought; she looked like that kind of woman.

I introduced myself and told her right out that I had found GG Garcia's body. "I've kind of gotten involved in figuring out who killed him, as my husband is with the police."

She looked a little stunned but didn't shut me down.

"I know that you were good friends with Andi Garcia and wondered if you had ideas about what happened to her husband."

"She didn't kill him; she didn't have that in her. Though she had plenty of reason to," Theresa said, her voice clear and sharp. She pulled off the big sunglasses. "And part of that was my fault. If you are involved in the investigation, you may have heard of my connection with them?"

"I heard you were close friends with Andi but not any longer." I'd leave it at that and see if she filled in any details.

She gazed out from the dog park across the road to the Atlantic Ocean, her eyes moist with tears. "Getting involved with him is by far the worst thing I've ever done in my whole life."

I said nothing, hoping she would explain.

"Even though Andi and I were close, I didn't know GG well. Except through her eyes, and that picture was not pretty. He wasn't home very often, certainly not during the day. And plenty of nights he stayed out altogether, which broke her heart. Of course, I ran into him at social events, and he was always complimentary and gracious. But then I saw him once or twice here at the dog park." She met my eyes. "Andi never came because she didn't want that dog in the first place. She didn't like him, and the feeling was mutual. Anyway, after some small talk, GG and I started talking more. At first it was him asking advice about his relationship, how to get Andi to lighten up and warm up."

"Getting involved with other women would not seem to be the way down that path," I said.

"You think?" She ducked her head and reached down to pet the dogs, who'd run over to get a sloppy drink of water from the pool by the water spigot and come back to touch base with us. "My marriage was on the rocks, and GG's attention helped me forget the unhappiness." She wove her fingers together, and I noticed the indented, white band of skin where a ring must have sat for a number of years. "We only got together the one time. It was a terrible mistake, and I regret it every day. I don't believe Andi will ever forgive me for going out with him, knowing how very much it would hurt her."

She patted a few stray hairs back into her bun. "It feels so much easier to look outside a problematic marriage for relief, rather than tackling what might be decaying inside your own home. Remember that," she said, glancing at my wedding ring and then back up at my face.

"I will," I said, sensing that she wouldn't go on until I promised. And almost feeling guilty for something I hadn't done. "What was he like, GG?" I asked. "I've heard so many stories."

She studied my face so carefully and for so long that I wondered if she'd heard.

"He was not a nice man," she said. "However, he had an irresistible energy, like a big magnet who drew people to him like metal objects. When he focused that energy on me? I couldn't help feeling exhilarated, like I was lucky to be with him, to feel chosen—and that exhilaration blinded me to the voices warning me not to get involved. On his side, he was my best friend's husband, and that didn't seem to matter to him one bit. He was a taker and a user and a cheat. Once Andi found out and freaked out, he dropped me as though that was all he wanted from an affair with me. Honestly, looking back on the whole sordid business, I believe he chose me *because* I was Andi's best friend. What better way to stab her heart? I was collateral damage. I was an idiot." She turned away, called to her dog, snapped on the leash. "After that, I hated the man, and hated myself too."

"Do you have any ideas about who killed him?" I asked quickly, before she could cut me off.

"Not really. The possibilities seem endless." She glanced at her watch, slid the sunglasses back on. "I'm late for church," she said, and strode off with her dog.

I collected my belongings and lured Ziggy back with the homemade dog biscuit. On the way home, I thought about what she'd said and how angry and sad she seemed. Would she have killed the guy? Maybe if her best friend Andi had asked her to, to prove her loyalty. But not because she valued the man so highly that she couldn't bear to let him go. In truth, she seemed much sadder about losing her friend than the murder of her married former boyfriend. But angry, so angry. I tried to picture her taking him to that deserted beach, clocking him on the head, and leaving him to die while the wind blasted him with sand. It wasn't out of the question.

Chapter Twenty-One

There he got out the luncheon-basket and packed a simple meal, in which, remembering the stranger's origin and preferences, he took care to include a yard of long French bread, a sausage out of which the garlic sang, some cheese which lay down and cried, and a long-necked straw-covered flask wherein lay bottled sunshine shed and garnered on far Southern slopes.

—Kenneth Grahame, *The Wind in the Willows*

We zipped back to Houseboat Row, and I parked in the scooter section next to our dock. I had enough time to wash up and lay out the crudités before Martha arrived. I boiled water for iced tea and then sliced up a stick of summer sausage and the cheeses—one deeply veined blue and the other a runny Brie—and arranged them on a maple cutting board that had been a wedding gift from Eric and Bill. Rummaging through the fridge produced a jar of kalamata olives, carrot and celery sticks, and a bunch of grapes. I added those to the board and stirred sugar and ice and lemon into the pitcher of tea. As I was cutting the baguette into slices, I heard Martha greeting Miss Gloria out on the deck. I wiped my hands on a clean dish towel and went out to welcome her.

"You were up and at 'em early," Miss Gloria said to me. Both of her cats sat beside her on the dock, as if looking to her for action.

"Dog park and sticky bun," I said, grinning. "And I regret to say I didn't save you even a bite. Thanks to Ziggy, I had a good chat with Andi Garcia's best friend. But come aboard," I told Martha. "I'll show you around the houseboat, and then we can get to work." I took the box from her and set it on the table between the lounge chairs. She had put the fragile old box into another one, much sturdier. Miss Gloria lingered on the dock, looking curious. "Come on," I said. "You'll be interested in Martha's box too. And I've got plenty of picnic food for a light lunch."

Miss Gloria and her cats scrambled onto our boat. "I'll wait here with my guys so Martha can get the whole picture without stumbling over us." T-Bone and Sparky jumped up onto the chaise longue that Nathan usually used, and Miss Gloria stretched out beside them. Evinrude nosed her extended fingers and settled into the crook of her elbow.

Martha loved the tidy layout of our home, especially the kitchen. "You could cook real meals in here," she said. "And your deck extends the space."

"She does cook real meals," Miss Gloria called in from the deck. "Lots of them. I'm a frequent beneficiary."

We settled under a big turquoise umbrella on the deck and began to eat the goodies I'd prepared.

"What's in the mysterious box?" asked Miss Gloria.

I explained about the balky drawer and finding the papers at the back of the corner cupboard. Martha began to pull out the drawings, handling them carefully in case they turned out to be valuable. Some were whimsical—such as ingredients jumping into a saucepan—and others were more traditional Key West scenes including boats and palm trees. All had been signed with the letters *CC*.

"Who is CC?" Miss Gloria asked.

I shook my head. "It's a mystery."

Then Martha reached for the handwritten pages at the bottom of the box. A black-and-white photograph fluttered to the deck. I picked it up, holding it carefully by the white deckled edge. Two willowy teens in fancy flowered dresses leaned against each other, pooching their lips for the cameraman. One was blonde, the other black haired, both radiating the gorgeous sheen of youth.

"Who are they?" Miss Gloria asked, getting up to examine the photo more closely. "I love the dresses and the hair. My older sister had the same look when she was going somewhere special. She always wanted to be older than she was—until she turned fifty, of course. They look like the best of friends, don't they?"

"One of them was probably the artist," said Martha.

"And the author of the diary entries," I added. I explained to Miss Gloria what we'd learned yesterday. "Read us the ones that are left?"

Martha began to read the last pages she'd found toward the bottom of the box.

Dear Diary,

I am so thrilled to be working at the club today. Everyone says my drawings are perfect. I volunteered to help prepare the cookbook recipes that the women have selected for the reception, and they asked if I would like to help serve. Tonight is a really fancy dinner party where the members will celebrate some of Key West's Navy celebrities and also a few authors and artists visiting Key West. I'm going to wear my pink watered silk dress with the sweetheart neckline. Mother says they have aprons for when I'm in the kitchen, and I'll be fine as long as I watch what the other ladies are doing and follow their lead. I guess that means smiling a lot and acting solicitous of the important guests. I'm nervous but so excited. I'll write more later.

Love,

CC

Dear Diary,

I hardly know how to write this, but I promised I would. The party was amazing. Candles everywhere and gorgeous flowers and the most amazing food. I met the commandant in charge of the Navy base in town—swoon-ably handsome, and he actually kissed my hand. And there was a poet who's apparently quite famous. Mrs. Higgs asked him to read some selections and I swear I didn't understand a word he said. Maybe when I'm older. Everyone had a lot to drink and had so much fun. There was music out on the patio and lots of people were dancing. I had finished serving dessert when Mr. Garcia asked if I'd serve the after-dinner drinks in the men's cigar room. He said I was the prettiest girl in the room and that I'd done a wonderful job. My nerves came rushing back again—how should I handle myself with all those men!

Now comes the hard part. On the way in, Mr. Garcia touched my back side. I felt a zing of excitement and immediately following that I was so embarrassed and ashamed. I am certain he didn't mean to touch me, I'm so clumsy. I must have bumped into him when I was clearing the drinks and replacing them with the new tray. I felt myself blush, a shade of red that spread out from neckline of my pink dress up across my neck and filling my cheeks, with rosy apples as my father would have said. I stumbled over myself apologizing for my clumsiness.

Mr. Garcia said not to worry, and he placed one hand low on my back and took my right hand with his left and pulled me in close. "You are beautiful just like your drawings," he whispered into my ear. Then he smiled, gave my low back a little squeeze, and let go. "Don't linger with these men. You are such a pretty little thing that I must take good care of you."

"Ewww," said Miss Gloria, pinching her nose with her fingers. "This Mr. Garcia was a lecherous slimeball, just like the man who died. I wonder if they're related?"

Now I was intensely curious to figure out what had happened to CC. "Is that the end of it?" I asked. "She didn't sign off on this entry or tell what happened during the rest of the night?"

"Nothing else written here." Martha pulled the final drawing from the box. This wasn't one that had made it into the book. It was dark and sad, and angry to the point of murderous, all mixed in together. Both the sky and sea in this drawing had the ominous cast of an approaching storm. On the porch of the Woman's Club, a woman's figure huddled with her head buried in her arms. The cookbook itself was cast onto the ground, open to the page with the flamenco dancers. It was signed with the same initials: *CC*.

"Wow," said Miss Gloria. "Where did that come from?"

"You know," I said to Martha, "this may sound odd, but that picture *looks* the way Theresa Martin *sounded* at the dog park—as though she'd been used for something awful and then cast aside. But she still felt like it was her fault. If something happened between CC and the senior Mr. Garcia, that would have been seventy years ago. Seventy years before GG Garcia screwed around with Theresa, ruined her friendship with Andi, and broke his wife's heart. But maybe the feelings are similar."

"Like I said, slimebucket," Miss Gloria added. "They have to be related, and that means disgusting behavior must run in their family. You don't know who CC is?"

Martha shook her head, as did I. "I think I read that the library is experimenting with Sunday hours." We looked at each other. "Want to pop over and have a chat with the Florida history maven?"

"Absolutely," Martha said.

"I'll opt out," said Miss Gloria. "The siren call of a nap awaits me. You can fill me in later. Thank you for lunch." She hopped off the boat, followed by her felines, and disappeared into her cabin.

I quickly cleaned up the leftovers from our lunch and stowed the small bits of remaining cheese in the fridge. Then I grabbed my helmet and offered my spare to Martha, and we set off for the library. I parked the scooter in the small lot at the back of the pink stucco building, and we went inside.

Mr. Hambright was considered by local Key Westers to be the national treasure of Monroe County. For thirty-five years, he had toiled in a small office at the back of the library, cataloging and digitizing photographs and other bits of island history. I knew this because we frequently turned to his historical archives, searching for digital photographs to illustrate our *Key Zest* articles. Before his current position, he'd served twenty-one years in the Navy and retired as a naval lieutenant commander. He was a tall, elderly man with an engaging presence and an encyclopedic knowledge of the history of Key West. If anyone knew who the mysterious CC was, I suspected it would be him.

We pushed open the glass door protecting the history room from the rest of the library. Mr. Hambright was seated behind an L-shaped desk, wearing a pink button-down shirt and blue striped tie, looking exactly like someone's grandfather. His desk was covered with papers, photographs, tins of cookies, sunglasses, scissors, and glue. I suspected that despite the disarray, he could instantly put his hands on anything he was searching for. We introduced ourselves, explaining that we were researching history of the Woman's Club, particularly during the time the first cookbook had been produced—me for an article, Martha for her foodie presentations.

"Please take a seat." He gestured to the two chairs in front of his desk. "How can I help?" he asked, folding his tapered fingers over his stomach.

I showed Mr. Hambright the old cookbook and leafed over to a page with artwork signed by CC. "My piece will focus on what this book can teach us about the history of Key West through its recipes and the women who developed them. I can identify and research the names of most of the contributors, but I'm not seeing any name to match the initials CC."

He took the book from me and paged through it. Then he set it on the desk, turned it so we could see the screen, and with a few strokes of his computer keys, brought up a set of old photographs. The first must have been taken at a launch party for the cookbook. The redbrick building was clear in the background. A group of ladies wearing dresses with cinched waists and full skirts falling below the knee had been arranged on the porch. They wore wide smiles and held up copies of the book. He pointed to the face of a beautiful young woman who was mostly blocked by the smaller women in front of her. Her hair was curled into victory rolls that hugged her delicate face, but unlike the other women in the photo, she wasn't smiling. She looked nervous.

"I think you're looking for Clementine Clark, although her name is now Griswold. She hasn't been Clark for many years, since she married Arthur Griswold when she was in her thirties."

"What can you tell us about her life?" Martha asked.

"I don't believe the marriage was a love match, as her husband was quite a bit older. She lives by herself and has been a widow for a number of years. I believe she had one daughter, now deceased, and a granddaughter."

I showed him the photograph that we'd found in the box.

"That's her on the right," he said, tapping the desk next to the picture. "The other girl might be Evelyn Garcia, née Marshall."

"You mean the mother of the man who was murdered?" I asked, and he nodded.

I felt a buzz of excitement. This young woman was still alive and might be able to resolve our curiosity about the hidden box, if she was willing to talk about what seemed like very dark days. I couldn't believe she and the elder Mrs. Garcia had been girlfriends. We chatted a little longer and then thanked Mr. Hambright for his help.

As we emerged from the cool library into the shimmer of afternoon heat, I noticed I had missed several texts. Nathan had alerted me that he'd gone in to the department for a few hours to work. My mother had invited us to dinner, the *us* to include Miss Gloria and my father-in-law. "We are just dying to meet him. Since you didn't answer me right away, I texted Nathan too, and he seems excited. Sam wants to grill, so there's nothing to bring."

Dinner at my mother's definitely sounded better than cooking after the busy week I'd had. Then I noticed a second text that had come in after the first.

"Lorenzo's coming too. I ran into him at the grocery store, and he seemed sad he hadn't seen us for a while. Helen hit it off with him famously, so maybe Skip will too."

I could imagine her sheepish tone if she'd told me this in person. No one who'd heard as much about Skip Bransford as she had would imagine him hitting it off with a tarot card reader, a man deeply in tune with the spiritual world.

"Family dinner," I explained to Martha with a grin. "It's bound to be a zoo. I will try to track down Clementine Griswold and ask if she'll talk to us. Maybe tomorrow morning?"

Chapter Twenty-Two

What you just dictated to me is the secret. As each Arcana is a mirror and not a truth in itself, become what you see in it. That tarot is a chameleon.

—Alejandro Jodorowsky, *The Book of Tarot*

I phoned Clementine Griswold when I got home and arranged to meet her at eleven the next morning. She hadn't sounded enthusiastic about my inquiry, but I persuaded her by assuring her that we would be brief, and that my focus was on the cookbook. Having the opportunity to interview someone who'd been there for the book's creation would add so much, I told her. I even agreed to show her the article before sending it to my editors, a strict no-no in my business. And I promised I wouldn't be sharing her personal history; I only wanted her memories and stories about the cookbook.

The remainder of the afternoon, I puttered around the houseboat, straightening things in the kitchen and working on my articles in my head. But the mystery of GG Garcia's death and the shock of finding his body on the beach kept circling in my mind, making it hard to concentrate.

I was drowsing on the deck in the sun when my phone rang an hour later. *Helen Bransford*, the screen read. I accepted the call because—mother-in-law . . .

"It occurred to me we hadn't chatted in forever," she said brightly, her tone shading toward chipper. "Is this a good time?"

"Sure," I said, "but Nathan's not here at the moment." *Bright* and *chipper* were not usually words I would use to describe her. What was up?

"Even better," she said. "How are you? What are you working on?"

I gave her the Cliff Notes version of the work I was doing, because she wasn't a foodie and wouldn't find a rundown of the restaurants I'd visited the least bit interesting. Then I told her about finding GG Garcia's body—that was in her wheelhouse. She was a forensic psychologist with tons of experience in crime scenes, among other things.

"It's in the jurisdiction of the sheriff's department, but the Key West police are working on it now as well. And no one quite knows what to make of it. Garcia has a terrible reputation in town for pushing through unpopular development projects and wooing married and younger women."

"Hmmm," she said. "A creep who had it coming? Are you certain he was murdered? What did you notice about the crime scene?"

"The authorities seem to believe he was killed, and both teams have been dashing around interviewing suspects." I told her about Ziggy's discovery, meeting Davis Jager on the scene, and the way the body had been splayed out with what looked like a head injury. "After the blow on the head, either he fell and hit the back of his head or he was struck again by the attacker. He suffered an internal bleed, and that's what actually killed him. We'd had a brief but intense and blowy thunderstorm after midnight, so lots of what might have been evidence was washed away."

"Tell me what you noticed about the man's body. What was he wearing? Could you get a sense of what he was doing on the beach at such a late hour?"

"Of course, that's a question we all want answered. Why was he there?" I paused, pushing my mind back to that gruesome scene, combing through the details to see if there was anything I could have missed. As far as I knew, none of the law enforcement professionals had asked the question about his clothing. It felt important to come across as competent in her eyes.

"Keep in mind that he was half-buried by the sand that had blown over him. And I was shocked and discombobulated. Anyway, Ziggy was digging and tugging on something denim. Then I saw the fingers." I shivered silently. "So a jean jacket or maybe a shirt in case it got cool, I'd say. Plus khaki shorts, a polo shirt, and slip-on casual shoes, like Allbirds. Dressed up a bit for Key West, now that I think of it. His head was bruised and he had a lump above the right eye. At the time, I thought it was hard to imagine that one lump killed him. But heads are fragile, right?"

"Right," she said. "It depends on exactly where the blow landed and what happened next. Anything else?"

I paused for a minute to riffle through my memories. "He had bruises on his legs as well. But those apparently looked older. Like maybe he'd tripped and fallen onto something?"

"If he was on a blood thinner," she said, "he would bruise easily. If Nathan's involved, remind him about the bruising."

"He is, and I will."

There was another pause in the conversation, and then Helen asked, "How is everyone getting along with the infamous Skip?"

I wasn't surprised that she was curious, although I was a little surprised that she was willing to ask. She had a lot of pride, and her ex-husband had shredded it with his infidelity. This explained why she'd called me and not Nathan. "He's a character," I said. "Quite charming so far. He seems to have a little insight into how he behaved in your family."

Helen snorted. I saw Nathan get out of his SUV in the parking lot and start toward our houseboat. "I spy Nathan. Do you want to say hello?" I asked. "We're about to drive over to Mom and Sam's place for dinner."

I handed the phone over as he stepped onto the deck. "Your mother." His raised his eyebrows but took the phone while I went next door to collect Miss Gloria.

"What was that all about?" he asked as the three of us hopped into his SUV.

"She was checking in. I told her about Garcia's murder, and she had some interesting questions. She's a smart cookie." I explained about the clothing and the bruises, keeping her questions about her ex to myself.

"So noted," he said, as he pulled onto Palm Avenue and headed over to pick up Skip on the other side of town.

"I can't imagine what possessed my mother to arrange this guest list," I said, slumping in the passenger seat. It had been yet another hectic day, and I had the feeling I'd need a surge of energy to field the possible drama. The more I thought about it, the more I grew sure that Lorenzo and Skip

Bransford could not be anyone's idea of a dinner party match made in heaven.

"It sounds perfect to me," said Miss Gloria, snickering in the back seat. "Lorenzo is always good at shaking people up. Besides, I haven't seen him in forever."

I could always count on my mother and Sam to act gracious, no matter what oddball guests I might bring over. Nathan's mother, Helen, had even stayed with them for several days last winter and ended up enjoying the visit thoroughly. If they'd objected to hosting her, they'd never said a peep to me. They were the most generous hosts I had ever met, and I tried to use them as role models.

Skip was waiting outside the Casa Marina. I hopped out of the front seat and moved to the back with Miss Gloria. "Thank you," he said, turning to smile at me. I smiled in return.

Nathan took the back streets through the Bahama Village and across town to my mother's neighborhood. As we rode, I explained that my mother and Sam were relative newlyweds too, and that Lorenzo read tarot cards at Mallory Square.

"Whether or not you believe in his power to predict the future, trust me, he's one of the most intuitive people I've ever met," I said, hoping to head off any conflict before it surfaced.

Miss Gloria patted Skip's shoulder and leaned forward to stage-whisper, "I'm a big believer, and I hope you will be too." Nathan and I laughed.

We drove through the gates marking the entrance to the Truman Annex and then a few blocks toward the harbor to the home my mother and Sam rented.

"This is a different neighborhood than your Houseboat Row," said Skip.

"For sure," Miss Gloria said. "Not nearly as homey as I prefer, but lovely all the same. And expensive," she added with a wink. "In case you were thinking of moving here too."

No one said a word after that. To my mind, a short visit with Skip Bransford seemed about right. Having him move to our island paradise would take some mental adjustment—maybe a lot. Nathan parked alongside the curb, and we all piled out. Sam was waiting on the porch, where he pumped Skip's hand and then Nathan's and kissed us ladies. He was quite a few inches shorter than Nathan's dad and less muscular. But he didn't seem the least bit intimidated.

"Lorenzo's already here," he said to me. And then he began to explain to Skip how this neighborhood had been built mostly on fill in the eighties, so it looked very different than it had in the days when Harry Truman spent time in the Little White House down the street. "Out on our back deck, you can get a little glimpse of the harbor if you stand in exactly the right place on the porch," he said with a chuckle. "If we have time after dinner, we'll take a stroll over there. They created a new park, including a water park for kids, and visitors and locals alike love it. There's often a big gathering of dogs and their owners in the morning, and the sunset viewers at the end of the day."

"Sounds charming," said Skip. "Like the rest of this island. Thank you for the dinner invitation on such short notice."

Miss Gloria raised her eyebrows at me, probably wondering the same thing. *Charming* didn't sound like a word he would often use; was he being sarcastic?

"We wouldn't even consider missing the chance to meet another member of our Nathan's family," said my mom, coming up behind her husband to greet Skip. "Come right in—it's cool enough to have a drink on the porch, I think, and then maybe eat inside?"

She hugged me and Miss Gloria, kissed Nathan's cheek, and led us through the back of the house to the deck. Lorenzo was seated in a lounge chair with a glass of something fizzy in his hand. He stood to greet us. In contrast to his usual work attire—black pants, a white shirt, a tie—he had on a plaid shirt and jeans. "And this is our dear friend Lorenzo," she added. "He is the wisest man on our island."

"That's quite an introduction," said Skip. He reached out to shake his hand but then pulled back, noticing that Lorenzo had bowed, his hands pressed together in namaste. "I'm Nathan's father. Not nearly so wise."

"The pleasure is mine," Lorenzo said.

After drinks and snacks and general conversation about how my father-in-law liked Key West and what life was like in Tallahassee, my mother waved us inside for dinner. Sam had grilled flank steak and sliced it thinly, then arranged it on a platter alongside skewers of Key West pinks. My mother had made a bowl of Sally Bell's knockoff potato salad and also sliced some good-looking tomatoes, layered them with fresh mozzarella, then sprinkled on fresh basil and drizzled olive oil over top.

"Don't worry," she said, looking at my face as I surveyed the spread. "I didn't fuss. But I was in the groove of making old-fashioned recipes, and I thought this potato salad would go perfectly with the steak. This version has lots of egg yolks and homemade sweet pickles and even a few chopped pickled jalapeños."

"Everything looks delicious," said Skip. "And thank you again for inviting me at the last minute." He sat in the chair Sam pulled out for him and folded his napkin over his stomach. "I am very grateful to have been received so warmly by Nathan's in-laws. And Nathan himself." He smiled at my husband, who barely grimaced in return.

"And we are glad to meet you," Miss Gloria said. "Shall I say grace?" After an unadorned but heartfelt set of thanks to God and her adoptive family, she turned back to Skip and Nathan. "And how is it going with Mr. Garcia's murder case?"

"This one isn't easy to crack," said Skip. "But I should let my son tell you what he can, as I'm only an outsider."

"What he said," said Nathan, looking grumpy. "We've done a whole lot of interviewing of a whole lot of people, but nothing has crystallized. Garcia did so many things to ruffle feathers in this town—the possibilities seem endless. But one strong murder suspect hasn't been identified."

I thought I'd better quickly fill them in with the new information I hadn't had the chance to discuss with Nathan. "I took Ziggy to the dog park this morning—I was wearing regular clothes this time, nothing weird—and I ran into Theresa. She's the woman who used to be Andi Garcia's best friend—until she succumbed to GG's charms and had an affair with him." I explained how genuinely sad she seemed about losing the friendship and how disgusted she was with her own weakness. "It was clear that she disliked him intensely at the end, but I'm not sure I see her murdering him. On the other hand, she sounded very angry about how her friendship had been ruined."

"A rat's nest," said my mother, as she delivered a plate of fresh fruit and cookies to the table. "Cookies," she said with a wink, "are courtesy of the reception on Friday. We made way too much food, as usual, and the president insisted I pack some of it up to bring home." She returned to the kitchen and came out with a chocolate cake, covered with lit candles. She settled it in front of Miss Gloria while we sang happy birthday. "We didn't have a proper cake the other night, and that seemed wrong," said Mom.

Miss Gloria beamed, blew out the candles, and got up to hug my mother. "Unnecessary but so sweet. Thank you!"

I took an oatmeal cookie and nibbled. "As for Theresa, it's almost as if she wouldn't have felt killing him was worth the bother, or the trouble it would cause. And she didn't believe Andi would have done it either."

"No one thinks their friends or relatives are capable of killing someone," Nathan said, with a dismissive wave. "If Garcia's wife is as high voltage as you describe, it's probably worth us paying her another visit."

His father nodded his approval. "One should always examine the spouse carefully in a case like this."

"Is there a front runner for a suspect?" asked Miss Gloria.

"Possibly this Entwistle fellow. He entered quite a few deals with Garcia and was burned more than once. Garcia had a knack for serving himself before others—from the looks of it, quite generously. We're going to have another chat with him tomorrow."

Nathan didn't sound as though he wanted to continue mulling over the possibilities with the present company.

"Did you get everything wrapped up at the Woman's Club yesterday?" my mother asked, noticing his grumpiness at the same time I did. "We felt terrible leaving that mess to you girls."

I laughed. "We're hardly girls. And it really wasn't a lot to do. And as a reward, we made a fascinating discovery." I described finding the old materials in the hutch at the Woman's Club, including an old photograph and the diary entries. "Tom Hambright, the historian at the library, identified the girls in the photo for us. One of them was Clementine Clark, now Griswold, who's still alive and well. I'm writing a piece about the old cookbook for this week's issue of the magazine, and Martha Hubbard wants to plan events using more vintage recipes, so we both are visiting Mrs. Griswold tomorrow. I can't think that any of this has anything to do with the murder, but it sure was fascinating history."

"You'll let me know if you turn up anything pertinent to the case?" Nathan asked, his eyebrows puckered with mild concern. "Any little bits of information you learn about Garcia could give us a shift in direction."

"You guys are really stumped," Miss Gloria declared. "It's not often you ask Hayley for advice."

I laughed out loud. "You nailed that one. Usually by now he's telling me to stick to my food writing and butt out because I'm putting myself in danger." I winked at Nathan to show him I was teasing and there were no hard feelings.

"But it's true," Nathan said. "You sometimes take unnecessary risks, and that gives me gray hair before my time."

"Do you ever read cards for a situation rather than a single person?" Miss Gloria asked Lorenzo. "I wonder if a reading would help the men solve the mystery of Mr. Garcia's death."

Nathan looked at her as though she might possibly have crossed the line into demented, and Skip's expression was identical.

Lorenzo ignored them both. "I've certainly intuited things about a place, so maybe it's not so different. Are you familiar with tarot cards?" he asked, fixing a quizzical look on my father-in-law's face.

"Not in the slightest," said Skip. "I warn you in advance that I'm a skeptic when it comes to anything woo-woo." He pushed his chair back a bit from the table and crossed his arms over his chest. This was the same defensive posture Nathan would have taken if he didn't like the way a conversation was going. "But don't let that stop you. Bring it on," said Skip, his chin jutting out, now tapping his knuckles on the table as if he were a card shark in Vegas waiting for the dealer.

I held my breath, but Lorenzo didn't seem ruffled. He smiled like a cherub, extracted a pack of cards from his back pocket where a man's wallet might usually be, and spread them on the table. To me they looked worn and wise and familiar and comforting. To Skip, I imagined they appeared like a children's game or, worse, an easy target for mockery. I almost blurted out how much his ex-wife, Helen, had appreciated Lorenzo's talents. But it was probably the worst idea ever to compare him unfavorably to his ex, so I bit my tongue.

"Usually when I'm giving a reading, I meditate for a moment first," said Lorenzo. "And then I ask my customer to think about the question they want answered. Next, the customer shuffles, which serves to transfer their energy to the cards. Finally, they cut the deck, and I deal them out." He looked around the table. As expected, my mother and Miss Gloria were most interested and encouraging, Sam a bit more neutral, and Nathan and his father skeptical.

"Since we are thinking about a situation rather than an individual person, I would suggest that we all close our eyes and focus on the question at hand. You might think that would be simple—who murdered this man? But allow yourselves to consider something wider if it comes to mind."

I didn't dare look at my husband and his father, so I closed my eyes and thought of GG Garcia. What kind of man had he been that had led him to the grim moment when I'd found his half-buried body? I opened my eyes to watch Lorenzo deal out four cards: the tower, the hanged man, the devil, and Justice. He made no comment on the spread but thought quietly for a moment.

"Justice," he said, touching the card featuring a king in a red robe sitting on a throne. The king had an upright sword in one hand and a scale in the other. "Justice reminds us that karma is real. Your past and your future may come together at this point. Justice tells us there is a consequence for every action and the present moment is exactly what you deserve."

"Wow," said Miss Gloria, "harsh. Every criminal or mean person should hear those words. I'm guessing that card was meant for Mr. Garcia."

Lorenzo nodded. "Perhaps." The second card was the hanged man. A man wearing a short blue dress and red tights hung upside down from a tree. "This one," he said, "often surfaces when a person feels they are in limbo. I advise people to let go in a situation like this. Try to lighten your grip, because whatever you are doing is not working right now."

I wondered whether the hanged man referred to Garcia or to the police. Possibly both.

The third card was a horrifying-looking devil with one hand held up and claws for feet. "The devil card often carries with it feelings of restraint and powerlessness. You may feel locked down, as though you have no moves, but you do hold the keys to your freedom. And those keys will unlock the door."

The tower was last. I'd often had this card dealt out to me, and I hated it every time. The illustration showed a tall tower that had burst into flames. The bodies of a man and a woman plunged toward the ground. They appeared to have flung themselves out the windows. It totally spooked me every time I saw it.

"The tower means destruction, obviously," Lorenzo said. "Your life is crumbling, going up in flames, and you don't have a way to control it. The card suggests that you let the pieces fall. Sometimes you have to tear down a rotten structure in order to allow something sturdy to be built in its place."

The table was silent as he finished. He sat back in his chair and looked around at us, his work done.

"Well, goodness," said my mother, "you have given us a lot to think about, as always. I should think Nathan will take this in carefully and determine whether it leads him in a helpful direction."

Lorenzo flashed a grin at her. "Questions?" he asked the rest of us.

"Okay," said Skip. "I'll bite. Here's one. What the hell does any of this mean? I have no idea what you're talking about, and I can't fathom how playing cards could help us with an active investigation."

Lorenzo merely smiled. "You're probably not alone. Some people find the readings very helpful and others not at all. I've learned not to take offense." He looked at the faces around the table. "Feel free to call or text if you think of questions."

I felt proud of him for choosing not to argue with or otherwise attempt to convince Skip, which I suspected would have been fruitless. I took a picture of the cards so I could think about them later without my thoughts getting contaminated by the negative energy from the Bransford men.

We thanked Mom and Sam again for the dinner and headed out to the car. Miss Gloria and I slid into the back seat, and Skip got in next to Nathan. He turned around to look at me. "I must say, you have interesting friends. I also have to be honest when I say I think those cards are hogwash. Though Lorenzo would probably do well with your sister and her thin places nonsense."

This last was directed to Nathan. Vera, his daughter—estranged, no big surprise—had been one of the writers on a gorgeous book about thin places in Scotland that Miss Gloria and I adored. She had described the places as points where the veil between heaven and earth was particularly thin, and she'd taken us to visit several of them.

"So you made clear," said Miss Gloria from the seat behind him. "Hayley and I find his readings remarkably revealing if we hold our minds open to what they might be saying. Vera's book is astonishing. We experienced a few of her thin places, and one day when I'm not so tired, I'll tell you about my time there."

That was a gentle scolding if ever I'd heard one.

Nathan dropped Skip off at the Casa Marina, and we continued home. I texted Lorenzo to apologize in case his feelings had been hurt.

No worries, Lorenzo texted back. *Your father-in-law has no faith, but I'm used to that and I don't let it bother me.*

But still it bothered me a bit that Nathan didn't accept the possibility of other spiritual realms, though he wasn't as rude as his father.

Later that night, I lay awake, my mind drifting through the packed week of events. Theresa's warning in the dog park surfaced. She'd said very definitely that if my marriage hit a rough spot, I should look inside for solutions rather than out. I scooched over until Nathan and I were bum to bum, so I could feel the rise and fall of his breath as he slept without waking him up. What would it take for either of us to get involved with another party? I'd been struck by the anger and sadness on Theresa's face and the bitterness of her friend, Andi Garcia. It made me even more determined to work out any glitches between Nathan and me as they arose over the course of our marriage. He wasn't a pushover. He didn't come from an easy family, good at talking about the tender patches of their soul. But I loved him desperately, and that should make the hard parts worth the struggle. Eventually I drifted off to sleep.

Chapter Twenty-Three

Emotions, particularly anger, are like fire. They can cook your food and keep you warm, or they can burn your house down.

—Cus D'Amato

The next morning, as I was making the bed, Nathan brought me a cup of coffee fixed exactly the way I liked it: strong, with lots of frothed whole milk on top. It wasn't as good as the café con leche served at the Cuban Coffee Queen, but it was delicious all the same.

"I wondered if you might take a ride with me to talk with Andi Garcia? I would do the interviewing, of course," he said. "But now that you've met her friend Theresa, it might be interesting to compare their stories. I'll talk and you stick to observing, okay?"

"What if she doesn't have anything to say to a big tough cop?" I asked, perching my hands on my hips and making a scowly face. Then I started to laugh. "Just kidding. I'd be happy to go with you, as long as I'm back by ten thirty or so to pick up Martha for our visit to Clementine Griswold."

On the way over to the Garcia home, Darcy Rogers called Nathan to confirm she'd be meeting him there. "Two sets of eyes are better than one when our leads have cooled," she said, her voice brisk.

"I asked Hayley to come with me too," Nathan told her. "She knows her role; she'll be mostly listening. She met Andi's friend Theresa at the dog park yesterday, so I'd like her to listen in and watch Andi's body language."

I could tell from the pause in the conversation that Deputy Rogers was not thrilled with this news, but Nathan hadn't left an opening for her to protest. Soon we were parked outside the Garcias' home on Seminary Street in the Casa Marina section of town.

Most of the houses in this neighborhood had walls around them and lots of tropical foliage grown for privacy, and the Garcias' place was no exception. We joined the deputy at the front of the property and went in through the gate. Inside, the grounds opened up to a huge and meticulously groomed lawn studded by exquisite tropical flowering bushes and trees. I recognized papaya, star fruit, avocado, mango, fig, and passion fruit. As my mother had said, it would have been a glorious setting for a party. How very sad that the last big party held here had been to celebrate a couple who didn't seem very happy together and were now separated permanently by the husband's death.

The two-story home was surrounded by wide covered porches on two sides, filled with comfortable seats and rocking chairs overlooking the lawn. More plants in stone planters were sprinkled here as well. Around the corner, I could see an enticing expanse of blue pool water, and beyond that, a guest house.

Andi Garcia met us at the door. "It's a bit warm out here, so I suggest we talk inside." She barely managed to eke out a smile.

We followed her through a tiled hallway to an air-conditioned porch at the back of the house. Rotating ceiling fans caused the chilled air to feel even colder. We sat on wicker chairs with striped cushions and declined her offer of coffee.

"I was hoping you would have come with news about my husband's murder. But I don't suppose that's the case."

Nathan shook his head. "Unfortunately, we are not close to an arrest at this moment. We had a few follow-up questions and hoped you might help us."

Darcy Rogers touched Andi's knee lightly and smiled with sympathy. "We understand how difficult this must be and apologize for the intrusion."

"What can you tell us about your husband's relationship with Mack Entwistle?" Nathan asked. "He was chosen to give a eulogy at the memorial service, so I assume they must have been close. Anything he and Mr. Garcia shared that might have caused problems between them?"

"I assume you are not talking about the women they shared?" Andi asked. Her voice was still polite, but the words were shocking, brittle, and harsh. "Though perhaps you are."

Both Nathan and Darcy looked as surprised as I felt.

Nathan quickly adjusted his expression back to neutral. "Could you tell us more about that? Perhaps they had similar tastes?"

"Similar tastes for jailbait," she said, practically spitting out the words. "With an occasional lapse into a mature woman with more experience in the sexual arts."

I bit my tongue to keep from exclaiming, *What in the world are you talking about?*

"This must be so painful. But important to the case, I suspect. I'm sorry to have to ask you this, but could you expand on that, please?" Nathan asked. "Which women did they share, and was there someone in particular who might have caused bad blood between the men?"

Andi pressed a hand to her forehead as if this was a difficult conversation, and I suspected it was. Layered on top of her grief and shock, she must be feeling humiliated and angry. She listed off the names of four women, none of whom I recognized.

"Mostly bartenders and waitresses," she added, "as that is where they spent most of their evenings. I exaggerated a bit calling them jailbait, but they were young enough to be my daughters. As for bad blood, my sense told me it was more a blood sport for the two of them—who could bed a girl more quickly. I don't believe either one of them cared particularly about the women." She looked directly at me as if in warning. "My husband was very, very charming. Handsome too."

"Is Mack Entwistle married?" Darcy asked.

"He was," said Andi. "His wife had had enough several years ago. I probably should have followed her lead. I thought—I hoped—maybe GG would grow out of it." Her gaze lifted, and she looked out the window at the pool behind the house.

Then she glanced back at us. "I didn't kill him, if that's what you're thinking. I was angry, for sure, and embarrassed. He should have behaved like an adult, but his mother never required that of him. Or her own husband, for that matter. She ruled the roost in every other way." She held out her hands to encompass the beautiful home. "Besides, I earned this and a lot more. And he would have fought tooth and nail to keep me from getting anything in a divorce." She stood up as if to see us out. "And besides that, I had to think of my son." Her face was lined with pain.

"Tell us about that," Nathan said.

"He was beginning to act like his father," said Andi softly, sitting down again and looking at her hands.

"In what way?" Darcy asked.

"In the way he treated women. Girls," she added. "He was not kind, and I felt it was important to stay with him and try to correct GG's influence. But he would not have killed his father; he loved that man."

"Do you know why he was so upset at the funeral reception?" Darcy asked. "I noticed him yelling at some women."

Andi studied the deputy's face. "He'd had a lot to drink. One of the girls was a former girlfriend, and apparently it didn't end well. He was upset that she came. That's all I could get from him. You could talk with him if you like, but he went back to school. He's been in Miami since right after the funeral. Not that I blame him for fleeing. Death is too hard on a young person."

Nathan took down his contact information.

Since neither Nathan nor Deputy Rogers had asked about Theresa, I did. "Theresa Martin," I said. "Was she one of the mutual conquests of your husband and Mack?"

Andi shook her head, her eyes shiny with tears. "My husband aimed that shot directly at me, and I'm not going to lie, it hurt a lot."

"I'm sorry," I said, wondering if I should mention how sad Theresa was about having made that choice. In the end, it would be up to them to sort their friendship out. I hoped they managed it. My own women friends meant so very much to me.

"Is it possible that Ms. Martin would have killed your husband? Did they have a falling out?" Nathan asked.

Her face grew stony. "She claimed they only slept together once and then he dropped her. I didn't really care; in my mind, once was betrayal enough. Would she have killed him? She's strong enough to have taken him on." She shrugged her slender shoulders carelessly. "I really couldn't say."

"Thank you for speaking with us. We'll be in touch if we have other questions or information about your husband's death," Nathan said as he stood to shake her hand. We returned to our cars, and I got back into the SUV with Nathan, feeling sad and—how else to say it?—slimed by what we'd heard.

"Do you think it's possible that Theresa killed him once she realized he'd used her to hurt Andi?" Nathan asked as he drove away.

I wrinkled my nose. "Maybe. If her friend asked her to. But I don't think that fits. Why would Theresa have ridden up to Geiger Key with him? It honestly didn't sound as if she had any interest in resuming an affair with him, even if he'd wanted her again." I swallowed hard, weighed down by the emotional damage that one man had wreaked. "I assume you'll talk to Andi's son?"

He nodded. "Tomorrow."

My phone rang when we were almost back to Houseboat Row. Though it was an unfamiliar number, I answered. "It's Al, Pizza Al," the man said with a laugh. "I remembered one other thing, and you told me to call, right?"

"Great. I'm going to put you on speaker phone so my husband, the detective, can hear."

"I told you about the scooter with two people on it. I remember that I did see that scooter leaving, but it had only one person on it this time. I'm sorry I didn't think of this earlier, I sleep hard when I finally get there. But I woke up when I heard that engine and went to the window to check it out."

"You knew it was the same scooter you'd spotted earlier?" Nathan asked. "How could you be sure?"

"On the way onto Boca Chica, it made a snapping noise, like there was a crack in the spark plug insulation or maybe the cap. Same thing an hour later, headed south toward Key West. Right before the storm moved in. I remember thinking the driver was going to be mad as a wet hen if he didn't make it home in time."

"No rider on the back this time?"

Al clucked his tongue. "Only the one person, but I can't be sure which one it was."

Chapter Twenty-Four

Anybody who knows me knows that when times get tough, the tough make pudding.

—Ijeoma Oluo, "Feminist Pudding," *The Book Club Cookbook Blog*

Clementine Griswold lived in a small home on a man-made inlet on Stock Island—an entirely different kind of neighborhood than the one where Nathan and I had visited Andi Garcia. Her street was located at the far side of Cow Key on the last road before the entrance to Island Farm. The farm had been established only recently on an enormous undeveloped tract of land, and the owners had plans to raise bees, provide outdoor events and experiences for adults and children, and launch kayaks and paddleboards from Lost Beach. A couple of weeks ago, I'd had my first visit to the farm, and the owner had persuaded me to go out in a double kayak so I could see everything from the water. I was glad I'd gone—the views were gorgeous and the paddling not as impossible as it looked. Especially on a smooth day with someone else in the captain's seat.

Next week, I was scheduled to attend one of their pig roasts to report on the food and the vibe. The homes on this street, though set close together, had privacy and a sense of openness from the lagoon on one side. Most had small docks with motorboats and kayaks floating beside them, and laundry flapped on many clotheslines, including Mrs. Griswold's, which sported beach towels, kitchen towels, and some clothing that looked like it belonged to a young woman. I suspected that some of Mrs. Griswold's neighbors were former Key Westers who'd been priced out of real estate on the island. She had a battered Toyota parked in her driveway, and we pulled up behind it.

Mrs. Griswold came to answer our knock after we spent several moments waiting. She seemed familiar—sharp blue eyes in a weathered face, though I couldn't exactly remember where I'd seen her before. Maybe she too had been at the memorial service, which would make sense if she was involved with the Woman's Club and knew Andi Garcia and the victim's mother. That was it—she'd been sitting on the left side, away from Garcia's family. Now I could also make out the features of the young girl she had been in the old photograph.

"Good morning, Mrs. Griswold. We spoke on the phone? I'm Hayley Snow," I said. "And this is my friend Martha Hubbard. Thank you so much for agreeing to chat with us."

"You may as well call me Clementine. Everyone does." She flashed a thin smile and invited us in. A ceiling fan spun lazily in the living room, causing a giant houseplant to rustle in passing. The walls were made of recycled Dade pine that I recognized from our houseboat renovation. Artwork nearly covered the wood walls, some of them drawings in charcoal and some paintings—the same style we'd seen both in the cookbook and in the hidden box.

"The artwork is gorgeous," I said. "Are you the artist?"

"Thanks, yes," she said, in a brisk voice that cut off further discussion. She led us toward a screened-in porch at the back of the house but stopped before we arrived. "I've made a banana cream pie this morning. Would you like a piece?"

I did want a piece; I'd been craving exactly that since reading about it in the cookbook. "I would love that," I said. "If it isn't too much trouble. I love having dessert for lunch."

"Me too," said Martha, grinning, and we followed Clementine to the kitchen to help. Her kitchen had an old-fashioned look, with black-and-white tiles on the counters and rag rugs scattered over the burnished wood floors. Even the table was vintage, with a Formica top and metal legs that looked like it had been taken from a 1950s diner. The room felt cozy and restful and very conducive to cooking and eating. There was a lacquered tray on the table containing three plates and three tall glasses, as though she'd assume we'd agree to her offer.

Clementine pulled a pie from her refrigerator. The peaks of meringue stood up perfectly, and a rim of graham cracker crust peeked out around the edges. My mouth watered in anticipation.

"If you're going to try to make this, don't use the pudding recipe from the original cookbook; use the later version," she said. "That early recipe called for fourteen to sixteen bananas. They were called ladyfinger bananas because they measured this long." She held up her thumb and forefinger to show a gap of what looked to be about three inches. "You might want to explain that in your article, lest your readers end up with gallons of unusable mashed bananas. And it's perfectly acceptable to use whipped cream rather than meringue, though it won't look so dramatic."

She cut three generous wedges of the pie, then poured three glasses of tea. "We'll eat on the porch," she said.

I picked up two of the glasses, and Martha followed with the tray. A low wicker table stood in front of two rockers and a love seat. The pie slices and frosty drinks arranged on the table, with the water and docks in the far background, would have been an Instagram sensation.

"Would you be willing to share the recipe for the Key Zest magazine?" I asked. "It would be really fun to include something from you, based on the recipe in the old cookbook."

"No pictures of me, though," she said, leaning away and holding a hand up.

I quickly agreed, pulling out the old cookbook and settling it on the rattan coffee table in front of us. Then I took notes about Clementine's recipe tweaks and snapped a few more close-up photos of the pie, this time with the cookbook arranged artfully in the background. As we ate, we chatted about cooking and exclaimed over the pie, which tasted rich and creamy—a perfect foil for the crunchy graham cracker crust. I replaced my fork on the empty plate and settled back in the wicker rocker.

"It's so peaceful here beside the water," I said. "You're close enough to everything, and yet it doesn't feel that way." I was thinking of our houseboat, also on the water, literally floating on the water. But the marina was bordered on two sides by busy roads; depending on the time of day and the flow of traffic, it didn't always have this removed-from-the-humdrum feeling.

"I'm lucky," she said. "We do sit low and thus are vulnerable to hurricane damage and sea level rise. But I wouldn't trade it for anything—and I hope I won't be alive if the neighborhood is flooded. Here, my neighbors are pleasant enough, and they leave me alone. My granddaughter visits me at least once a week, often more. And often with her friends, which is lovely."

She showed us a photo displayed on an end table. A young woman stood on the dock leading to the lagoon wearing cutoff jean shorts and a halter top. Another girl with blonde braids wound atop her head was bending over a double kayak, as if to launch it.

"Ida loves being out on the water as much as I do." She gestured at the two kayaks bobbing alongside her dock, one single, one double. "We've had developers sniff around and try to buy us out, but so far we've held the line. The more they offered, the more tempting it has been to some of my neighbors." She was scowling now. "But this is my home. I've lived here since my husband passed and I've enjoyed making it my own, without answering to anyone else's taste. Where would I move? Where would I go? You may know as well as I do that senior housing on the Keys is both scarce and unappealing."

Once Martha had finished her pie and declared it far and away the best banana cream pie she'd ever eaten, Clementine said, "You mentioned that you had some questions about the old cookbook. I don't know that I can tell you anything useful. Other than a few cooking tips, like buying the right bananas. That publication was long ago and meant nothing to me really."

I knew that couldn't be true—if in fact she had been the author of the diary and the artist in the cookbook. Or at least it hadn't been true years ago. People did change and move on and forget things. As my friend Eric would have reminded me, suppression of unpleasant memories was practically an epidemic in this country. How else could we survive in this world? I shifted my backpack to my lap.

"You had some drawings included in the first edition, right? They were really quite good, and professional, compared to some of the others." I opened my copy to the page where her flamenco dancers were featured and watched her reaction.

She pushed the book back across the table, a blank look on her face. "That was a phase, pretending I could draw. I'm by no means an artist. I gave that up long ago."

I exchanged glances with Martha—I doubted this was true either. She had similar artwork all over her living room walls, and she had told us she was the artist. I took the box we'd found in the cupboard from my backpack, opened the lid, and removed the diary pages and placed them in front of her.

Her face drained of color, leaving her skin papery white. She leaned away from the table, as if the papers were contaminated. "Where in the world did you find that?" Her reaction told us everything—she was shocked to see those pages resurface.

I told her about discovering the box at the back of the hutch. "Can you tell us anything more about what happened that night? Or how the box ended up in the cabinet?"

"It was so long ago, I don't remember. I was young and so silly. Who knows what I wrote? I have no memory of any of it. It's not important." She crossed her arms, frowning, and shook her head. "It has no bearing on my life today."

Then I showed her the photograph of her with another girl, placing it on the table right in front of her.

"What can you tell us about this girl?" Martha asked.

Clementine pushed the photo back across the table with the tip of her forefinger. "Pffft," she said. "I didn't know her well. Even back then she was self-absorbed, not a person to rely on. I learned that soon enough. It's not important, and I can't imagine why you're dragging this up now."

"It's very important," I said. "Because of Mr. Garcia's murder. The police are having a difficult time solving the case, so the net is being cast wide."

It wasn't entirely true that the authorities were interested in her, but Martha and I certainly were. We waited her out, staying quiet, listening to the sounds of her neighborhood—birds squabbling, a band saw whining, the sloshing of waves against the docks.

When she finally spoke, her voice was barely above a whisper. "We were best girlfriends until this happened. We did everything together."

"She was GG Garcia's mother, right? I spoke with her at the memorial service," I said. "Tough old bird, though I'm sure she was grieving in her own way."

Clementine grimaced, and I suddenly pictured the fury on her face as she looked at the row of Garcia's bereaved family. "I wouldn't know. We haven't spoken in years."

"Did you hide the box in the cupboard?" Martha asked, keeping her voice gentle.

"No," she said. "No. It can only have been Evelyn. But she never told me, and we've never spoken since."

"Can you tell us why she hid them? You wrote the diary, did you not?"

"She was a nasty piece of work, and most disloyal. I was distraught about what Mr. Garcia Sr. did later that night after the party. I finally broke down and told her what happened. But Evelyn informed me that that miserable man had promised to get engaged to her, as soon as he got divorced from his present wife, and she wouldn't believe me. Or perhaps she did believe me, but she wasn't willing to give up a marriage to a wealthy and important man. She told me I was jealous and mentally sick and trying to ruin everything for her. I dropped it. Who else would have listened? Certainly not his family, and probably not mine. They wouldn't have survived the shame."

"I'm so sorry for what he did to you," I said, once her words had trailed off to nothing, guessing that Garcia must have assaulted her.

"As I told you, we were best girlfriends until this happened," Clementine said. Her face looked brittle with the effort to stay calm. "I'd been keeping the notes along with the diary in a box at the club, in one of the bottom drawers that wasn't used by the members. That way I could write things down and add drawings when the ideas were fresh. Evelyn knew that. After that night, it was gone, and she never spoke to me again. Nor did I try to ask her about it. It's quite possible she hid the box." She gestured at the papers on the coffee table.

Martha said, "This has happened over and over to us women. Only recently have our stories been heard, and even so, not often enough. And not soon enough to undo the damage." She paused, her expression full of compassion. "If you want to tell us what happened that night, we're willing to listen. Sometimes," she added, "it helps to purge the poison."

Clementine studied her face and seemed to find it reassuring.

"There was more that night than what I wrote. He touched me again later. The second time, I believed it couldn't be accidental—he must have felt a special connection with me. Perhaps one day he would even divorce his wife—who was, let's face it, bossy and a shrew of a woman. I was so naïve and silly. At the end of the evening when everyone was drunk, he asked me to help him carry some boxes of leftover cookbooks to the shed behind the club. He shut the door behind us, and that's when I felt a spike of fear. He grabbed my arm and twisted the skin of my forearm until I squeaked with pain.

"'You've been teasing me for months,' he said. 'Now I can no longer be responsible.' He pushed my face up against the wall and lifted my skirts. 'One word,' he said, 'and I will tell them the truth: you made every bit up because you're a jealous little vixen.'"

Martha and I both reached for Clementine's hands, but she pulled away from the contact.

"I realized this was true when I tried to speak to my friend Evelyn, who then told me she was his fiancée-to-be and insisted he was a gentleman and never would have touched me. If she wouldn't hear me out, no one would. After that, I assumed I'd never marry. I never wanted to marry. I was ruined. If anyone else found out about what happened, they would surely have blamed me. I would have been shunned." She kept talking as though the dam had broken and the whole story needed to pour out.

"But my mother was so sad not to have grandchildren. When I was thirty-five, she told me old Mr. Griswold had approached her and would like to wed me, so I agreed. I figured he'd be too old to bother me, and it wouldn't hurt to inherit his money. Then my daughter was born, and then Ida, the light of my life."

She pointed to the photograph of the two girls with their kayaks. "That's it, end of story. No murders involved. May I say without prejudice that I was not sorry to hear about GG Garcia's passing? He was a dreadful man, exactly like his father. But I'm an old lady; I certainly couldn't have killed him and dragged the body to that beach. If my granddaughter should hear about this—any of it—she would be devastated."

* * *

By the time I got home to the houseboat after processing Clementine's shocking news with Martha, I'd received a text from Nathan asking me how the visit had gone. I settled on a deck chair and called him right back.

"It was more dramatic than I expected," I said, once he answered. "And complicated. It turns out Clementine was sexually assaulted by GG Garcia's father when she was only a teenager. Her best friend was GG's mother, Evelyn Garcia—remember her? She was the cranky old lady in black lace with a cane that she thunked to emphasize her words. Of course, they weren't yet married at the time he assaulted Clementine. Anyway, she was the only person Clementine told about the episode. It turns out Garcia was about to dump his current wife and get engaged to Evelyn, which Clementine didn't know. Evelyn certainly wasn't willing to believe her friend's awful story about her new fiancé—it would have destroyed her future."

"That's disgusting," Nathan said. "Like father, like son."

"Unfortunately, in this case, yes. I can't think what this could have to do with the murder, but it was heartbreaking and awful to hear about what she's been through and how long she kept it inside. Did you get a chance to meet with Mr. Entwistle?"

Nathan groaned. "We did. He was as slippery a character as I've ever interviewed. He's exactly the kind of man who would file a lawsuit protesting his mother's will when she gave too much to charity. I wouldn't put it past him to have murdered his friend. The more we learn, the sleazier he looks.

"What's on your schedule for this afternoon? Are you sure you don't mind if I play another nine holes of golf with my father in the late afternoon? I know this is probably not what you had planned for the day . . ." His words trailed off.

Actually, it was a perfect plan. I was so far behind in my work that it wasn't funny. Everything was due tonight, and the thought of all I had left to do made my stomach grind and my head pound. Besides, I liked the idea of Nathan continuing to do something that wasn't work-related with his father. Skip wasn't perfect, but he was blood, and he was trying, and that did count for a lot. The game of golf had taken on a symbolic and negative meaning for my husband, and I felt glad that he might be shaking that off for good. Although this turn of events did make me wonder how long the man was planning on staying on the island.

"That would be fine with me. I'm desperately behind with the articles I owe Key Zest, so I couldn't pay you much attention anyway. What about dinner?"

"Supposing I pick up a pizza from Clemente's on my way home? After I drop my father off," he added quickly. "Pepperoni and peppers so we can say we ate vegetables? Just you and me and maybe some mindless television."

"Heavenly," I said.

After he hung up, I reached for my notes and computer, and dove into the work for several hours. I'd just sent everything to Wally and Palamina when I heard the rumble of my husband's car.

As we ate the pizza and a salad that I'd put together from Miss Gloria's little back deck garden, I asked him about the case. "Does it look like you have enough to arrest Entwistle?"

"Darcy Rogers is following up on his alibi. He's having some trouble remembering which woman he was with. We're a little stumped by Pizza Al's memory of two people on the scooter, one small and one bigger. Both of those men are big. Were big," he corrected, "in Garcia's case. I can't see them hitching a ride together, on a small scooter, to a beach in the middle of nowhere in the middle of the night. And then one came back alone? Hard to make sense of that."

"You'll figure it out," I said. "You always do. Darcy seems like a sharp cookie, if a little gruff."

"You think?" he asked, adding a laugh. "How did you make out with your writing?"

"Good," I said. "The piece about restaurants off the rock is solid. I'm very happy with the story of the old cookbook and the Key West history it tells. As a bonus, I was able to get Clementine Griswold to agree to allow us to run her recipe for banana cream pie. I got some killer photos." I showed him the best, edited to look absolutely mouthwatering.

"I don't suppose you brought a piece home?"

"I was too busy interviewing my prickly baker—it would have been a stretch to ask. Sorry." I leaned over to kiss him. "I do have some stray cookies in the freezer."

Chapter Twenty-Five

At night, fruit falls to the grass with a soft thunk *and in the morning she finds the oranges split and stormed by ants.*

—Naomi Wood, *Mrs. Hemingway*

Tuesday morning, I woke to an urgent text message from Palamina. They loved the articles but needed a few follow-up items. Did I have a photo of the Geiger Key Fish Camp with a perspective of the whole scene, including the tiki hut roof and the picnic tables on the dock? *Once in a while, a picture really is worth a thousand words*, Palamina had added at the end.

Unfortunately, no, I did not. The two times I'd visited Geiger Key this past week, I'd been focused on (a) eating and making notes about the food and (b) figuring out who'd murdered Garcia. I needed to zip up the keys and take that photo. My boss wouldn't demand it, but she'd be disappointed if I didn't come through.

A second, longer message arrived. They were thinking of leading with the article about how the food and recipes in a cookbook could give insights into history, but could I work on the first paragraph or two? Maybe I could flesh out the line I'd written stating that an amateur cookbook could be read as an autobiography of the times.

What exactly did that mean? Could I touch on the fact that women were overrepresented in cookbooks, as a rule, especially one like this? What did this cookbook tell us about the role of women in Key West during that historical era? How did the book speak to gender roles, class, politics, religion, and the world view of its authors? Last but not least, could I wrangle permission from the old woman to take her photograph?

I knew what all the questions meant: pressure. With a front-page placement, all eyes would be on the piece, and that was a compliment but also a challenge. As for the autobiography bit, I'd have to think fast about what that meant. I'd known when I sent in the article that I'd skated on the surface of those deeper questions, and I wasn't convinced I could dive more deeply without a lot more time. But honestly, now it sounded as though Palamina was looking for a doctoral dissertation rather than an article. I flipped through the pages of the old cookbook until I found the section called "Vegetables and Luncheon Dishes." The introduction began:

> *When noon sneaks up on you do you wring your hands, set out the peanut butter jar and hope for the earth to swallow you, or are you one of those fabulous housekeepers ready with a souffle, fruit tarts, fresh cookies, a rose sprigged apron and a gleaming smile when the nominal head of the house comes in at twelve o'clock?*

For sure, the description spoke of different times with different expectations for women. Later today, I'd work on making the connection between the times and the recipes clearer.

Meanwhile, I doubted that Clementine Griswold would agree to more publicity. But I could try. First stop, Geiger Key. I swallowed my coffee and a quick bowl of granola, dressed, and hopped on the scooter. The humidity hung thick as the steam from a hot shower. At least I hadn't spent a lot of time arranging my hair.

At the restaurant, I parked the scooter and walked past the vacant host stand, looking for the best view for my photo. Many of the tables were busy with people eating plates of bacon and eggs and biscuits and sipping bloody Marys. If life ever slowed down, I would love to bring Nathan here for a leisurely breakfast as a treat. Standing as close to the water as I could without falling in, I took pictures from multiple angles. Across the dining area, I spotted Amelia, the waitress with the blonde braids. Maybe she would have noticed something the night Davis Jager was attacked. I waved at her in a friendly way, but instead of responding in kind or coming toward me to say hello, she ducked into the kitchen. I could have sworn she'd seen me. The more I thought about it, the more it bothered me. Maybe she knew something she was afraid to share. I went to the bar and asked the bartender if I could have a word with Amelia.

"Hang on a sec, and I'll see if she's busy," he said, stepping away from the bar toward the kitchen. "She was here a minute ago, but she appears to have stepped out," he said when he returned. "I could take your name and number."

He was a lousy liar. His face had flushed pink, one eyebrow twitched, and he couldn't quite meet my gaze. She must have asked him to make me go away. Suddenly I remembered where I'd seen her last: she'd been sitting with Clementine Griswold at the memorial service along with another young woman, probably Clementine's granddaughter, Ida. I'd also seen them both in Clementine's photo by the water. I remembered them leaning close together as if to support each other during the service, and at the time I'd assumed they'd been close to the Garcia family and were feeling sad about GG's death. But if they'd been close to the family, wouldn't they have stayed longer at the reception? Why had Garcia's son Derek screamed at them and demanded that they leave? I now knew that Clementine was not a close friend of the family—quite the opposite. She nursed the embers of an old rage that could be traced back to her teenage trauma.

Could Amelia have been one of GG Garcia's very young conquests and Derek found out about it? I felt a shiver of disgust mingled with fear. Had she gone to Clementine for comfort and support and found a kindred spirit? More likely she'd talked to her friend Ida, and Ida had convinced her to tell Clementine. I had a strong feeling that Clementine would know the truth about whether something had happened to Amelia, though I wasn't so sure she'd share that with me.

I sent a photograph of the restaurant to my boss and texted Nathan to tell him I was planning to swing by Clementine Griswold's house on Stock Island to try for a follow-up photo and ask a few more questions.

* * *

I pulled up in front of Clementine's cottage. Mid Tuesday morning, the neighborhood was quiet. I tapped on the front door but got no answer. I peered into the living room and noticed that the overhead fans were spinning and the light was on in the kitchen. She had to be home. Either she didn't want to speak with me, or she was outside near or on the water. It seemed worth a try to walk around the house and see whether she and the boats were there.

As soon as I rounded the corner of the house to the backyard, I noticed Clementine out on the dock on a teak bench, her face tipped up to the sun. She looked sturdy for a woman of nearly ninety, but tired or sad, more like an old woman than she'd appeared on the previous visit. I tried to make enough noise walking toward the dock that I wouldn't startle her.

Her eyes flew open, and the look on her face when she recognized me was not welcoming. I started to talk quickly.

"I'm so sorry to pester you again, but I sent the article in with your excellent interview about the cookbook, and my boss pleaded with me to get a photo. I wondered if you might consider that?" I held my phone up and grinned.

She pushed herself up from the bench and sidestepped closer to the water. "No photos," she said firmly. "I don't want my dirty laundry or wrinkled mug aired in the local rags."

"Understood," I said, tucking the phone into my pocket and holding up empty hands. "If I could ask one question, though? I tried to chat with your granddaughter's friend Amelia up in Geiger Key, but she disappeared the moment she saw me. That made me wonder—and maybe this is a crazy idea—but I wondered whether she might have been one of GG Garcia's conquests?" Even as I asked the question, I wondered why I'd ever imagined she'd tell me. Especially as I saw a look of dismay on her face morph into panic.

She leaned down and scooped up the kayak paddle lying beside her on the dock. Was she planning to hit me?

"There is no need for you to take this any further," she said. "He got what he deserved, end of story." Then she hopped into the smaller of the two boats, sat down, and took off paddling, faster than I could have managed.

I texted Nathan a second time and told him I needed help, that Clementine had disappeared, headed toward the mangroves across from Twelfth Avenue, possibly taking with her the secret of the murder.

I think it might have to do with the blonde waitress at the marina. Amelia.

Clementine's yellow kayak had reached the other side of the inlet, and she disappeared through the cut and headed left. The only other boat tied to this dock was the two-person kayak—the same kind I'd ridden in exactly once, as a deadweight passenger. But I couldn't just let her go. At least I could try to follow her and point out her route when the sheriff's or the police department arrived—hopefully by sea. I grabbed a paddle and stepped in gingerly, wobbling and almost pitching into the water. Once I'd crouched low and regained my balance, I untied the rope and pushed away from the dock.

Navigating a two-person kayak alone turned out to be even more difficult than I'd imagined. With each stroke I took on the left, the front of the boat lurched right. If I dug the paddle in on the right, attempting to correct, it went the other way. I zigzagged awkwardly across the lagoon, feeling a bit sick to my stomach. Muscles in my arms and back screamed their protest at such an unfamiliar workout.

By the time I reached the cut through the edge of the mangroves, I saw no sign of Clementine. There was no boat in view in the water to the left, and directly across the water were hotels and other commercial buildings. I could either try paddling across the choppy open water—the idea of this made me instantly queasy—or go left along the tangle of mangroves leading toward Cow Key. I didn't know Clementine well, obviously, but my guess was she'd hide out in the wilds.

After paddling across a short expanse of open water, I nosed into a field of exposed mangrove roots, what the locals called dead man's knees. Using my paddle to push off the partially submerged wood cones, I slowly advanced the unwieldy boat. The little channel grew more and more narrow, the arch of the mangroves closing in from above. I gave a fierce push to break loose of the roots and force my craft around the corner.

I almost ran Clementine over; she was hunkered down in the vegetation, betrayed by her bright-yellow kayak. She brandished her paddle, and I paddled backward so as not to get too close and spook her any further.

"Clementine," I said, keeping my voice soft, as though I were talking to a nervous cat, "I know there must be a good reason that you did what you did. Maybe you wanted to protect the girl from the agony you endured. I believe that's still what you want most of all, to protect Amelia. It will only make things worse if you hurt me. Please consider coming back to the dock and talking to the police."

Her eyes got wide, and she stood up abruptly. I stood too and whirled around to see what was behind me. It wasn't Amelia at all. Instead, it was her granddaughter, Ida. She had approached soundlessly in her own single kayak and now held her paddle cocked behind her head as if she planned to take me out.

Clementine called out. "No, don't hit her. We can't kill someone else. It will only bring us down to his level, and we deserve better. We'll tell the truth, and if I go to jail, so be it."

"No one's saying you'll go to jail," I said in a soothing voice, trying to hide my fear. The young woman appeared terrified, angry, and unconvinced.

"Please, my dear, put the paddle down," Clementine said. "You're worth so much more than this. We all are."

I heard the putter of a motorboat engine navigating the mangroves and gave Clementine a wavery smile. "That's the police. They will help us sort this out."

The girl sank back down in her kayak, and the paddle clattered beside her. She began to weep, great buckets of noisy tears.

"We're back here," I called to the boat. "It's Hayley Snow. Mrs. Griswold and her granddaughter are here, and I think—I know—they are ready to talk."

A small sturdy motorboat came into view, with a sheriff's department deputy at the helm and Nathan and Darcy Rogers on board. I felt the tension flow out of my muscles and relief rush in. I collapsed abruptly to the kayak's seat. Within minutes, Nathan and Darcy had persuaded the two women to board the law enforcement boat and then tied their two kayaks to the stern.

"It's getting to be a heavy load," said the deputy at the helm, looking at me and the two-seater kayak and back at Nathan.

"I'll help Hayley get back," Nathan said. I crab-walked to the forward seat, and he took my place at the rear. "I didn't realize you had boating expertise," he teased as he propelled us out of the mangroves and across the water toward Clementine's dock. You are full of surprises."

I dipped my paddle in rhythm with him—if an eighty-nine-year-old woman could navigate her own kayak, I could certainly do my part. I knew Nathan had a lot more than boats on his mind, and that I'd hear it later. By the time we reached Clementine's home, the officers had helped the two women out of the boat. They were hunched together on the bench beside the dock.

"Before we decide what's going to happen here, supposing you explain the facts of how GG Garcia died," said Darcy Rogers, her lips pinched, arms crossed over her chest, and her legs spread wide. She looked fierce and unforgiving.

"My life was ruined by that awful man's father," Clementine said, circling an arm around her granddaughter's thin shoulders. "Now he was doing everything in his power to ruin Ida's. I could not allow that to happen."

"Ida, not Amelia?" I asked. They nodded in unison. "But Amelia is a true friend," Clementine added.

"So you killed the man?" the deputy asked.

Clementine glared, her lips clenched tightly together as though she was finished spilling the story. I couldn't imagine that the old woman would tell Deputy Rogers anything, the way things were going. I glanced at Nathan, and he nodded back.

"Let's back up a bit first," I suggested, looking directly at Ida. "How did things get started between you and Mr. Garcia?"

The girl's face colored. She looked down at her lap and toyed with a silver ring. "I saw him from time to time over this past year when I was waitressing, and I was nice to him. That's it. I'm nice to everyone—that's the secret of good customer service. He kept complimenting me and telling me I was the most beautiful girl on the island. He acted like he was confiding his troubles in me, how his wife had become a withholding, critical nag and he was so lonely."

"She had just been dumped by her boyfriend, his stupid son, Derek," her grandmother interjected. "Maybe you saw him at the memorial service—he got drunk and was hanging all over a fifteen-year-old girl. Disgusting. Then he had the nerve to yell at us to leave." Clementine snorted. "My Ida was feeling so low and hurt. She felt like she was lacking, just like that kid told her."

"While you were dating Derek, did you have any contact with his father?" I asked.

Tears gathered in the corners of Ida's eyes and spilled down her cheeks.

I took that as a yes, but feared she'd shut down if I pushed too hard. I sat down cross-legged on the dock so we wouldn't all be standing over her, looking official and unfriendly. "Go ahead and tell us the rest," I said to Ida. "Take your time."

"I'd met him from time to time when I was working at parties. Soon after Derek broke up with me, I was waitressing at a private party and Mr. Garcia was one of the guests. Everyone drank way too much. I'd snuck a few drinks too, and my defenses were down and I started to feel so depressed. Mr. Garcia found me in the kitchen cleaning up, and I was crying. He said his son didn't deserve me and that he was a stupid kid to throw away something so amazing." She stopped talking, and the tears came faster.

"I know this must be so hard," I said. "But it's important to tell them everything."

In fits and starts, she explained how he'd started by rubbing her back, dabbing her tears dry, and smoothing her hair. "He said his son was a fool if he didn't want to give me sugar. And then he kissed me."

With the long braids and tearstains on her cheeks and her lips quivering, she looked about ten years old rather than her eighteen.

"But that kiss was so light and quick, I could almost imagine I'd made it up. I felt better than I had in a long time, like maybe something wasn't wrong with me, maybe it was wrong with Derek." She lifted her chin in a slight show of defiance. "Mr. Garcia wasn't pretending; he was interested in me. He asked whether I was applying to college and how I'd feel about leaving the island. He said it could be a shock, but it would be good for me to get out into the world. That sometimes an island could be too small to hold a light like mine. He told me again that his son was an idiot and I deserved a man who knew how to treat me right."

She began to cry harder and dropped her head into her hands. Garcia's words sounded completely right, but the man had told her these things as a way to take advantage of her, not build her up. It made me feel sick to my stomach to watch her pain.

"Sounds like you had been feeling so vulnerable but then he treated you well, like you were special. You began to feel better than you had in months and months." I felt terrible about pushing her to keep talking, but getting the truth was too important. "Maybe he took you to some nice places? Or bought you things?"

She sat up straight, her eyes haunted with the memories. "This ring." She held out slender fingers, showing a silver filigreed ring with a purple stone in the center. "He said it was fit for a princess. That night we drove up to Islamorada, and he took me to the most wonderful dinner. He ordered a bottle of super-expensive champagne. Then he asked if I wanted to see the yacht he'd recently bought." She paused, and I was afraid she'd stop talking.

"Things got out of control?" I asked.

She nodded. "He was so sweet and kind at first, but when I said no, he said I must have wanted this or I wouldn't have come with him. He would hate to have to tell everyone what a terrible person I was and how I tried to ruin his marriage."

"You believed him, that it was your fault," I said.

"Of course she believed him," said Clementine. "She was eighteen and had way too much to drink, and her self-esteem was shaky because of that awful boy. A lot of girls have problems at this age. They look so confident and so gorgeous, but inside, they are desperate for attention."

From the emotion in her voice, I suspected she was remembering her own experience as well.

"I knew it was wrong," Ida said. "But he kept pushing to meet me again. He said he was falling in love with me and he was going to tell his wife he wanted a divorce. I agreed to meet him at Boca Chica Beach a few times after that."

"My sweet girl was devastated, and she was losing weight and she looked like the walking dead. Finally, I persuaded her to tell me what had happened. All I could think was, he was exactly like his father before him, and the world had had enough of his family's poison. I kept telling her to cut him off, she owed him nothing."

"I told him I'd never see him again." Ida kept her gaze focused on my face, not looking at her grandmother or any of the cops. "Then he said if I didn't continue, he'd post the photos he'd taken."

"Photos? Did he actually have photos?" Deputy Rogers asked. Her eyes had narrowed to slits.

"He did. He showed me a few, and they were disgusting and embarrassing. He had a camera in the bedroom of that stupid yacht. I couldn't risk him going public. It would have leaked all over town. You know what it's like here; it would have ruined my life." She looked only at me, her eyes imploring me to understand. "I asked him to return them to me, but he refused. So I finally told my grandmother."

Clementine picked up the narrative. "I figured it all out. We'd turn the tables and show the world what a slimy sleazeball he was. She would pick him up on her scooter at the parking garage and drive him to the Geiger Key beach and spread out a blanket and pour wine as if it was a tryst that she welcomed. Amelia and I paddled in ahead of time and hid in the bushes near the driftwood hut."

I must have looked surprised, because she added, "I'm still pretty good with a boat, as you saw. I take my sit-on-top kayak out several times a week by myself. I don't want to end up an old, crippled lady who can't make her way down the sidewalk without a nurse to lean on. Besides, I had Amelia to help. As the crow flies, it's only about five miles from that beach to Cow Key.

"Ida would get him talking, maybe even get him to tell how he'd double-crossed his pal Entwistle with the development plans. Then she would tell him the affair was over. We knew he'd try to force her to do what she didn't want to, and we planned to video that too. Before things got out of control, Amelia and I would step out of the bushes with the phone and confront him. We would threaten to post everything on social media. He deserved to have everyone know he was a complete scumbag, a man who forced himself on young women, cheated on his wife, and swindled his partners. Unless he left my Ida alone, we'd tell the world."

Her hands were balled into little fists, tight as knots on a nautical rope.

"Maybe you'll think it sounds gruesome and over complicated," her grandmother continued. "But for me, it wasn't enough that he should be humiliated alone on this beach. I thought he needed to hear what he'd done to my sweet Ida and what his father did to me. I knew he wouldn't take responsibility for the damage, but he should fear us because we held him responsible. We'd make him promise never to contact her again."

"What happened next?" I asked, looking at Ida.

The girl's face flushed. "We arrived at the driftwood hut, and he grabbed me right away." Ida covered her eyes and groaned. "He was grinning like a wolf, and he started to tear my clothes off and tell me it was a little late to be acting coy, that he knew I wanted this."

"Rather than something that he'd already taken." Clementine hugged her granddaughter. "That disgusting piece of dog crap," she said. "He made me want to barf, and then whack him senseless. Amelia and I burst out of the bushes, and I told him we were onto his disgusting game and now everyone was going to know what a pig he was. He would deserve the humiliation and the backlash he got once the community knew. Amelia held up her phone with the video we'd taken. End of story."

I wondered how terrified Clementine must have been as a girl when GG's father did the same thing to her. Only she'd had no one to tell, and she believed it was her fault, and gradually that history had filled her with poison from bottom to top, like a fund-raising thermometer.

"But you claim you didn't kill him?" I asked gently.

"We didn't mean to," Clementine said. "That buffoon pulled up his pants and struggled to his feet. He grabbed a big piece of driftwood from the hut and began to swing it at us. I do believe he would have beaten all three of us to death to get that phone."

"But he didn't . . ." I nudged.

Ida said, "No. He hit Amelia's arm with his wood, and her phone went flying over the Navy's fence into the base. He was like a wild animal, and I was afraid he'd kill my grandmother. I grabbed a piece of coral rock, and that made him even madder, and he lunged at me. I had to stop him or he would kill her."

"You threw the rock?"

She looked down at the slats of the dock. "Yes. He lost his balance and fell hard. But he sat up quickly. He was so angry; he said I hadn't heard the last of him."

"We cleared out," said Clementine. "The storm was coming in, and we had to get home because we'd arrived in a kayak and on a scooter. I told Ida to drive to my place and we'd meet her there—let him figure out how to get his own ride back to Key West. The worst that could happen would be he'd have to spend an uncomfortable night in the rain."

"I never meant to kill him," Ida said. "I didn't think I'd hit him hard enough to do that much damage." Her face had grown pale, but her eyes were dry and her lips set. "He was fine when we left." I believed every word she said.

The tears shone in Clementine's eyes as she looked at her sad but determined granddaughter. "I take full responsibility for not informing the authorities. Then you found him before I got the nerve to call." She tipped her chin at me.

Darcy Rogers asked, "If you hit his head with a rock, why have our search teams not found it?"

A memory of the rock cairns we'd seen on the way to investigate the murder site flashed to my mind. "You built it into one of those cairns, right?" I asked.

Clementine nodded. "I picked the rock up on the way to the water. We hid the evidence in plain sight."

She held out her hands for handcuffs, but Deputy Darcy Rogers shook her head.

"Maybe you killed him, maybe not. Garcia was on a blood thinner, and when he fell back, he hit his head. That blow caused a subdural hematoma, which bled into his brain. My team is searching the Navy property now. If you ladies are lucky, we'll find that phone to confirm you hit him in self-defense."

Now I remembered a post on Facebook a year or so ago about GG having heart surgery. There was nothing private about his medical process. He'd posted all kinds of photos on Facebook—him with the surgeon, him with the flowers he'd been sent, him squeezing the nurses on the cardiac ICU unit.

None of them looked happy about it. I knew from my own grandfather's experience with serious heart issues that he'd been prescribed Coumadin afterward, which came with stern warnings about the risks of heavy bleeding, both internal and external.

Deputy Rogers turned her gaze to Ida. "That's not to say you behaved correctly, leaving an injured man on the beach without alerting the authorities. But right now, it's enough that all three of you stay here in town while we sort out the details."

Chapter Twenty-Six

Instead of "sweetness and light" let us use "sweetness and lime" for our dessert motto, as the delicate sharpness of the lime seems just the right note to strike in the finale of a tropical meal.

—*The Key West Cookbook* by the Members of the Key West Woman's Club, 1949

Both Wally and Palamina were waiting for me in their shared office. I didn't even have to bring my own chair in, as it had already been set up. How much trouble was I in this time? It felt like feeding time and the lions were waiting in the Colosseum.

"We have good news and bad news today," Palamina said. She wasn't frowning, though I knew from past conversations that didn't necessarily mean much. Her family heritage was a vertical wrinkle in the forehead that emerged in the forties, and she'd been hoping to head that off by avoiding negative facial expressions. She'd made a copy of my article about local food and the cookbook and how reading these recipes and trying the old-time ingredients connected us to our ancestors and helped new generations understand the challenges in the lives of the older folks. It was sitting on her desk.

"Your off-the-rock review is solid, but this piece is outstanding," she said.

Wally was nodding. "You've come a long way since you first started. Further than I imagined possible."

Sheesh, talk about a backhanded compliment. "Thanks, that means a lot." If they liked my work, what was wrong? Why did they both need to see me?

Then Palamina smiled. "Wally's decided to leave the island, and we've decided to offer his managerial position to you. We'll still need the weekly food criticism and other features, but you'll also work with me in planning the editorial calendar and brainstorming issues and hiring new writers as we can afford them. Are you interested in that?"

"Would I be sharing your office?" I blurted that out before I could stop myself. The two of them looked shocked, but I could hear Danielle giggling in the anteroom. "That was so rude. What I meant to say is, I'm thrilled with the offer, but sad to see Wally go."

"Terrific." Palamina stood up and shook my hand, and Wally did the same. "You can stay in your nook for the time being. If we decide to take in some new hires, I'll figure it out. We'll probably need to find new space. Can you start tomorrow at nine? We'll talk salary then as well."

"Thanks so much for your confidence!" I turned to face Wally. "I wish you all the best on the mainland. We'll miss you here." I *would* miss him, the way Pooh would miss Eeyore. Wally and Eeyore were two fellows who could see the glass half-empty even if it was spilling over the top. But they were lovable in their own curmudgeonly ways.

A text flashed in, and I glanced at my phone. "I'm due home half an hour ago. But I can't wait to get started." I gathered my belongings, accepted joyous congratulations from Danielle, and left the office. I heard footsteps behind me.

Wally had followed me down the stairs and stopped three steps above me. "Hayley? Can I speak to you for a moment?" He continued to talk without waiting for an answer. "I wanted to say this before I lost my nerve. I'm sorry for acting like a grouch lately. It's just that if you don't mind me being blunt, you don't seem that happy in your marriage, and I can't help feeling like we were the ones who belonged together. I messed up, and you'll always be the one who got away."

He looked at me with big cow eyes, as though waiting for me to agree with his assessment. And then what? Fling my wedding rings to the carpet and ride off into the sunset on his Jet Ski—if he had one? I didn't know whether to laugh or cry.

"That's so sweet," I said. "But I don't think it's accurate. First of all, even though Nathan and I have some fiery moments, I love him dearly and he loves me, and we are committed for a lifetime."

Wally's face fell, but he nodded. I thought maybe a bit of relief was mixed in with the disappointment and embarrassment on his face.

"Second, I was on the rebound from dreadful Chad when we met, and not in any shape to be in a serious relationship. You suffered because of that. Besides, we were always better as friends, don't you think?" I added. "Hopefully that can continue. I think 'the one' for you is out there somewhere, probably in Miami, exactly where you're headed."

I ran back up the stairs to give him a quick hug. "Take care, and stay in touch."

* * *

Skip was waiting with Nathan on our houseboat. They had beers in front of them—beers in the middle of a weekday?—along with a bowl of nuts. My father-in-law's luggage was stored to the side. He was either moving in or moving on. I liked him better than when I'd first met him, but I sure wasn't ready for another roommate.

I sat down with the men, placing my backpack beside me.

"Our little detective arrives," said Nathan's dad.

I met Nathan's gaze, unsure whether to laugh or object or ignore him.

"To be serious," Skip said, "you're good at reading people, and not everyone has that skill."

"Thank you."

"Maybe you could explain to a nonlocal the backstory of why GG Garcia was killed. I understand about the affair, and how the old woman couldn't bear the idea of him defiling her granddaughter, but the plan she came up with seems so extreme. When I was a detective, I always wanted to go deeper and not accept the obvious."

I sneaked a glance at Nathan to see whether he was feeling this comment as a slam on his work. He appeared to be calmly listening.

"Clementine and Ida didn't actually murder him," I said. "Darcy Rogers said that based on the video they found on

Amelia's cell phone, his death would probably be ruled accidental. Besides that, he wasn't dead when they left him. They believed he was fine—just stunned enough that they could get away. The autopsy confirmed that he died much later in the night than when Pizza Al heard the scooter head back to Key West."

"No, right, but Clementine would have killed if she had to, and she certainly planned on getting her revenge by social media. Tell me more about your theories on that," said Skip.

I gave a quick nod but took a few minutes to organize what I'd been thinking. "Key West—and maybe this is true for a lot of islands—is different. We live on such a tiny patch of land. Everything here is limited: what grows on the land, the land itself, the creatures in the water around the island. Many times over in Key West's history, people have exploited the available resources until they're exhausted. Take turtles, for example—they're on my mind because of the cookbook—they were hunted and produced into foodstuffs and exported until they were gone. They vanished from the island, and now they're endangered around the world. Same with sponge farming. People got greedy about pillaging sponges for export and weren't careful about conserving them for the future."

Skip had a look of impatience on his face.

"More recently, it's been the island itself. Garcia and his father were guilty of this—developing every available inch without thought to how it would affect life on the island and the resources that we all need to share. Trying to jam a resort on that little spit of land on Geiger Key? That was crazy. This family has never cared about conserving resources, whether it's wildlife or property or people."

"Yes, but that's not what got him killed." Skip was frowning at me, his forehead creased as though I wasn't quite making sense.

"Honestly, I believe they treated women with the same disregard—as things to be used and discarded. That's exactly and specifically what got GG Garcia killed. I'm not a psychologist, so I can't tell you whether Garcia's behavior was caused by genetics or environment."

"Maybe some of both," Skip said.

I nodded slowly. "But as we saw in the diary Martha and I discovered, his father behaved the same way with Clementine when she was a young woman. I suspect there were others. Used up and tossed aside like the turtles and the sponges."

I pulled the old cookbook out of my pack. "I've been writing about this cookbook all week but only just noticed the inscription from mother-in-law to daughter-in-law." I showed them the crabbed writing on the title page: *For Andrea, Best regards, Mrs. Gerald (Evelyn) Garcia*. The words had been slashed through with a black magic marker. Best regards? What mother-in-law wrote that to a new daughter in her family?

"I don't know this for sure, but I suspect Andi Garcia defaced this inscription and gave the book to the library when she'd had enough of her husband's behavior. She might also have realized that *his* mother knew exactly what he was doing, because she'd watched her own husband do the same thing. I think she's recognized that her son has been acting similarly and she plans to change that."

"You are one smart cookie," Nathan said, his voice full of admiration. "Who else would make those connections? Andi

Garcia has already started working on the kid. She demanded he come home and talk with us, so we interviewed him this morning. He confessed that he attacked Davis Jager in the Fish Camp parking lot. Jager was blabbing at the bar about Derek's father, and Derek was worried he knew too much and would spill a lot of dirty secrets."

"But didn't Davis Jager think two people struck him?"

"We'll continue to talk to Derek, but I'm guessing the two-people theory was a function of how much Jager had drunk. He was probably seeing double that night, too."

"She's not only smart," Skip said. "Your Hayley is brave as well. But she's not foolhardy. She's an asset to you in your work, the way your mother would have been in mine, had my ego not gotten in the way. I hope you'll come to see that clearly."

His Apple watch buzzed with a text. "My Uber is here," he said as got to his feet, still graceful for a tall, older guy.

"We'd be happy to give you a ride to the airport," I said.

"No worries; I've taken enough of your time. It's been a pleasure to meet you," he told me. "Nathan is a lucky man, and I hope he doesn't blow it."

Nathan looked furious for a moment but tamped that down.

"I'm so glad to meet you too," I said, reaching on tiptoe to peck Skip's cheek. "We hope you'll come back for a visit that doesn't involve work. You barely had a chance to experience the joys of our island."

"Thank you," he said, adding a grin. Then he shook Nathan's hand, picked up his luggage, hopped onto the dock, and strode off to the parking lot. We followed him partway down so we could wave good-bye.

"Thank god that's over," said Nathan, watching him disappear into the waiting car. We returned to our home and settled into deck chairs, our animals beside us. I studied my husband, cocking my head a bit, certain I had a quizzical expression on my face. But Nathan didn't say anything else.

"He's a little testy, but I kind of enjoyed him," I said finally. I wondered how to word my question so as not to set off my occasionally edgy husband. "I guess I don't quite understand all that's going on with you two, but I should think you'd be glad to reconnect with him. He is your father."

Nathan was silent for a few moments. "Here's the thing. Look at what happened with the Garcia men. The grandfather was a disgusting man who molested a teenager and essentially ruined her life. By all reports his son behaved the same way, and in the end that got him murdered. Killed, anyway." He picked up my hand and stroked the palm.

"My father may have his strong points intellectually, and he's a charmer. But he too had serious flaws. He was distant with his own family as I was growing up and obsessed with work. Despite what he told you, I am quite sure he cheated with more than one woman while he was married to my mother. I don't ever want to be like him. Having him around reminds me of that probability."

"Nathan," I said, taking both of his hands in mine. "I don't think it's a probability for you. It's certainly not a foregone conclusion. Infidelity and coldness are not hardwired into the genes."

"You said it yourself," Nathan argued. "It's both nature and nurture. I got half my DNA from my father—strike one. I watched him betray my mother over the years, whether

I understood it as such at the time or not—strike two. And I experienced the distance firsthand—strike three. Those are the things I learned."

"No," I said. "I'm not buying that. You are not your father. Eric always tells me that the reason people get stuck repeating the past is that they refuse to acknowledge that it's there, or that it could have any effect on the present. As long as we talk and share how we're feeling throughout our marriage, even during the low points, I think we'll be fine. Remember what Steve Torrence told us in our premarital counseling? The couples who talk, even when it's painful, are the ones who survive." I quirked a smile. "There are similarities between you and your dad, and I like some of them, a lot. He's adorable for an older guy, and he can be very funny when he lightens up. He cares so much about protecting people, same as you do."

I leaned in to give him a good, long kiss. "What do you say we have an early dinner and early to bed? Just us?"

He reached for my hands and pulled me closer. "What say we just skip the dinner?"

Recipes

Mojito With Simple Syrup

Hayley and I have both sampled our share of mojitos on the island—all in the name of research, of course! One of the ingredients that makes for the best drinks is simple syrup. The sugar is completely incorporated by simmering it in water. Infusing the syrup with fresh mint takes the flavor up a notch.

Servings: 5

Ingredients

1/2 cup sugar (I used Domino's golden sugar)
1/2 cup water
1 bunch mint leaves, washed and dried
1 lemon
5 to 6 key limes
Rum
Club soda

To make the simple syrup:

Combine the sugar and water in a small saucepan and bring to a low boil. Simmer until the sugar has dissolved. Move the pan from the heat and add several sprigs of mint (I used two and I would double it next time). Let the syrup cool to room temperature.

To make the mojitos:

In each of five highball glasses, add one lemon slice, several lime slices, and 0.75 ounce simple syrup. Muddle this (bruise it) using a pestle or wooden spoon. Add 1 to 2 ounces of rum, depending on how strong you want the drink to be.

Fill each glass with ice, then club soda. Float a mint sprig on top.

To make the drink nonalcoholic, simply omit the rum.

Banana Cream Pie

One of the plot strands in this book has to do with the Woman's Club in Key West, which is a gorgeous old home on Duval Street. I took a tour of the building in the spring of 2021 and was the happy recipient of the 1988 version of their cookbook. I had also found an earlier edition of the book on eBay that had been published in 1949. Oh my, the recipes and stories in those cookbooks had my mind racing with possibilities! This banana cream pie was served to Hayley and Martha Hubbard while they were probing a suspect. I chose to make a graham cracker crust, but any crust is fine. The recipe is based on the version in the 1988 cookbook.

Ingredients

For the crust:

1 package graham crackers (nine sheets)
4 tablespoons butter
2 tablespoons sugar

For the filling:

3 eggs, room temperature, separated
4 tablespoons sugar
3 tablespoons cornstarch
Pinch salt

2 teaspoons water
2 cups whole milk
1 teaspoon vanilla extract
1 tablespoon butter
2 ripe bananas

For the meringue:

3 egg whites (see above)
1/4 teaspoon cream of tartar
2 teaspoons sugar

Directions

Preheat the oven to 350 degrees.

To make the crust, smash or whirl the crackers to crumbs. Melt the butter. Stir the butter and sugar into the crumbs and press this mixture into the bottom and sides of a 10-inch pie pan. Bake for 10 minutes and let that cool.

For the filling, separate the eggs and set the whites aside. Beat the yolks with the sugar, cornstarch, salt, and cold water until thick and smooth. Heat the milk until it's about to boil, then cool for a few minutes and stir it slowly into the egg mixture. Cook this mixture over low heat, stirring constantly, until the pudding thickens (about 5 minutes). Let that cool a bit and then mix in the vanilla and butter.

Slice the bananas into the pie crust. Spread the pudding on top of the bananas.

For the meringue, beat the egg whites in a clean bowl with the cream of tartar until soft peaks appear. Continue beating while slowly adding the sugar until peaks are stiff and glossy (about five minutes).

Mound the meringue onto the pudding, arranging it into peaks.

Bake for 10 to 15 minutes or until the meringue begins to brown. Refrigerate the pie for 3 hours before serving.

Party Sandwiches With Egg Salad, Cucumber Watercress, and Pimento Cheese Layers

My mother used to make three-layer finger sandwiches for holiday parties, and that was my inspiration for Janet Snow's canapes. I've offered you recipes for three different fillings, but you can mix and match or replace them as your tastes dictate. You will choose two fillings for each three-decker loaf. Ask a bakery to cut your loaves of bread lengthwise—that makes sandwich construction a snap.

Cucumber Watercress Filling

1 16-ounce tub whipped cream cheese, softened
1/2 lemon, zested
2 tablespoons fresh dill, chopped finely
1 bunch watercress
1 large Persian cucumber, finely sliced
1 loaf nice white or wheat bread, sliced lengthwise

Mix the zest and the dill with the cream cheese and stir well. Taste to see if the seasonings suit; I didn't feel the need for added salt or pepper. You could also add fresh chopped chives.

Wash the watercress, spin it dry, and detach it from the stems. Set it aside.

Wash the cucumber, cut off the ends, and slice it thinly. I used a mandolin, which made a tedious job super easy. I left the skin on for a nice touch of green.

Lay open two slices of bread, and spread both with the cream cheese mixture. Press a layer of sliced cucumbers into one side and a layer of watercress into the other.

Close the sandwich.

Curried Egg Salad Filling

12 boiled eggs
1/4 to 1/2 cup good mayonnaise
1 tablespoon amazing maple or other tasty mustard
1 heaping teaspoon good curry powder
1 to 2 tablespoons finely chopped fresh dill

Peel the eggs and mash them finely with a pastry cutter. Add the mayonnaise, mustard, curry powder, and dill, and stir well. Taste for seasoning. Spread on the top of the bread covering the cucumber watercress layer, then add another slice. Or replace either of those fillings with pimento cheese.

Pimento Cheese Filling

(This recipe is based on one shared by my niece's father, chef Harry Williams.)

6 cups shredded sharp white cheddar (avoid preshredded cheese)
4 ounces Greek cream cheese (this is half cream cheese and half Greek yogurt—more protein, less fat)

7 to 8 ounces roasted red peppers in oil, chopped
1 bunch scallions, mostly the white parts, cleaned, chopped, and sautéed in a tiny amount of butter
1/2 cup mayonnaise, more if needed (I used Hellmann's)
Dash hot sauce

Grate the cheese. Combine it in a large bowl with the cream cheese and beat until well mixed. Add the red peppers and scallions; mix well. Add the mayo. If the mixture isn't the right texture for spreading, add more mayonnaise, plus hot sauce to taste.

Spread the filling on top of the layer of bread covering the egg salad or the cream cheese, then layer with the third slice. Wrap the result in a damp, clean kitchen towel and then plastic wrap; refrigerate for an hour or longer. Cut the sandwiches into fingers and serve.

Pat Kennedy's Homemade Pigs in a Blanket

My good friend Pat has a large family, and she loves cooking for them. Her retro recipe for pigs in a blanket is always in demand, exactly as it was at the funeral reception.

Ingredients

For the dough:

3/4 cup butter
3/4 cup sugar
1 1/2 tsp salt
1 cup boiling water
2 packages dry yeast
1 cup lukewarm water
2 eggs
6 cups all-purpose flour

For the pigs:

1 package Hillshire Farms Lit'l Smokies (Pat says you can use other small sausages, but they aren't nearly as tasty)
Small chunks of cheddar cheese (optional)

Directions

In a large bowl, blend butter, sugar, and salt; then add boiling water. Cool.

Dissolve yeast in lukewarm water; add to above and mix in.

Mix eggs with a fork or spoon; add to above mixture.

Blend flour in gradually, 1/2 cup flour at a time, beating well. (A large stand mixer makes this easier!) Cover dough bowl with plastic wrap; place in refrigerator for at least 4 hours before using. You can leave it in the refrigerator for up to 10 days. Punch the dough down and then take portions out to use as desired.

When the dough is ready, flour your hands, then take a small pinch of dough, roll it out into a wormlike shape, and roll it around one Lit'l Smokie with or without a chunk of cheese inserted into a split in the sausage. Place shaped rolls on a lightly greased (Pam-sprayed) baking sheet. Cover with a tea towel. Let rise 4 hours on the counter.

Bake 10 to 12 minutes in a 375-degree oven. Check to make sure the bottoms are browned.

Serve when just slightly cooled with a dark grainy mustard on the side.

Pat says: They go fast! The dough has to be made in advance but comes together very quickly. Once mixed, it can be refrigerated for up to 10 days. When making the pigs, there is always dough left over, so I use the extra to make dinner rolls or sometimes cinnamon rolls for breakfast. These are totally delicious but homey and irresistible. The secret is the dough. No Pillsbury crescent rolls could ever compete.

Sally Bell's Knockoff Potato Salad

When my husband and I drive to Key West, we have one must-stop lunch place: Sally Bell's Kitchen in downtown Richmond, Virginia. When you walk in, you feel like you've fallen back to an earlier time, with grandmothers in aprons and hairnets preparing you a southern lunch. You choose your preferred sandwich and cupcake, and then potato salad, a deviled egg, and a Parmesan wafer are added. The packaging is adorable—each lunch comes in a little white cardboard box, tied up with string.

We love everything about the lunch but especially the potato salad. I wondered if I could make something that tasted like Sally Bell's potato salad, which is a little sweet. I started with Vicky Yates's recipe and then tweaked it. We liked the results a lot. Janet Snow serves this to her guests when Hayley's father-in-law comes to visit.

Servings: 6–8

Ingredients

2.5 pounds medium red-skinned potatoes, washed, with bad spots cut out (about 7–8)
1/2 cup mayonnaise
3 tablespoons good pickle relish with juice or chopped sweet pickles

1–3 tablespoons chopped candied jalapeños, to taste
2 stalks finely minced celery
1 1/2 tablespoons Dijon mustard
1 teaspoon sugar
1/4 teaspoon freshly ground black pepper plus more to taste
1/2 teaspoon salt
2 tablespoons chopped red onion
2 tablespoons chopped flat-leaf parsley
5 large hard-boiled eggs—just the yolks, folks
Paprika

Directions

Cut the potatoes into quarters, cover with water, and simmer until tender when pierced with a knife, 20 to 30 minutes. Drain. Place potatoes in a large bowl and let cool slightly.

Meanwhile, whisk mayonnaise, pickle relish, jalapeños, celery, Dijon mustard, sugar, pepper, and salt in a small bowl for dressing. Add onion and parsley.

Using a large wooden spoon or potato masher, coarsely smash potatoes. Add egg yolks to potatoes and coarsely smash them together. Then gently mix in the dressing. Cover and chill.

Dust the top of the bowl with paprika.

Acknowledgments

Bits and pieces of this story are very real, as usual. My dear writer friend Ang Pompano alerted me to the existence of the Key West cookbook, written and published by the women of the Key West Woman's Club in 1949. I was able to find a copy on eBay, and as I read through the pages, my imagination caught fire like the hibiscus described in the book's foreword. I'm grateful to Dawn Martin, the president of the Woman's Club, who gave me a tour of their gorgeous building. If you have the chance to visit Key West, do take a tour. It's located right on Duval Street, though you could walk by it a million times on your way to dinner and never imagine it's there. I'm grateful to have had the chance to study both of the club's cookbooks—the snippets I used in this book are real, including the description of the lunch conundrum in chapter twenty-five. However, the murder and the old grudges you'll find in this mystery come only from my imagination—not from the real cookbook or the real people in the Woman's Club!

Geiger Key is a real place as well, and a lovely spot to walk your dog or take a picnic lunch. Thanks to my sister, Susan Cerulean, and her husband, Jeff Chanton, for the sparks of inspiration we found there. John and I adore the food at the

Geiger Key Fish Camp, so do make a visit if you have a car and a couple of free hours. Thanks to Eric and Bill for turning us onto it, and for their plot ideas and inspiration.

Annette Holmstrom is a real person too, and graciously shared her love of book collecting and tips for what to look for when sorting through old books. Carrie Jo Howe spent many entertaining hours with me at the Higgs Beach small-dog park with her dog, Vana, and my nutty Lottie. Thanks to Martha Hubbard for endorsing the idea of her character in a second book. I am always grateful to my friend Ron Augustine, on whom Lorenzo is based. They are both wise and insightful men. Thank you to Pat Kennedy for sharing her pigs in a blanket recipe—you will be grateful to her as well after you try the recipe.

My Facebook friends made so many amazing title suggestions, and for each of those, I'm grateful. Special thanks to Ruth McCarty for the one that was chosen. Thank you to the Key West police officers who contributed to plot ideas and corrected my errors, especially Chief Sean Brandenburg, Steve Torrence, and Randy Smith.

Angelo Pompano and Chris Falcone are amazing readers, writers, and most important, friends. Thank you, guys, again! Thanks to Paige Wheeler, my fabulous agent, and the folks at Crooked Lane Books who brought this book to life. These include Matt Martz, Madeline Rathle, Melissa Rechter, cover artists Griesbach and Martucci, and independent editor Sandy Harding, whose comments always lead to a stronger book.

Thank you to my dear friends, the Jungle Red Writers, Hallie Ephron, Hank Phillippi Ryan, Rhys Bowen, Deborah Crombie, Julia Spencer-Fleming, and Jenn McKinlay. They are such a talented, funny, and unfailingly supportive group of friends! And I am so grateful to you, my readers, and to the bookstores and libraries who bring my work into the world.

Aa always, my thanks to John.

Lucy Burdette
December 2021
Key West